DETOUR

A Big Rig Thriller

DEVORAH FOX

Mike Byrnes and Associates, Inc.
355 Keewaydin Lane
Port Aransas, Texas 78373

Also by Devorah Fox
The Bewildering Adventures of King Bewilliam series:
The Lost King, Book One
The King's Ransom, Book Two
The King's Redress, Book Three
Detour, Book Four

Naked Came the Sharks with Jed Donellie
Masters of Time, A Science Fiction and Fantasy Time Travel Anthology
Magic Unveiled, An Anthology
Murder by the Book, A Mystery Mini
One Bad Apple, A Mystery Mini
The Zen Detective

http://devorahfox.com
ISBN: 0-9778245-8-6
ISBN-13: 978-0-9778245-8-8

DEDICATION

to Barbara Sanchez and Mike Byrnes.

AUTHOR'S NOTE

This is a work of fiction—mostly. Some of the locations mentioned did at one time exist and a few still do. They are used fictitiously and no endorsements or criticisms are intended or should be derived from their portrayal. Use of any trademarks or service marks does not imply any affiliation with or endorsement by them.

While every attempt has been made to represent faithfully the job of commercial motor vehicle operation, this work of fiction is not to be taken as a driver's instructional manual. Those seeking further details about CMV driving are invited to read *Bumper to Bumper, The Complete Guide to Tractor-Trailer Operations*, the textbook mentioned in the story. It's still in print as of the first publication of *Detour*.

All the characters and events are the product of my imagination. Any resemblance to actual events, places, or persons living or dead is purely coincidental, with one exception: President William Jefferson Clinton did hold a Town Hall at the Haviland Middle School and stopped at the Franklin D. Roosevelt National Historic Site in Hyde Park, New York, the afternoon of Friday, February 19, 1993. Any other details of his visit in this story are my invention.

THANKS

I am grateful to:

Barbara Sanchez, for inspiration.

Beta readers Alice Marks, author of *Missing* and *Breaks,* and Michael Stephen Daigle, author of the Frank Nagler Mysteries, whose support means so much; industry professionals Andrea Dobson, Mike Green, John Rojas, and David Kolman for their valuable time and expertise, and Joyce Walters and Phyllis Harp for their close attention. Any errors that remain are mine.

My Street Team of Chip Cooper, Alan White, Ellie Killian, Joyce Walters, Theresa Guettler, Orville Ballard, Diana Knowlton Vondra, Hanna Brodie, David Abbe, and Andrea Dobson, who relentlessly cheer me on.

Indie Author Masterminds and Indie Author Promos, as well as my Facebook, Twitter, and Goodreads friends, too numerous to list, ever ready with advice and encouragement.

Bill Urbin, National Park Service, for sharing his photographs from President William Clinton's visit to the Franklin D. Roosevelt National Historic Site.

The Art Center of Port Aransas, the Estelle Stair Gallery, and the Family Center IGA for their support.

and Mike Byrnes, always.

CHAPTER ONE

RALEIGH, NC, Wednesday, February 10, 1993

Even over the cellular, the urgency in Debbie's voice could not be missed. "Ah, come on, Archie. This is an excellent opportunity to spend some serious time with my family."

"Debbie. Baby. I ...," Archie Harlanson stammered, making a last ditch effort to get out of this trip.

"I know you think they don't like you."

"I know they don't. They don't think I'm good enough for you." *And they might be right.* Marvin and Miriam Stenowitz's beautiful and brilliant daughter probably did deserve a moneyed Big City doctor or lawyer, not some humble country-boy truck driver struggling to make a go of it as an owner-operator.

"Oh, don't be silly, my parents aren't like that. They just haven't had a chance to get to know you. This visit will give them that chance."

"Shit." Archie downshifted so abruptly he almost ground the gears. "Not you, Deb. Got a four wheeler in front of me driving like he's all alone out here." The car's driver wove in and out of the lanes as if playing bumper cars on I-95. "Honey, I'll make it if I can, but you know how these things go. Got loads to haul."

Archie could hear her draw a breath, rallying for a new onslaught. "We'd be together for Valentine's Day."

Archie sighed. "OK, OK. I'll meet you there, how's that?"

"Great." Her smile was audible. Archie pictured the way the corners of her Cupid's bow mouth would turn up.

"You know how to get there? Salt Point, New York?" she asked.

"Babe, if there's a road leading to it, I can find it."

"Isn't that the truth?" Debbie's soft chuckle told him all was forgiven, for now at least. "See you Thursday then," she said. "I love you, Super Man."

"Me too, babe." Archie grinned. He loved the way his handle sounded on her lips. It always made him sit a little taller in the saddle. The nickname had been her idea. He felt it was bigheaded and he got a lot of ribbing about it from other truckers but he stuck with it to please Debbie.

He pressed the end-call button and laid the cellular phone on the truck's passenger seat. Last year when he'd first gotten the Nokia 101, one of 1992's hottest gadgets, he thought three hundred bucks mighty steep for something the size of a candy bar. Debbie urged him to get it, thinking it could be a useful work tool. It would never replace the CB; the cellular phone didn't work everywhere. But it did sometimes come in handy. Like now, when he could call one of his load brokers to see if there was a drop and hook from Raleigh, where he was now headed to Salt Point, New York, where clearly he was headed after that.

He downshifted another gear and prepared to pull the next grade.

CHAPTER TWO

POUGHKEEPSIE, NY, Thursday, February 11, 1993

Archie dictated into his tape recorder, "Under drifting snow, U.S. 9 is a barely discernible dark ribbon through the monochrome Currier and Ives print that is lower upstate New York in February."

The landscape was pretty but Archie had to wonder why he was going north when everyone who could would head for the warm sunny south that he just left. *Must be love.*

"The Kenworth W900L is handling the road well. And with the cab's noise reduction package, it's so quiet, you can almost hear the rustle of pines, the whisper of snowfall." *Well, almost.*

In deference to the weather, he drove slightly below the speed limit. His fellow motorists, however, were in general going too fast for conditions. Speeding, slowing, passing him left and right, they fussed at him, trying his patience, but he resisted the temptation to respond in kind. *Might as well get used to it.* For the next few days he'd be fussed at plenty.

A crackling came over the CB followed by a deep, drawling voice. "Breaker one-nine, this is Lizard Lips. I'm liking this big red Kenworth I'm seeing. Does she ride as fine as she looks? Over."

"Super Man, here," Archie replied. "You bet, Lizard Lips. This baby kicks butt."

"Superman, eh? Faster than a speeding bullet?"

Archie chuckled. *No speeding for me.* For the most part, he kept within posted limits. Sure, speeding could get you to your destination quicker, but not quick enough to justify the fuel overhead. "Let's just say that if I had to change a tire, I wouldn't need a jack."

The other trucker guffawed. "More powerful than a locomotive, huh? Say, that rig looks brand new."

"It is." The trailer Archie pulled was payload but assessing the tractor's hauling ability was on the evaluation checklist for the article he was writing "on spec."

"You've seen our product review stories," the magazine's editor had told him. "Report on your new vehicle as if you were writing one of those. Then we'll see if we want any more of your work."

"You can read all about it in *American Big Rigs* in a few months," Archie told the other trucker. *I hope.*

"I'll look for it. Enjoy the ride."

"Thanks, Lizard Lips," Archie said. "It'll be the only part of this trip I will enjoy," he muttered as he stowed the mike.

He dropped his loaded trailer in Poughkeepsie, which was as close to Salt Point as the broker could get him, and continued north. Bobtailing without a trailer, much less a loaded one, meant the vehicle had less traction. Slick with snow and black ice, the road surface was especially slippery without the weight of a load to hold the tractor on it, and Archie took curves and turns with extra care. Once past the city limits, the divided highway narrowed to a throughway clogged with local traffic and he geared down. Hugging the Hudson River to the west, Archie's route took him past the poured concrete buildings of Marist College, gleaming white as snow banks, glass windows glittering like sheets of ice, and the more traditional brick and marble of The Culinary Institute of America, shrouded in snow and sheltered by trees.

Wrestling with stop-and-go traffic, he inched past Franklin Delano Roosevelt's Hyde Park home, now a national historic site, braking for drivers who paused to admire the mansion set back from the road on park-like grounds.

One four-wheeler had skidded off the highway entirely and stood alongside her compact car, flapping her arms. Archie spotted a cleared spot on the shoulder, slowed, and pulled off the pavement. He flipped on his hazard lights to warn other drivers, jogged over to the stranded motorist, and made a quick assessment of her predicament. "Give me a minute. I think I can help you," he said, and set out warning devices to ensure that traffic would give them a wide berth. Getting her back on the road was a simple matter of pushing the small car just enough to get a couple of wheels onto pavement dry enough to give the tires some traction. Nothing anyone else couldn't have done if they'd only take the time to stop, he thought. *Rack up another point for the Heroes of the Highway.* He had also successfully delayed his Salt Point arrival just a little longer.

Advising the motorist to use caution when merging back into traffic, Archie watched until she was safely on her way then got underway himself. He reached the junction of Route 9 with County 41, paused, and sighed. Buck up, Super Man, he told himself, although he felt about as bold as Jimmy Olsen. Times like these he would light up a cigarette, but he'd quit when he'd met Debbie, a non-smoker. Instead, Archie popped a CD into the player. Tom Cochran's recent Top 40 hit, *Life is a Highway,* had become his go-to road tune.

Archie turned onto the winding two-lane blacktop leading to Salt Point. Narrow paths leading to gable-roofed clapboarded houses and tidy churches punctuated the stands of snow-dusted pines lining the road.

Slowly rounding the tight corner that was the junction of Hibernia Road with the turnpike, Archie immediately found himself in front of the Stenowitz home. He brought the tractor to a stop, his air brakes giving out a deep exhalation. *A nasty corner.* The intersection apparently was also the edge of the Stenowitz property, but the border of thick pines concealed the residence on the other side. Archie had assumed there was a field beyond that line of trees and would have been taken by unfortunate surprise if someone had pulled out of the driveway just as he came around the bend.

A low density neighborhood, homes zigzagged along the road. Now Archie had a problem. The Stenowitz acreage went right to the road so there was no curb, no sidewalk, and no shoulder to speak of. To leave a factory-fresh tractor in the street would invite disaster. He had no choice but to park in the driveway, blocking the garage door. Setting the parking brake and shrugging into his down vest, he locked the truck and started toward the house. Cinnamon-colored shingle siding and forest-green trim made the house look warm even under a gray winter sky. The front walkway had been shoveled and now bore just a dusting of snow. Clear patches of an iced-over pond centered in the front yard gleamed like a mirror. A good inch or two of snow frosted the limbs of the property's mature trees.

Archie climbed the steps to the covered front porch and scraped his shoes on a mat emblazoned with the word "Welcome" in a variety of scripts and languages. Before he could knock or ring a bell, Miriam Stenowitz met him at the door. In her trim tweed skirt suit she looked more formal than Archie would have expected for a Thursday afternoon.

"Archibald," she said. "We heard you pull up."

"It's Archie, Mrs. Stenowitz," he said, stepping into the small foyer. "Not Archibald."

She frowned, and her dark eyes glittered with the same hard brilliance as the leaded glass light in the heavy carved oak door. "Oh, yes. I remember Deborah telling me that. Now, uh, before I take your, uh, vest— about your truck, you simply can't leave that there. No one will be able to get in or out."

"Well, I know, but there wasn't any other place."

"Marvin, dear, Archibald is here," Miriam hollered. "And Marvin, we have a problem," Miriam padded off down the hallway, her high heels denting the clear plastic runner protecting a beige wall-to-wall carpet. Archie stood for a moment, abandoned in the foyer, then followed.

"Debbie not here?" he asked as he trailed Miriam Stenowitz. Photos in faded sepia, in high gloss black and white with serrated edges, in satin finish Kodachrome, depicting generations of the Stenowitz family decorated the eggshell walls. Toward the end of the hall before it branched off were pictures of Debbie and her younger sister Caryn as babies, as toddlers and schoolgirls, preteens and prom queens, high school and college graduates. Conspicuous in its huge gilded frame was the wedding portrait of Caryn and her husband Elliot.

Archie wondered, if he and Debbie got married, would her parents display their picture as proudly?

At the very end of the hall, a small spotlight beamed down on an empty frame soon to hold a photo of Marvin and Miriam's proudest achievement, their first grandchild, due any day now.

"Elliot, Caryn, and Debbie have gone shopping for a few last minute baby things," Miriam told Archie. "I thought they'd be home by now, but maybe the weather's got them running a bit late. I hope they're not ... Marvin. Dear." Miriam Stenowitz stopped in the doorway to her husband's den, hands on hips, tapping her foot.

At a tall walnut office armoire fitted with a keyboard tray sat a big man dressed in a gray sweater vest over a blue oxford shirt and brown trousers. Marvin Stenowitz, his bulbous nose practically glued to the glass screen of a computer monitor, held up a cautionary finger. He clattered some keys, clicked a mouse then cried, "Yeah" with all the gusto of a football fan whose team has just scored a touchdown.

Turning away from the computer, he said much more calmly, "What seems to be the problem now, Miriam? Oh, hello, Archie. I see you made it all right." He got up from his brown leather desk chair and extended a broad hand.

Archie barely got to shake it before it was snatched away again. "Yes, sir. Thank you for inviting me."

"Yes. Well, Deborah thought you should be here."

"This is what's the problem," Miriam said. She propped a knee on the sofa under a street side window and jerked up the mini blinds with a mean yank of the cord. She pointed to the huge red tractor filling the driveway.

"I see. Archie, I'm afraid you simply can't leave—" Before Marvin could finish, the phone rang. He reached behind a stack of papers and brochures piled high on the desk and picked it up. "Elliot? Something the matter? No. How can that be?"

"What? What?" Miriam said.

Marvin waved his hand for silence then ran it through his dark but thinning hair. "What's that, Elliot? OK, OK, just stay calm, we'll be right there." He hung up.

"Don't tell me. Not an accident." Miriam cried, her fist pressed against her mouth.

"Not an accident," Marvin assured her. "On the way back, Caryn went into labor. They're at the hospital."

"Oh my God," Miriam said. "I'll get my coat." She scurried down the hallway and began pulling coats and boots from the closet. "Caryn's overnight case. We need her overnight case," she said, dropping the armful of overcoats and charging up the stairs instead.

Marvin squeezed into a small teak hall chair to pull on his boots.

"Miriam, I'll go get the car out," he yelled toward the stairs. "Don't forget to turn on the alarm when you come out." He tilted his head toward the driveway. "Archie?"

"I'll go move the truck."

Archie brought the tractor as far down the driveway as possible without actually putting it into the road and shifted into neutral to wait. The garage door opened and Marvin backed out the Stenowitz's black Lincoln. Miriam emerged from the house, her coat not yet buttoned, her scarf haphazardly wound around her neck, and picked her way painstakingly on the icy sidewalk in fur-trimmed high-heeled ankle boots. Halfway down the drive, she turned, baby-stepped back to the house, and came back out, this time with the floral-patterned overnight case.

Marvin stuck his head out of the car window. "The alarm?"

Throwing up her free hand, Miriam made one more trip back.

His wife finally aboard, Marvin backed the Lincoln further down the drive. He leaned out of the window and gestured for Archie to give him more room. Archie backed into the road, the corner intersection in his blind spot no matter how much he adjusted the mirrors. A loud blast from a car horn greeted his maneuver. A Ford Bronco driven by a man wearing a red and black plaid cap with ear flaps passed Archie and nearly clipped Marvin Stenowitz as he cleared the driveway. The Bronco driver threw Marvin a middle-finger salute. Miriam flailed both hands in reply.

Sighing, Archie pulled back up the drive.

Marvin signaled "A OK" and tore off down the road.

Stunned, Archie sat half in, half out of the Stenowitz driveway.

CHAPTER THREE

RHINEBECK, NY, Thursday, February 11, 1993

Archie followed the nurse's pointing finger to Caryn Jordan's room at Pilgrims Medical Center. A patchwork quilt lay over the usual white sheets on her hospital bed, and the windows were curtained in a coordinating plaid fabric. A wooden bureau rather than a metal one, a cradle, and a rocking chair for the new mother all contributed to a homebirth atmosphere. There were a couple of comfortable chairs for visitors but they were empty. Everyone stood crowded around the bed. All of them except a man that Archie recognized from Caryn's wedding photo, her husband, Elliot. He stood shifting from foot to foot, talking into the room phone, and nervously running the fingers of his free hand through his brown hair.

"No, Aunt Esther, she just started. The contractions are minutes apart yet. Yes, we'll keep you posted."

"Archie," Debbie cried as he walked into the room. A big smile brightened her face and delight warmed her milk-chocolate brown eyes. "I'm so glad to see you." She broke away and came over to hug and kiss him. All conversation came to a halt.

"I see you found us," Marvin said.

"If there's a road leading to it, he can find it," Debbie said.

"Fortunately for me there are only two hospitals in the county with maternity wards," Archie whispered to Debbie.

She frowned at her parents. "What'd you do, run off and leave him without telling him where you were going?"

Miriam threw up her hands. "Deborah, I didn't do it intentionally. You can't expect me to think clearly at a time like this, I'm having a grandbaby. You do forgive me, Archibald, don't you?"

"Of course, Mrs. Stenowitz," he said through clenched teeth.

"Oh, call her Miriam. You don't have to be so formal. Does he, Mom? Archie, you're practically part of the family."

Miriam Stenowitz frowned.

Debbie hooked Archie's elbow and drew him closer to the bed. "And the mom-to-be, my sister Caryn."

"Caryn," he said, extending his hand.

"I was hoping I'd be on my feet for at least part of your visit, but ..." Caryn gave him a wan smile. "Sorry, I must look a mess." She patted her hair.

A little flustered, a little anxious, but certainly not a mess. Fluffy brown hair with blond streaks, round brown eyes, and a little button nose, Caryn was cute version of her big sister. Similar features, but on a smaller scale, as if in having Caryn, Miriam had produced a compact model of Debbie. Caryn had Miriam's fine-boned features whereas Debbie took after her father and was built on a sturdier frame: tall with thick hair, full lips, and an unflinching gaze. With envy in her voice, Debbie would say that her younger sister got all the looks but Archie didn't agree. Debbie had presence that he found appealing.

"And Elliot," Debbie said.

Caryn's husband was slender with an office-worker's pallor that today seemed even more pronounced. "No, Aunt Isobel, she just started," Elliot said into the phone. He shuttled the phone from his right hand to his left to accept Archie's handshake and continued his conversation. "The contractions are five minutes apart, yet. Yes, we'll keep you posted."

"Now don't have that baby just this minute, OK, Caryn?" Debbie said. "I need a few moments with my Super Man."

She led him out into the hospital corridor where she kissed him longer and more lovingly. "I'm sorry I wasn't at the house to meet you but Caryn was all *shpilkis*. Sorry, that's Yiddish for 'ants in your pants.' So we took her shopping for a distraction."

Shpilkis. *I'll have to remember that one.* Every now and then Debbie let fly with a foreign phrase that somehow said it all in a succinct and colorful way, the Yiddish ones especially. To Archie, the Yiddish saying that roughly translated to "Don't hit me with the teakettle" communicated so much more than the more timid, "don't bug me."

"So tell me, how was your trip? How's the new truck?"

"Thing rides like a dream and it's loaded: cruise control, stereo cassette and CD player, TV, refrigerator/freezer, on-board computer. And you should see the sleeper. Seventy-four inches, it's like a mobile home. C'mon, I'll show you." He took her hand.

"Deborah," Marvin's voice rose above the buzz inside the birthing room.

"Sorry, Archie. Let me go see what my Dad wants." Debbie smiled sheepishly. "I have a feeling it's going to be a little crazy around here for the next couple of days."

Only a couple of days?

CHAPTER FOUR

RHINEBECK, NY, Thursday, February 11, 1993

With a sigh, Archie wedged his six-foot frame into a too-small chair and settled in for what promised to be the longest of long hauls.

The chairs in the birthing room were not built for extended periods of sitting. Too short in the seat, too low in the back to support his legs or his lumbar. He'd be better off sitting in the truck's driver's seat for sure. Fully adjustable with arm rests and an air-ride suspension, the seat felt as if sculpted for his butt. He would definitely have to comment on that in his review. He shifted and wriggled, trying to redistribute his weight and keep his legs from going to sleep, rotated his neck and shoulders, and flexed his back.

"No, Aunt Lilly, not yet. But the contractions are getting closer," Elliot said into the phone. He looked at Caryn for confirmation.

She let out a yelp in acknowledgement. Her face was flushed and her hairline was dark with perspiration. Elliot had raked his own hair into short spikes.

Marvin rose halfway out of his chair. "Are you all right, punkin?" he asked.

"She's fine, Daddy. Caryn, you're doing fine," Debbie said, wiping her sister's brow with a damp washcloth.

Archie got up and limped over to the window on cramped legs that felt about two inches long. "Snow's still coming down," he reported.

Miriam stopped knitting, looked up and frowned, then took up her needles and started again, the aluminum needles clacking furiously.

At the rate she was going, she'd have the baby's entire wardrobe done within the hour, Archie decided. Taking his seat again, he reached for a foam cup on the end table, thinking some caffeine would ease the pounding in his head. The cup was empty.

Sighing, he picked up a *People* magazine from the stack at his elbow. It looked familiar and he realized he'd read it hours ago. He'd read every magazine in the room.

He stood up. "Debbie, I'll be right back."

All eyes turned to stare at him. Elliot broke off his report to Aunt Lilly and Caryn paused in mid-yelp.

"Where are you going?" Debbie asked.

"Just need to get something from the truck," Archie answered, backing out of the room. *So that's how the person who took the last remaining lifeboat off the Titanic felt.*

Outside, the night air was icy but he took a deep breath, clearing his lungs of the birthing room's disinfectant-and-sweat smog. Snowflakes falling and melting on his face felt refreshing. He climbed into the cab and reveled in the muffled quiet for a moment. The cab's huge sleeper, no less luxurious than a first class cabin on a cruise ship, beckoned. He'd left the bed in the couch position. Softly lit by the courtesy lamp, the plush gray velour upholstery and puffy blue and teal chintz toss pillows tempted him. He sat down and brushed his hand across the deep pile.

"Sleep," it whispered. "Sleep."

Groaning, he picked up his notebook and trudged through the snow back into the hospital.

"... seconds apart, Aunt Esther," Elliot was saying in the phone as Archie returned to the birthing room.

"How's she doing?" Archie asked of no one in particular.

From deep in the huddle, Caryn bellowed in answer.

"Well, maybe I'll go somewhere and work on my magazine story."

Five pairs of eyes fixed themselves on him and Archie thought no more accusing looks could be found outside a firing squad.

"... later, that is. Maybe," he finished.

"Ooooh, Mom, this is getting serious," Caryn moaned, her forehead wrinkled in worry and pain. Debbie dabbed away tears.

"Caryn, baby," Miriam said, patting her hand.

"I'll go get help," Debbie dashed from the room and returned with a nurse who elbowed her way in to take measurements.

"You're dilated ten centimeters now, Caryn," the nurse reported. "You can start pushing." She pulled the comforter back from the foot of the bed and racked the stirrups into place.

"I guess that's our cue to leave," Marvin said.

"No reason to," the nurse said. "Caryn can use all the support she can get."

"Oh," Elliot and Marvin said in unison, looking at the floor.

"Archibald." Miriam pointed at him with a knitting needle then waved him towards the door with it.

"I'll just go wait out there," Archie said.

"Why don't you go, too, Marv, get some rest. It's been a long night. I'll stay with her," Elliot offered.

"No, no. I'm fine," Marvin replied. "But you look like you could use a break. You go on, Elliot, I'll stay."

"Oh, no. I'm her coach. I'm staying. But if you want to go get a cup of coffee ..."

"I'm fine, but maybe you ..."

"No, not me. I'll stay right here."

"How nice for Caryn to have such wonderful support from the men in her family," the nurse said.

"If they want to be supportive, let them have the damn baby. I want to go home," Caryn shouted, straining against the pillows.

"Now, dear, you'll go home soon enough." With a practiced smile, the nurse headed for the door. "I'll go get Doctor."

"Elliot, I've changed my mind, I don't want to have a baby. Make it stop," Caryn wailed.

Elliot turned a shade paler and ran his hand through his hair, now sticking out on all sides.

"I'm never going through this again, understand?" Caryn sobbed.

Archie slunk out to the ward lobby, where the acoustics were superb. He could clearly hear Caryn screaming alternately, "Mommy" and "Elliot, you stinking sonofabitch, I hate you."

Archie crossed over to the window and watched the snow drift through the orange glow of the parking lot's sulfur lights. He looked longingly at his truck.

"Still snowing, huh?"

Archie turned to face a haggard Marvin Stenowitz.

"I would have stayed, but Caryn threw me out," Marvin explained. He took a seat.

"Elliot Jordan, it will be a cold day in hell before you ever touch me again." Caryn's voice rang out from down the hall.

Elliot came staggering into the lobby.

"Oh, God, it's awful," he said, both hands buried in his hair.

Marvin closed his eyes, pressed his palms together, and intoned some Hebrew or Yiddish phrase, followed by "Thank you, God, for not making me a woman."

There's a prayer for that?

"Amen," Elliot said with feeling.

"Elliot, get your goddamn male ass back in here. You're not getting off that easy."

Muttering "Damn, I could use a cigarette," Elliot slunk back to the birthing room.

Archie sat and picked up another magazine.

*****

"It's a boy."

Archie pried one gritty eye open. Debbie stood at his knee. Her face was drawn, lines etched deeply into her forehead and under her eyes, but her eyes shone.

"Mother and son are doing fine," she continued.

Archie smiled. "That's great, Debbie. Can we go home now?"

"Home? You mean back to the house?"

"No, I mean home home. Tampa."

"Archie, don't be silly. Didn't you hear me? It's a boy. We're staying for the *brit.*"

"The brit," Archie echoed, still groggy.

"The ritual circumcision? You said you understood it's important, that you would stay."

Right, Archie thought, realizing he'd been hoping for a girl. Debbie had explained how her new nephew would be inducted into the faith. As upsetting as a baptism could be for babies, it had nothing on what this little guy was in for.

"And I better get busy," Debbie said. "We've got just barely eight days to pull it together."

Eight more days. More than enough for me and the Stenowitzes to get acquainted. But it would take a lifetime to win them over.

Archie let his eyelids drop.

CHAPTER FIVE

SALT POINT, NY, Friday, February 12, 1993

Archie woke to a strong smell of oil paint. He shivered. The cold light coming from a north-facing window didn't contribute much warmth and neither did the colorful quilt that covered him, it being more decorative than functional. The cot he'd slept on was too short to support his feet. He lifted his head to see that he was surrounded by canvasses, easels, empty frames, palettes, turpentine-filled jars of brushes.

An artist's studio?

No, just a sun porch in the Stenowitz house, converted into a workroom to accommodate Miriam Stenowitz's landscape-painting hobby.

Struggling to bring his cramped body to a sitting position Archie upset the flimsy cot. It slid out from under him and skidded into an easel, sending it and the canvas it supported crashing to the floor.

He heard "What on earth?" and the floor creaked under approaching footsteps. Debbie appeared in the doorway, her flannel travel robe belted crookedly over a sleep tee. "Oh, Archie."

"I'm OK," he grumbled, picking himself up and brushing at his thermal underwear. He righted the easel and propped the canvas back on it. "I hope this is."

Debbie examined the painting and declared it unharmed.

Archie rubbed at his tailbone.

"Archie, you did hurt yourself."

"No, I'm fine. It's just that—"

"The cot wasn't very comfortable, was it?"

He shook his head.

"I'm sorry about that. I should have warned you. When we got home last night, Mom told me she didn't feel right about us sharing a room. I would have debated it with her but I was so tired."

"We all were."

"I'll take it up with her today."

Archie nodded. He ran a finger along the side of the painting-in-progress, a rural road winding past a small horse farm with a red mansard-roofed barn and a white fence.

"Pretty," he said. "I think I drove past this yesterday."

"You probably did. Mom does a lot of local landscapes. They're getting popular in The City. It would be great if more people knew about them."

"I'll bet." He cocked his head left and right, looking at the painting from different angles. "It gives you a peaceful feeling. Like just at daylight, before the rest of the world is up."

"Thank you," came Miriam's voice from the doorway. "That's just the effect I was going after." She came into the room. In contrast with her appearance yesterday, she looked calm and collected in a green quilted satin robe and matching heeled slippers.

She noticed the overturned cot. "Oh, Archibald, I'm sorry. I can see this isn't a very good arrangement for you but I can't think where we're going to put you. Elliot and Caryn have the second bedroom and Deborah's in the third." She folded her hands over her stomach. "Now I know how things are for you and Deborah in Tampa, but I'm afraid I just don't feel it's proper."

"Mother."

Miriam pressed her lips together. "Deborah, I know you think I'm hopelessly old fashioned, but that's how I feel." She beamed a stern look at Archie. "I think you understand, don't you?"

"I understand perfectly." *Do I ever. It's going to be a very long eight days.*

Miriam nodded and smiled. "Good. Meanwhile, everyone is up and on the move and it's about time we all were. We have a busy day ahead of us. Breakfast is ready when you are."

Archie cleaned himself up as best he could in the powder room. His duffle bag and Dopp kit were still in the truck which was still in the hospital parking lot. He hadn't thought to grab them when Marvin insisted that Archie ride home in the Lincoln and leave the truck behind. Scruffy-jawed, in yesterday's flannel shirt, jeans, and boots, he joined Debbie and Miriam, still in their robes, at the breakfast bar. Marvin was nowhere in sight but the sounds of computer keyboard clicking and clacking suggested his whereabouts.

A dent had been made in what had been a big spread of assorted bagels, flavored cream cheeses, and smoked fish. A clean empty coffee cup and a full glass of orange juice marked Archie's place.

"Make you an omelet, Archibald?" Miriam offered.

"No thanks, Mir ... Mrs. ... Ma'am," he said, but Miriam went to the range and started scrambling eggs anyway.

"Just eat it," Debbie whispered. "She'll be offended if you refuse her food."

The phone rang.

"I'll get it, Mom," Debbie said.

Archie sipped his juice, scanned the headlines of the *Poughkeepsie Journal,* and tried to read upside down what was written on several legal pads scattered amongst the baskets of bagels. Lists, lots of lists.

"That was Edna and Frank," Debbie announced. "Elliot's parents," she said to Archie. "They'll be here tomorrow, in case we need help."

"Tomorrow? They can't come tomorrow," Miriam cried. "I won't be ready for them. The house isn't clean, I have nothing in the refrigerator."

The reason why there was nothing in the refrigerator, Archie thought, was because it was all laid out on the breakfast bar.

"Take it easy, Mom. I'll help. That's what Archie and I are here for, to help."

Archie did the best he could to smile agreeably with a mouth full of eggs.

"So, what's on the agenda today, Mom?" Debbie asked.

Miriam replied, "Elliot's bringing Caryn and the baby home from the hospital this afternoon."

"So soon?" Archie asked. To Debbie, he whispered, "Can I have more juice?"

Miriam said, "Yes, it's outrageous. A woman barely gets a chance to catch her breath and they send her home with a new baby. That's why I wanted Caryn here, so she can take her time about recuperating and I can take care of her." She picked up Archie's bagel plate as well as his juice glass and coffee cup although he was about to pour more. He wolfed down his omelet for fear it would be snatched away too. "So, I've got to get the house cleaned and bake and—"

Debbie said, "Mom, don't panic. I can clean."

"—get dinner started," Miriam continued. "We really should have all the family here for the baby's first Shabbat but it's so last minute and people can't get a flight out on a Friday and with this weather everywhere messing everything up. Esther and Isobel won't be here until Sunday and Lilly—Marvin, when is Lilly arriving?"

"Well, they'll all be here next Friday, Mom," Debbie said.

"Friday?" Archie said, working the math in his head. To Debbie he whispered, "Shouldn't eight days be Thursday?"

"The baby was born after sundown," Debbie said. "Twilight, to be precise."

"Oh." That *Fiddler on the Roof* song had it wrong. It wasn't "Sunrise, Sunset." Jewish "days" went from sundown to sundown.

"Now that's going to be a busy day, what with the seudat after the brit and then Shabbat," said Miriam.

"Mom, take it easy. One Friday at a time."

"You're right." Miriam picked up one of the legal pads. "Let's see—I've got the chicken defrosting, the gefilte fish chilling, green beans to almondine, challah ... oh, I've got to pick up a challah. Marvin, Marvin, I need you to pick me up a challah."

From the other room, Marvin hollered back, "Miriam, I'm working over here." An investment counselor, Marvin had moved his successful New York City practice to the Hudson Valley. With a phone, a fax machine, and now the Internet, her father could really work from anywhere, Debbie had explained.

"Oh, and it's snowing. Still. Can you believe it? We need to keep the driveway and the walkway clear."

"Mom, don't worry. I can shovel. Archie can shovel."

"I, uh, I need to get my truck," Archie said. If it kept snowing like this, he was going to have to chain the tires, never a fun task.

Miriam replied, "Marvin will have to take you. Marvin," she called. "Archibald needs to get his truck. You'll have to drive him back to the hospital. Where are you going to park it, Archibald? You can't leave it in the driveway, we're going to have people coming and going all weekend."

Dressed for the day in slacks, a crew neck sweater over a collared shirt, socks and loafers, Marvin appeared at the breakfast bar.

"I'll work something out," Archie said.

Marvin reached for a bagel half. "All right, Miriam, but the hospital's in Rhinebeck and the bakery's in Kingston and I don't have time to do both today."

Miriam frowned. "Marvin, we can't have Shabbat without a challah."

"I can go to the bakery once I get my truck," Archie said. "Just point me in the right direction."

Miriam smiled with surprise and pleasure. "Why, thank you, Archibald. That's one problem solved."

*****

"Thanks for letting me leave that here last night," Archie said.

"Glad I could help," replied Emmet Benhopf. Pilgrims Medical Center's security chief tugged the hem of his blue twill bomber-style jacket down over his round belly. "You will be moving that today though, won't you? 'Cause over the weekend, I can't be responsible."

"I understand. I'm moving it now, as a matter of fact."

Emmet smiled. "So would now be a good time?" he asked. "I got a break coming up."

"Now's as good a time as any," Archie replied. Regulations prohibited unauthorized passengers but as the owner-operator, Archie figured he could decide who qualified.

Carefully navigating narrow roads quickly filling up with snow, Archie gave the security chief a ride in the Kenworth all the way into Hyde Park to Haviland Middle School where Emmet's wife worked in the principal's office. Franklin Delano Roosevelt himself had been involved in the planning, building, and dedication of the school and it looked it, with its stately red brick, gabled roof, white trimmed windows, columned portico, and steeple. Emmet would not be satisfied except that his wife got to work the truck's air horn to the delight of all her co-workers.

On the way back to the hospital, Archie asked, "Say, what's a nice motel around Salt Point? One with truck parking?" Near as he could tell, the closest truck stop was back south of Poughkeepsie, and on the other side of the Hudson. He didn't see himself making that drive twice a day.

"Thought you were staying with your in-laws."

"They're not my in-laws."

"Aw, you and your girl, you look so together, I just figured you was married."

Archie smiled. "Her parents' house is getting pretty crowded. Out-of-town guests coming in the next week. And there's no room to park the truck. So, what would you suggest?"

"That's easy," said Emmet. "Ain't none in Salt Point. Closest is Hyde Park. There's only two open this time of year, The Super-Stay and the Hyde Park Manor. Both on 9, practically within spittin' distance of each other. Why anyone needs two motels that close together?"

"Competition?"

"Competition," Emmet agreed. "The Super-Stay's OK. It's one of those national chain places, you know the kind."

Archie nodded. He'd probably spent a night in a Super-Stay on a long haul or two.

"I'd try the Manor. The Soons, they run the place. They're good people and they could use the business."

*****

The Hyde Park Manor was a vaguely U-shaped facility separated from the neighboring Super-Stay by a small wooded area about a mile wide. Both properties sat directly across Route 9 from the Franklin Delano Roosevelt Home. The Hyde Park Manor had two wings of rooms, the right one backing up to the woods, with the lobby between the two wings.

Nisha Soon held down the reception desk.

"Rooms? You need rooms? No problem," she said, the slurring of her Rs and Ls being the only sign of an Asian accent. "The Hyde Park Manor is not exactly what you call busy this time of year. Not that this isn't a nice place," she hastened to add. "Come, I show you."

She called for her daughter, Trini, to mind the front desk and grabbed a huge ring of keys. Archie followed as Nisha pointed out the various amenities.

"Here in the lobby we always have coffee and tea available." She pointed to a self-serve coffee bar. "And here is where you will find our complimentary continental breakfast buffet, six to nine, during the season. This isn't the season so you can take your time about getting out here."

She was right; some of the morning's buffet was still in evidence. An opened box of Daisy Donuts, from which one was missing, and a half-gallon jug of orange drink remained on the bar. A large empty glass pickle jar labeled TIPS held a single dollar bill. It looked lonely and when Nisha turned her back Archie tucked another one inside.

She led him outside past the newspaper machines which offered *The Poughkeepsie Journal* and a local shopper. The dispensers were empty. There were also dispensers for the big city papers: *Barron's, The Daily News, The New York Times.* They were full.

Nisha took him to the right wing of rooms and opened one for his inspection. The basic double bed flanked by night stands, a small table and chair, a bureau, not fancy, but clean.

"We have satellite," she said, pointing to the television. "We get better reception than people around here get in their homes."

"Well, this is nice but I don't need a room. All I really need is a place to park my truck. Do you suppose? ..."

"Sure, you can leave it here, park it on the side there. No one will bother it." She locked the door to the room. "Now, we don't have a restaurant on the premises but the Town and Country's just a mile down the road. Food's just like home cooking and they're the only place open for breakfast this time of year. You tell them Nisha at the Manor sent you, your coffee will be on the house. They serve lunch and dinner, too, or you could go to Coppola's, that's just across the street. Nice place—eat by candlelight. And for the best pizza in town, also the only pizza in town, you must try Giorgio's Honest Italian."

"Sounds authentic," Archie said. He was here in New York, he was duty bound to have New York pizza.

Nisha smiled. "It is. It's the most authentic Italian pizza my husband Pacifico knows how to make."

*****

Archie's errand to get challah bread sent him to Kingston. The trip over the Kingston-Rhinecliff Bridge cost him a toll but it was worth it for the view of the Hudson River. From that perspective, the river's history as a major transportation artery was easy to appreciate.

Even more rewarding was when he stepped through the door of Frieda's European Bakery and became eight years old again, the aromas of sugar, vanilla, and baking bread were that magical. Facing the door, cases of cakes, cookies, and pastries stood about half full. Along the wall, shelves of wire baskets held breads in various shapes and colors.

Archie stepped up to the counter. "I'd like a challah bread, please." The name for the traditional egg bread without which, apparently, no Friday night meal was complete, began with a guttural consonant that was somewhere between an "H" and a gargle. Try as he might, he simply could not pronounce it with quite the finesse that Debbie and her parents managed. You have to be born into it, Debbie told him.

The woman behind the counter was Frieda herself, according to the name plate pinned to her floral print dress. A small woman with salt and pepper hair, she wore bulky orthopedic shoes and the white apron over her dress bore stains in various shades of chocolate, strawberry, and grape. "Plain or poppy-seed challah? The sweet ones are all gone. You want a sweet one, you have to get in here before noon."

"I'll remember that. Plain, then."

"Sliced or unsliced?"

"I'm not sure," Archie replied, certain he would get it wrong and irrevocably alienate Debbie's mother.

Frieda said, "Unsliced stays fresher longer."

"Make it unsliced." The long loaf was golden in color, glossy with an egg-wash glaze, and braided from six ropes of dough. Debbie had told him that there were many explanations for the design. One, she said, was that the six strands stood for the days of the week that weren't a day of rest because God had spent them creating. The braiding represented His work's culmination and the intertwining of all the elements of Creation.

"Smells great in here," Archie said.

Frieda smiled. "That's the vanilla. I'm baking cookies."

Archie took a deep breath. "Mind if I stand here and just inhale a while? I haven't been in a bakery since I was a kid."

Frieda said, "That's too long." From a tray, she took a thick round cookie glazed half with chocolate, half vanilla, and handed it over the counter. "Come more often."

"Ma'am, you've just taken thirty years off my life."

"That's what a good cookie should do. Sit, enjoy. Would you like a cup of coffee to wash that down with?"

"I would, thanks." Archie took his beverage and snack to a table in the bakery's dining room. When he was finished, he brought his cup back to the counter and pulled out his wallet to pay for the bread. He pointed to a large heart-shaped cookie with pink frosting. "I think I'd better have one of those also."

"For your Valentine?"

Archie nodded and Frieda winked.

A man pushing a cart of baked goods to restock the shelves entered from a door behind the counter between the bread racks. Balding and pale, he was thinner than Archie would have imagined possible for someone who worked in a bakery.

"Say, that your truck?" the man asked. "It's a beaut. I used to drive long haul, but the doc said if I didn't give it up I'd drive myself into an early grave from stress. Isn't that right, Frieda?

"That's right, Lyle."

"Hey, I'd really like to get a look inside."

"It would be my pleasure."

*****

Archie crawled back to the Stenowitz house through the seemingly ceaseless snow. Warm air scented with fragrant cooking aromas greeted him when he opened the door. Blue "It's a Boy" balloons and cheerful floral arrangements crowded the entry hall. Carrying his duffle and a change of clothing inside, he made his cautious way through the house in search of Debbie. As he passed the kitchen, Mrs. Stenowitz blocked his path.

"Oh, Archibald. Thank you for getting the bread." She took the bakery bag and set it on the kitchen island. "I wonder, would you be so kind as to tackle the driveway and the walk? Marvin worked on it when he got back from the hospital with Caryn but this snow just doesn't seem to want to quit."

"Not a problem," Archie said. *So much for surprising Debbie with the heart-shaped cookie.* Well, he would give it to her after supper.

Though it was cold enough to snow, he worked up quite a sweat shoveling. Wanting little more than a hot shower and a change of clothing, Archie stowed the snow shovel in the garage and went upstairs to see where he might get cleaned up.

From a bedroom to his right he heard Caryn's strained voice. "Debbie, I had no idea. God, I hurt so bad. The only position I'm comfortable in is lying on my side, or my stomach. Edna and Frank will be here tomorrow. Mother's got Elliot calling the entire family tree to come for the brit and I can't even sit up, much less stand."

He heard Debbie reply, "Stop stressing. The brit's a week away. You'll feel much better by then. Anyhow, no one expects you to be hostess with the mostest. Just be a new mother, that's all. Not worry is what you are going to do. I'm here. You need something, you ask me."

"Some visit this is turning out to be for you. Not to mention Archibald."

"Archie. Don't worry about him, my Super Man is a patient guy."

"Superman? That's quite a claim. How'd he get a nickname like that?

Debbie replied, "It's his CB handle. I gave it to him. My Man of Steel." Debbie chuckled and Archie could almost hear her wink. "I'm talking about his equipment, of course. You know, his truck."

Caryn chortled. "Deborah, you slut. Oh, don't make me laugh, it hurts too much."

As tempted as he was to continue eavesdropping, Archie cleared his throat. Debbie stepped into the hallway.

"Oh, there you are," she said. "Did you find everything OK? Of course you did. Say, are you feeling all right? You looked flushed, you're perspiring."

"I was shoveling."

Debbie gave him a hug. "Aren't you just the sweetest?"

"Your sister doing OK? I should go in and say 'hi,' see the baby."

"Mmm, not such a good idea. A little later, maybe. She's really in no mood for company. She's going to be OK but she did have to have an episiotomy."

"Episi ... what?"

"I'll spare you the intimate details. Just take it from me, she's not a happy postpartum camper. So, what would you like? A hot shower? A bath? Can I bring you a coffee or maybe a beer?

A bath and a beer? Archie thought he might just make it through till next week.

Cleaned and changed, Archie made his way downstairs and found that someone had been busy in the dining room. With its white table cover and cloth napkins, the dining table looked like a winter landscape. Soft light from the crystal chandelier gleamed in silver-trimmed white china and polished silverware. A few inches of red wine turned cut-crystal goblets into ruby jewels. A soup tureen and platter holding a roast chicken sat at the center. In ornate silver candlesticks, two white candles yet to be lit stood at one end of the table.

In the kitchen, Archie found Debbie tossing a salad and Miriam placing the bread on a tray. Elliot sat at the breakfast bar making notes on a lined yellow tablet.

"Work?" Archie asked.

Elliot grimaced. "No one told the idiots of the world that I'm on paternity leave. Some fool got himself arrested for possession." Elliot shook his head. "You have got to be some kind of dumb ass to get pulled over for a traffic violation with pot in your car. Well, if it weren't for dumb asses I wouldn't have a job so ... Let's see who was dumber here, my client or the cops who arrested him without due process." He shrugged and returned to scribbling.

"Archibald, thank you for that cookie," Miriam said. "How did you know I needed a snack? But wouldn't they slice the bread for you?

Archie sighed. *So much for my early Valentine's Day surprise for Debbie.* "I didn't know what you would want and Frieda recommended unsliced."

"Let me fix that for you, Mom." Elliot pulled a bread knife from a wooden block and tackled the loaf. His first slice came out crushed and ragged. "Damn it," he grumbled.

"Oh, don't feel bad, Elliot," Miriam said. "I've never had much luck with that knife."

"Maybe it just needs sharpening," Archie said. He saw that the knife block included a tapered honing steel. "Let me see."

With a frown, Elliot passed him the bread knife. Archie took the knife in one hand and the steel in the other. With short light strokes, he tackled each of the teeth in the knife's serrated edge, flipped over the knife, and polished off the burrs, smoothing the back. "There, that should work better for you." He handed it to Miriam.

A skeptical look on her face, she pulled the knife through the oblong loaf of braided bread. A neat slice fell onto the bread tray. The look on her face was worth the price of admission, Archie thought.

She wrapped one portion in a white cloth and placed it on a small tray with a wine glass. "Elliot, dear, take this up to your wife." Miriam wrapped the remainder of the loaf in a white cloth and brought it to the dining table. "Marvin," she hollered, "call it a day. It's almost Shabbat. I'm lighting the candles."

Shabbat, Archie had learned, was the day of rest Jewish-style, and observed not on Sunday but from sundown Friday to sundown Saturday.

Marvin came to the table from the den, Elliot from upstairs, and everyone sat except Miriam. She draped a lace scarf on her head and stood at the end of the table where she lit the candles. She waved her hands as if to pull the light to her, then covered her face and murmured something in Hebrew. She lowered her hands and Archie thought her face looked slightly more serene. Smiling, she picked up the candlesticks and moved them to the buffet.

Marvin lifted his wine glass and said another cryptic prayer, then unwrapped the bread. He looked at Archie with a stern expression. "What, they wouldn't slice the bread for you?"

Before Archie could explain, Miriam said, "It's not a problem, dear. Elliot, could you cut a slice for Marvin?"

Frowning, his lips pressed together, Elliot drew the knife through the bread. When an even slice dropped onto the plate, he tackled the rest of the loaf with gusto, smiling proudly.

"Thank you, Elliot, that's perfect. See, Marvin? I think we'll be getting unsliced from now on. It will stay fresher longer."

Marvin passed the bread plate and said yet a third prayer. Archie was all for saying grace before a meal but was glad when the Stenowitzes started reaching for food dishes. Miriam whisked the wine glasses and bread plates off to the kitchen. At the sound of water splashing, Marvin said, "Miriam, come sit down already."

Miriam returned and they ladled soup from a tureen into bowls. "Is the soup too salty?" she asked. "It's too salty, isn't it?"

Debbie sighed. "It's fine, Mom, it always is. I wish I could make soup this good. Yours is the best. Isn't hers the best, Archie?

Faced with a question impossible to answer, Archie pretended his mouth was too full to speak.

Miriam said, "You think Caryn's going to find it all right?" She half rose from her seat.

"Mom, she'll be fine," Debbie said. "I'll go check on her in a minute. Now relax."

Instead of relaxing, Miriam cleared the soup bowls and took them into the kitchen.

Marvin cried, "Miriam, will you leave the dishes and come sit down?"

"I just hate to leave a sink full of dishes," came the reply from the kitchen.

Marvin hollered so he could be heard over the running water. "For five minutes you can leave them. Relax already, spend a little time with your daughter. It's not as if we get to see her every week." He picked up the carving knife. "Elliot, would you care to do the honors?"

"My pleasure." Elliot stood, took the carving knife, and tackled the chicken, tearing at the meat.

Having watched his father a thousand times, Archie knew the best way to carve up poultry was to remove the thigh and leg pieces first then separate the white meat from the breastbone so that nice uniform slices could be cut from the breast. "Maybe that knife could use some sharpening too."

Elliot seemed reluctant to part with the utensil and Archie had to almost forcibly wrest it from the man's hand. He took it into the kitchen and gave it a few swipes with the sharpening steel. Back at the table he severed the leg joints, made the starter slice against the breastbone, and returned the knife to Elliot who still managed to butcher the job.

Miriam returned to her seat and passed plates down the table. "You're right, Marvin." To Debbie she said, "We see so little of you, dear, you live so far away and you're always so busy working."

Debbie was the customer service manager for a carrier, which was how she and Archie had met. She researched a shipper's complaint and Archie had been the driver on that load. The graceful way she handled the matter impressed him.

"It's so good to have you here, dear. You, too, Archibald. And right after dinner, we'll figure out what to do about the sleeping arrangements. I can see that the cot in my studio isn't going to work. Perhaps the couch in the den? Marvin, you won't mind if Archie sleeps on the couch in your office, would you?"

"Problem's already solved, Ma'am. I'll spend the night in the truck. I can park it at the Hyde Park Manor."

Debbie, who had been making up plates for her sister and brother-in-law, looked up. "You did what? Aw, Mom, now look what you've done. You've made Archie feel like he's not welcome here."

"I did no such thing."

"That's OK. There's plenty of room in the sleeper."

"Room for me too?" Debbie asked.

Archie smiled. *Valentine's Day might not suck after all.*

Miriam pouted. "Deborah, I need you here with me and Caryn. I'm sure Archibald understands."

Debbie's head swiveled between her mother and Archie.

"I believe I do," Archie said. In his mind's eye, the pink-frosted heart-shaped cookie from Frieda's fluttered away on Cupid's wings.

CHAPTER SIX

HYDE PARK, NY, Saturday, February 13, 1993

Archie woke feeling not quite as refreshed as he would have liked. The Kenworth's sleeper was first rate; he had no complaints about that. The sill was high enough that he hadn't even had to duck to get into the sleeper berth and he couldn't criticize the mattress's cushioning. Tinted and curtained windows kept the interior sufficiently dark. For the trucker looking to spare the cost of a motel room, it was more than adequate. Still, it was just a sleeper in a truck. Local limits on idling meant he couldn't run the truck's heater. The auxiliary power unit did a good enough job of keeping the cab warm but it was noisy. Turning it off just let the cab get too cold during a below-freezing night. It sure wasn't the bed at home that he shared with Debbie.

All the same, it was a job well done. Reporting on the sleeper berth was on *American Big Rig's* vehicle evaluation checklist. Now he'd be able to write up that experience.

He loosened up with some calisthenics on the cab floor and some exercises for his back, making a mental note to comment that the cab offered enough room to do that. He threw on a pair of sweats and headed for the Hyde Park Manor lobby. Light snow had added to yesterday's accumulation. Archie spied a shovel leaning against the wall alongside the lobby entrance and gave the walkway a quick clearing, the least he could do in return for the use of the Manor's parking lot.

There being no guests, the little lobby was deserted. Nevertheless, Nisha had provided the "complimentary breakfast": a carafe of coffee and a box of donuts. Archie filled a Styrofoam cup of coffee from the pot and selected a glazed raised. It certainly wasn't the spread that Miriam Stenowitz set out. On the other hand, no one snatched Archie's plate before crumbs could hit it, either.

He availed himself of the lobby's men's room for a "cat lick" bath. The Kenworth had plenty of amenities but it was a working truck, not an RV; it didn't have a head or a shower. At the motel's sink, he swabbed his armpits with a washcloth, shaved, brushed his teeth, and rinsed his hair, ducking under the warm air hand blower to dry. A real shower would have to wait until he got to the Stenowitz's.

Back at the truck, he started the engine and got the heater warming the cab while he caught up his logbook. He was racking up a lot of off duty time. Too bad he couldn't bank it against long hauls whose delivery deadlines made taking the legally-required breaks impractical.

Archie checked all the gauges, and tested the air brake system. He turned on all the lights and stepped outside to confirm that they worked. In the thin light of a chilly morning, he walked around the truck inspecting the tires, wheels, suspension, brakes. It was a new truck and he didn't expect to find anything out of order, but you never knew and anyway it was mandatory. The inspection took longer than usual because he kept stopping to wipe spots off the bright work of which there was a lot. His equipment wouldn't be giving him any trouble today, that was for certain.

He spotted a dark Buick Riviera entering the parking lot. It parked at the main entrance and the driver stepped out. Of medium height, in a gimme cap pulled low on his forehead and a puffy dark blue parka, he wasn't remarkable. After only a few minutes in the lobby, he emerged munching on a donut and got back into his car. Asked about rates, Archie guessed.

He watched the guy pull back onto the highway then turn into the drive leading to the FDR Park. *Tourist?* Unless the man was a winter weather nut or a rabid history buff, he had picked a fine time to be vacationing in Hyde Park.

Archie headed down the road. In the rear view mirror he spotted the Buick leaving the grounds of the FDR Park. *That had been a short tour.* Maybe the place was closed for the season or the guy just wasn't that big on history after all.

Archie headed north toward the Town and Country diner. It was hard not to notice the southbound traffic, a veritable caravan of white utility trucks. *Some big installation? On a Saturday? Maybe a major outage? In any case, someone was getting a lot of overtime today.*

The sight of the diner made Archie smile. There was just something delightful about classic roadside eateries. *Was it the architecture, the quaint glass block walls, and the chrome grille work? Maybe it was the curving roofline that conjured up images of a railroad dining car and inspired thoughts of more leisurely, pampered travel. Or perhaps it was the thought of strong hot coffee in a substantial ceramic mug, and the prospect of a close-to-home-cooked meal served by a good-natured gal who would call him "Hon" and "Dearie" while a jukebox played old country-western tunes or doo-wop.*

The aroma of warm buttered toast greeted him when he stepped into the foyer. The cashier/hostess station was busy with diners settling their tabs. Past the hostess station stretched the coffee shop with its booths parallel to the street side at the left, the counter and grill opposite, the kitchen behind that. The heads of cooks with their hair covered in bandanas, netting, or caps could be seen on the other side of the pass-through window. Music from a country radio station in the kitchen competed with the cooks' chatter. To Archie's right, a short hall led to a dining room and catering hall with tables and chairs.

The Saturday morning breakfast crowd filled the booths: families with kids scarfing up pancakes and waffles, couples splitting oversized omelets. At the counter, farmers, ranchers, and homeowners in work clothes took a break between early-morning chores or trips to the hardware and feed stores.

Archie grabbed a vacant counter stool and picked up a menu illustrated with a silhouette of FDR's profile, a cigarette holder clenched in his mouth. A waitress came by with the coffee pot and a cup.

"Good morning. What can I get you?" asked Bonnie, or so proclaimed the engraved black plastic nameplate pinned to her pink uniform. In her early twenties, she had dark hair and eyes. She wore several pairs of earrings and pendant necklaces, all bearing charms, crystals, ankhs, and amulets.

"I'd like the waffle special, please. And, uh, milk."

"Coming right up." Bonnie turned to the cooks at the grill behind her and hollered, "One checkerboard special." She grabbed a tulip-shaped glass and filled it with milk from a chrome dispenser. "No coffee? You're sure?"

Archie shook his head. "I'm sure."

"Let me guess," said Bonnie. "You're staying at the Manor and you've already had plenty?"

"That's right? How'd you know?"

Bonnie smiled. "I'm psychic. Also, I read auras, palms, and tarot cards."

Gee, who would have ever suspected? "And what's my aura tell you today?"

Bonnie screwed up her face in concentration. "Give me a minute." She went down the line of diners at the counter, refilling coffee cups, then came back. "It's a little brown today. You're tense."

"Could be too much of Nisha's coffee."

"Nah. You're stressed."

Intrigued, Archie leaned an elbow on the counter. "Yeah, what am I stressed about?"

Bonnie replied, "Give me your palm."

Archie held his right hand out.

"No, the other one."

Archie shrugged and extended his left hand, palm up.

Bonnie took it in her strong hand and traced his palm with an index finger, its nail long and painted with a custom job and studded with a tiny silver half-moon. "Problems with your love life. Am I right?

Archie jerked back his hand and picked up the clean coffee cup at his place. "Maybe I'll have that coffee after all."

Bonnie shook her head. "Ought to have a nice herb tea. Got a camomile with some soothing properties I can offer you.

"You're the doctor."

Bonnie pushed the swinging door into the kitchen, and reappeared a few moments later with a tea cup. "It's my own special blend. I grow and dry the herbs myself." She grabbed his breakfast plate from under the heat lamp and a metal pitcher of syrup and set his breakfast before him. "So, that your rig out there?"

The older man at Archie's right followed her glance.

"It's a beaut," said Bonnie. "Looks new. You deadheading?"

"At the moment. I'm on a working vacation. I'm writing a review."

Bonnie's eyebrows went up. "You're a writer? A journalist?"

"You could say that," Archie replied. *She could say that. No one else was likely to.* "Actually I'm in the area for a few days visiting. The Stenowitzes in Salt Point. Know them?

Bonnie shook her head. "Can't say that I do."

"Hibernia Road and County 13? Right on the corner there?"

"Oh, the old Studebakker place."

Archie said, "Whatever. Marvin Stenowitz, he's an investment counselor. Moved with his wife up from New York City to get out of the rat race. Runs his business via computer."

Bonnie nodded. "Hudson Valley Mutants."

"How's that?"

Bonnie chuckled. "Transplants. You know." She winked and moved off to take a new order.

He poured syrup on his waffle.

"So, you're a journalist who writes about trucks?" said the man to Archie's right.

"More a trucker who writes," Archie replied. Even as a kid he'd thought he'd like to be a reporter. Like most boys his age, he was a fan of *Superman,* but he was almost as interested in reporter Clark Kent and the goings-on at the newspaper as he was in the superhero. A veteran, Archie spent his GI bill pursing a journalism degree, one night-school course at a time, while making a living with the more practical heavy-vehicle driving experience he had earned as a Navy motor transport operator. He never did complete the degree, but the dream hadn't died. He hoped that his story for *American Big Rigs* would be the first of many bylines that could shoehorn him into a journalism career. He held out his hand. "Archie Harlanson."

The man returned the greeting. "Good to meet you, Archie. Leonard Peerman. Local or long-haul?"

"Long haul. Owner-operator."

"Now that's not an easy job. You gotta drive and have a head for business. Bet you've eaten in your share of truck stops and diners, but you won't get any better food than right here at the T&C."

Archie would be inclined to agree. Too bad he wasn't reviewing restaurants instead of trucks. Both the bacon and the waffle had been crisp and the eggs cooked to over-medium perfection.

In his plaid flannel shirt, puffy vest, and plaid wool cap with ear flaps, Leonard Peerman reminded Archie of his late father and his Midwestern contemporaries. They spent their Saturday morning breaks holding down counter stools just like these, albeit in the Kozy Korner café a thousand miles and a time zone away. "You farm?"

"Used to. Got to be too much for an old guy like me. Sold it. Kids didn't want it. They'll be a lot happier with the money I got for it." He set down his newspaper, a copy of the *Daily Freeman,* and picked up his cigarette. "Looking to invest it, parlay it into something worth leaving, so I'm watching the market every day."

"If you want a little help with that, my father-in-law's an investment counselor."

"So I heard you say."

"Well, he's not exactly my father-in-law, not yet."

"She hasn't said 'yes,' your girl?"

"I haven't asked her yet. I thought, maybe tomorrow."

Leonard Peerman winked. "Valentine's Day."

"Anyhow, if you want investment advice, her dad's just over in Salt Point. Marvin Stenowitz. The way Debbie tells it, he does know what he's doing."

"I'll look him up. What was that name again?" He patted his vest, then looked across to the fellow at Archie's left. "Hey, fella, can I borrow your pen a minute?"

The man handed it over. The farmer wrote "M. Stenowitz Salt Point" on his newspaper and returned the pen. "Thanks." He stubbed out his cigarette, laid some money on the counter, picked up his meal ticket and newspaper, and slid from his stool. "And thank you," he said to Archie.

"Don't mention it. Good luck."

On the other stool, the man who had lent the pen to Leonard Peerman picked at a bismark with his left hand and scribbled on a lined yellow tablet with his right. He caught Archie eyeing the imposing looking camera perched on the counter next to his plate. "Some game, huh?"

"Excuse me?"

"Last night's high school basketball game?" The fellow correctly read Archie's baffled expression because he said, "Oh right, you're not from around here." The young man laid down his pen and held out his hand. "Name's Lincoln. Linc Haybens, *Valley Voice*."

"Archie Harlanson. So you're a reporter?" Linc Haybens didn't look like a reporter. More like a college athlete. Say, track. And older than a student. Maybe a coach. His puffy black Afro was definitely more seventies than nineties but it did balance his lean, angular face.

Haybens nodded and took a sip from his coffee cup. Tapping out a cigarette, he offered the pack to Archie, who shook his head. The reporter lit up.

"I thought reporters use those little itty bitty notebooks." Archie pictured Clark Kent and Lois Lane flipping back the covers of narrow lined pads spiral-bound across the top.

Haybens shrugged. "My handwriting's nasty. I need more room to scribble. Otherwise I get back from an interview and find I can't read what I wrote."

"Why not record the interview?"

"A lot of people don't like being recorded. And it's annoying to scroll through a tape to find the bit that I want. Handwritten notes are easier."

"So you cover sports?"

"Sports, events, new businesses. I do features. You know, a longer in-depth article on a particular topic. Whatever I think will make interesting reading." He took a drag. "The *Voice* is a weekly and by the time the paper comes out on Thursday, what was happening a week ago is old news." He grinned at Archie. "An out-of-towner with a flashy red rig might be enough for a story. Whatcha picking up?"

"Nothing at the moment. I'm just in the area because my girl is having a baby. I mean, her sister is."

"A new baby?" Haybens' eyebrows went up. He parked his cigarette and for a moment it looked like he was about to reach for his pen to get all the details, but instead he snagged another bite of bismark.

"Do you write about the arts at all?" Archie asked.

"Yeah. Gallery openings, new exhibits, art festivals. Why?"

"The new baby's grandmother is a painter. Landscapes. I don't know much about art but I think they look good and I guess she's getting to be pretty popular."

Haybens narrowed his eyes. "And you think you can suck up to her by getting her some publicity."

"Well, I just thought—"

Haybens elbowed him in the ribs. "I'm just giving you a hard time. Seriously, you might be right. That might make a nice story. What's her name?"

"Miriam Stenowitz."

Haybens made notes on his lined tablet.

Bonnie topped up the reporter's cup. She pointed to Archie's empty plate. "Done with that?"

He nodded and she swept the plate into a bus basin under counter. "Can I get you anything else?"

"More tea?"

"Like it, huh? I told you." She winked. "Be right back with it."

She checked on the other diners at the counter and fetched another cup of tea. She propped her elbows on the counter and leaned forward. "So, you being from Florida, where do you fit in with these Stenowitzes?"

"How'd you know?" Archie asked.

"About you being from Florida? Told you, I'm psychic. I'm good, aren't I? Well, here it is the middle of February, but you've got a tan. You don't have a New York accent so you weren't just at the beach on vacation. You've got a bit of a Midwestern twang though, so Florida's not your home state."

"You are good."

"And your truck has Florida plates," Linc said with a wink.

Bonnie socked his biceps.

"As for fitting in with the Stenowitzes, I don't," Archie said. "Yet. I'm engaged to one of the daughters. Or, well, I'd like to be engaged."

Bonnie pouted. "Too bad for me. So that's why you're here in the dead of winter when you could be in the Sunshine State? You're going to ask for her hand in marriage? Oh, just in time for

Valentine's Day. That's so romantic." She clapped her hands together under her chin.

"Well, I dunno. I don't think her parents like me much. Anyway, her sister just had a baby. That's what we're here for."

"And you sort of don't know what to do with yourself with all this family hoopla."

"Too true."

"I'd say just stay out of the way. A new baby in the house, the baby's gonna get all the attention, there's not gonna be much left for you. But don't take it personal. Just keep telling them what a jewel the little one is. As for your girlfriend's parents, if they love her, all they really want to know is that you'll do right by her."

Archie doubted that was all there was to it. "So speaking of Valentine's Day, where around here can a guy get a gift?"

"Around here?" Bonnie scoffed. "Try Rhinebeck, north on 9G, then head for East Market Street. Lots of nice shops there. Jewelry, art, clothing, florists. Me, I like the Mystic Moon. They've got wonderful mellow meditation tapes, some heavenly scented candles, really sweet wind chimes, crystals—" Bonnie drifted off for a moment, window-shopping in her mind's eye.

Archie laid some money on the counter. "Thanks for the tip."

Bonnie pocketed the money. "No, thank you for the tip."

"And the tea. Kinda took the edge off my nerves. You got something to fix my love life, too?

"Trust me. No potion's gonna fix what's wrong with your love life. That's up to you." She peeled his breakfast tab off her order pad and laid it on the counter.

Archie finished his tea.

Linc Haybens said, "Fixin' to leave?"

Archie nodded.

Haybens put out his cigarette and grasped his camera. "Would you mind if I took some pics? Might make a nice photo in the *Voice*."

"That desperate for news, huh?"

Haybens grinned and shrugged. "Not a whole lot going on around here under normal circumstances, much less the dead of winter."

"There isn't something special going on at the FDR Park?" *Maybe the place* wasn't *open after all.*

"Not that I know of."

"I guess I'm it then," Archie said.

Haybens grabbed his yellow pad and camera. "Do I get to work the horn?"

Archie paid for his breakfast, pocketed the receipt, and took the reporter on a tour of the Kenworth. Haybens was properly appreciative and snapped away with his camera. "It's a digital camera," he explained. "I can take just about as many pics as I want," he said. "I don't have to worry about film or developing. I can burn 'em to a CD if you want copies."

"Could I use them with the story I'm writing for a magazine? That might really impress the editor."

"You're a journalist too?"

"Wannabe. For a trucking trade journal. It's a review of the truck. It's my first story, just a sample, so they can see if I can write."

"On spec."

"Yeah, that's it. They're not going to pay me for it or anything."

"Byline only."

"Right. Dumb, huh?"

"Not at all. Byline stories on spec is how lots of freelancers break into writing. Do you have it all written yet?"

"Some of it."

"If you want, I'll take a look."

Archie tried not to goggle. "You would do that?"

"Sure. We freelancers have to stick together. Well, actually we don't since we're competing for jobs. But what the heck."

"And I can use the photos too?

"If you'll credit me. Which, come to think of it, wouldn't hurt my portfolio. Just tell me where to send the CD."

"I can meet you here tomorrow if that works for you," Archie said.

"See you then." Haybens headed across the parking lot for his car, a black Honda Civic. Its dull dingy finish told it had seen many miles and had been too many times rode hard and put away wet.

Archie figured it was late enough in the morning that he wouldn't be disturbing anyone, and punched in the numbers for the Stenowitz residence on the cellular phone. Unable to get a signal, he left the truck and ducked back into the Town and Country to use the payphone in the lobby. He was grateful when Debbie answered.

"Archie, I feel so bad about last night but you know, it's a madhouse here," she said. "Mom's making herself crazy, obsessing about every detail."

"Anything I can do to help? You need anything from here? I was just about to head that way."

"Actually, you stay put. I'm coming out there to get you. There is no way you can park that truck here, not with everyone who's coming. I'll be there in twenty minutes or so."

Wondering what she could have in mind, Archie busied himself with paperwork in the cab, looking up now and then to monitor the traffic in the T&C parking lot. The breakfast rush being over, more people went then came. At last he spotted a silver Chrysler Le Baron with Debbie behind the wheel. She parked, met him alongside the truck, and hugged him as close as her bulky winter coat would allow. "You spent the night OK?" she asked.

"Well, considering I had to spend it without you," he said.

"I'm so sorry about that but I don't think this is the week to get into a squabble with Mom. Especially since—OK, here's my idea. You take me back to the house then you can keep Mom's car. Otherwise you'll be spending a fortune in fuel driving back and forth."

She was right about that. "You're sure she won't mind?"

"She'd never admit it but it will give her a good excuse not to leave Caryn, much less have to drive in the snow. Dad or I can run errands for her."

"Sounds good."

Debbie followed him to the Hyde Park Manor where he parked the truck and they rode together to Salt Point.

"So how is your sister doing?"

"Poor Caryn," Debbie said. "She's still, as the doctors like to say, uncomfortable. Uncomfortable, hell, she hurts. And of course she's not getting any rest, the baby needs attention about every two hours."

"Cries a lot?" Archie asked.

"Kinda seems that way. Just doesn't stay asleep for very long. He's keeping Caryn and Elliot pretty busy. His parents are on the way, Frank and Edna. So Caryn's all wound up about them coming.

Frank and Edna, well, she's sweet but Elliot's her baby. Caryn's sure Edna doesn't think she's good enough."

I know the feeling.

CHAPTER SEVEN

SALT POINT, NY, Saturday, February 13, 1993

It looked like Elliot's parents had already arrived; an Oldsmobile sedan with Connecticut plates stood in the Stenowitz's driveway.

The new guests wouldn't lack for something to eat. Miriam had cut the remaining bagels into thin slices, toasted them, and loaded them with spreads, making snack-sized bites, accompanied by bowls of tuna- and egg salads. Cups and glasses stood ready to be filled from pots of tea and coffee and pitchers of juice. Another platter held one slice of what appeared to be French toast.

Debbie noticed him eyeing it and said, "Oh, you missed the best French toast. Mom made it with leftover challah bread. There's nothing better."

"Archibald, let me make you fresh," Miriam said.

Full of the Town and Country's eggs and waffles Archie was about to decline, but caught Debbie's warning glance. "That'd be great."

Despite his complete lack of appetite, Archie managed to clear his plate. "Debbie was right," he said. "This is really good." It was, too: a rich combination of egg bread soaked in egg batter. Archie could almost feel his arteries clogging with cholesterol. It was for sure he wouldn't need to eat for the rest of the day.

Caryn's husband Elliot got his reedy build from his father Frank, a tall, almost gaunt man. Frank ran his Connecticut furniture store with his wife, Edna, who managed the office staff. The weather had made their drive stressful and Frank was at the breakfast bar settling his nerves with a drink, a Bloody Mary if the celery stalk sticking out of the tall glass of tomato juice was any clue.

"Frank," Debbie said, "this is my Super Man, Archie."

"Archibald," Frank said, holding his hand out. "It's great to meet you. We've heard so much about you from Debbie."

"Archie, please." He shook the man's hand.

"My wife will be down in a minute. She's with the baby. It's a blessing, our first grandchild. A boy. Another lawyer in the family." With his thin frame and drawn face, Frank looked tired but his eyes were bright with joy.

Archie wondered if he and Debbie were to have a son, would Marvin be as proud to have another trucker in the family?

The doorbell rang and Miriam raced to open it to a middle-aged man in a dark overcoat and fedora. "Rabbi Davis," she said. "How kind of you to come. All this way, and in this weather."

The rabbi knocked the snow from his hat and shoes before stepping over the threshold.

Archie tried not to stare. It wasn't that he expected the rabbi to be generously bearded and dressed in frock coat and iconic broad fur hat. Still, priests at least had Roman collars to tell you who you were dealing with. The rabbi's attire gave no hint.

Introductions were made all around. "And this is Archibald Harlanson, our oldest daughter Debbie's friend," Miriam said.

"Archie." Archie held out his hand.

"Scott Davis," the rabbi said. His smile was warm, friendly, and confident, and his handshake firm. He could just as easily be a school principal or a restaurant owner. "I gather that you and Debbie get the prize for traveling the farthest. All the way from Florida."

"That's nothing for Archie," Debbie said. "That's all he does all day. Drive."

"I'm a trucker," Archie said, trying to give it as much weight as if he were saying "I'm a brain surgeon" or "I'm a nuclear physicist."

"Really?" said Rabbi Davis. "Now there's a job I don't think I could do. Coping with people all day."

Archie felt his eyebrows rise in surprise. Usually when he told people what he did for a living, they got excited about the equipment, recalling childhood days playing with toy trucks, or they would express envy about having nothing else to do but tour the country. While Archie did enjoy the adventure of traveling to new places, it wasn't as if he was on a continuous vacation road trip. Some of his destinations were not exactly worthy of mention in a Fodor's guide and interstate driving could prove less than scenic. Other people would frown and grumble about how a truck had once made a trip difficult for them.

While commercial driving was about the equipment and the open road, the important part was the people: the shippers who entrusted him with their cargo, the mechanics who kept his equipment in service, the truck stop personnel who made every minute of his brief breaks count, the dock workers who helped him to stay on schedule, and the other drivers with whom he shared the road. *The rabbi was right; being a trucker was about dealing with people all day long.* Archie regarded the man with appreciation.

"But Rabbi, dealing with people is exactly what you do," Miriam said.

"Yeah, but not while we're all moving at sixty miles an hour."

Debbie chuckled. "Archie's very good at it. He's been accident-free his entire career. Considering the gazillion miles he's racked up, that's saying something. I can barely back out of a garage without banging my side mirror."

"Please, have something to eat," Miriam took the rabbi's elbow and drew him toward the kitchen. "You must be famished after Saturday morning services and you obviously haven't had time for lunch. Can I get you some coffee, or maybe you would like a little schnapps? It's so cold out."

"It was nice of him to come," Debbie told Archie. "That way we won't have to go to the temple in Poughkeepsie to discuss the brit."

"He's the one who's going to do it?"

"Well, Elliot could do it or should do it. Let me say that strictly speaking, the father should do it. But a lot of modern fathers are intimidated by the whole thing—"

"No kidding," Archie murmured.

"So they can designate a *mohel,* someone specially trained in the procedure and the rituals. Mohels aren't rabbis and not all rabbis are mohels but Rabbi Davis is."

The whole idea of the circumcision and the attendant ceremony made Archie think of wizards and magic spells and things equally shrouded in mysticism and occult power. There was, however, nothing arcane about Scott Davis who looked like just a neighborhood kind of guy.

"Debbie, I know you just got back but I need you to go to Rhinebeck for me. I need some things from the drugstore for Caryn."

Salt Point was more densely populated than Archie's rural Midwest hometown but was equally as lacking in supermarkets, pharmacies, convenience marts, even liquor stores.

Debbie's eyebrows went up and Archie could hear her sigh. "Why don't I go get that?" he said. Bonnie's advice to stay out of the way was starting to make a lot of sense.

"That's a very nice offer, Archibald, but didn't you leave your truck back in Hyde Park?"

"Mom, he can take your car."

Miriam frowned.

"Aw, come on, Mom. It makes perfect sense. You're going to have more cars here than you'll know what to do with. Daddy's, Elliot's, and now Frank and Edna's and Rabbi Davis's. What happens when Aunt Esther and Isobel and Lilly get here?"

"What if I need to go somewhere?" Miriam asked.

"I'll take you in Daddy's car. I'm here for you, Mom, as well as Caryn."

Miriam still looked unconvinced.

"Certainly you're not worried about Archie having your car," said Debbie. "Mom, he's a professional driver. He knows what he's doing. It's what he does for a living. He has a special license and everything."

"He does?"

Archie smiled. He wondered just how much Miriam—or any of these four-wheelers—would want to know about commercial driver licensing. Just last year, a federal law went into effect that required drivers to have a "CDL." Drivers like him in every state had to pass tests to prove that they knew how to do what they had been doing for years, for decades, for an entire career. Archie had passed the first time out but a lot of otherwise good drivers didn't. The new regulation sure made life difficult for a lot of veteran truckers.

"So, Mom, one less car to play musical chairs with," Debbie said.

Miriam fluttered her hands. "Yes, yes, all right."

Debbie winked at Archie and he tried not to smile. Debbie Stenowitz had handled her Mom as smoothly as she did disgruntled customers at work.

*****

Navigating around and parking on Rhinebeck's East Market Street was a whole lot easier in a passenger car than a semi. He quickly found the items on Miriam's list at a drugstore but didn't rush to head back to Salt Point. Archie wasn't much for shopping but had to admit that there was something relaxing about strolling past the brick storefronts with colorful merchandise displayed in their windows, shops with names that were by turns hippie-dippie or quaintly olde-timey. There was even a shop with things for babies and new moms. Maybe he was still under Bonnie's mystic spell because a small tub of "magic" salve sounded like it would be soothing for Caryn, as would "bottom balm" for the little one. He bought a toy pickup truck for Debbie and at a confectionary shop, chocolate hearts to fill the bed.

Not far from the shopping district was a building that Archie found fascinating. Like so much else he was running into, it had the FDR touch. Of fieldstone with a colonial look to it, two chimneys and a wide front porch, he thought it might be a bed and breakfast. It turned out to be the post office. A sign mounted on the wall explained that Roosevelt had taken an interest in the design of post offices in the county and had had a hand in this one which had been built during his administration.

Equally quaint was the Beekman Arms which claimed to be oldest continuously-operating inn in the country. With its beamed ceilings and open hearth fireplace, its Colonial-style restaurant looked like the ideal setting for a romantic Valentine's Day dinner. Archie discovered that he wasn't the first person to have come up with that idea and the place was completely booked for that night.

"Damn." Archie leaned conspiratorially toward the hostess, a prim young lady in a white blouse and slim dark skirt. "I was thinking I might propose to my girl."

The hostess gave him a sad smile. "You and about half the guys we already have reservations for. We'll put your name on a waiting list. Give us a call again tomorrow and we'll see what we can do. You never know, we might have cancellations."

Maybe it was the way the afternoon sun glinted off the gems in the picture window but something about Candelmann's Jewelers caught his eye. Studded with rubies and other red-colored stones, the window throbbed with Valentine's Day enthusiasm and beckoned him to enter. As Archie strolled past the display cases, a man not much older than he said, "Hi, I'm Bill Candelmann. Anything I can help you with?"

"Is there such a thing as a pre-engagement engagement ring?" Archie asked, unable to take his eyes off one item.

The man chuckled. "Not quite ready to take the big leap?"

"I am," Archie said. "I'm not sure that she is."

"What you want is a promise ring."

Archie looked up from the case. "Yeah, I do."

"Obviously, you're not the one who's hesitating. You've got no problem saying 'I do.'"

"What about that one?" Set in a twining band that was more pink than gold, a gleaming pink stone heart was so warm and friendly that Archie couldn't stop smiling. "Is that a promise ring?"

"You've got a good eye for jewelry. It is."

"I've never seen a pink stone like that. Is it a type of ruby?"

"That's a morganite, a fairly recent discovery. It's a beryl. Same family as emeralds and aquamarines but it's got some different minerals in it. That's what gives it that peachy pink color. And the band is rose gold."

"I didn't know gold came in colors."

"Oh it does. Yellow, of course. Various shades of red as you can see. That has to do with how much copper is alloyed with the gold. There's also purple, white, green, blue, black."

"There really is black gold? I thought that meant oil."

"There's definitely black gold. Very popular with the guys. And Goth chicks. I can show you a few. Black gold rings, not chicks."

"No, thanks. That pink one though. With the morganite."

Bill Candelmann took the ring from the case and handed it to Archie. He would have been willing to swear that it felt as warm as it looked.

"Except, I don't know her size."

"Not a problem," said the jeweler. "When you find out, you can bring it back, or bring the lady in and we'll size it to fit. That's our promise."

Having dawdled as long as he reasonably could, Archie headed back to the Stenowitz home to find the extended family crowded into the kitchen where Miriam prepared dinner. Archie leaned on the breakfast bar. "How are you holding up?" he asked Elliot.

"I think it's just starting to sink in. I'm a father."

He did look a little shell-shocked. He'd raked his hands through his hair so much he probably never would get it to lie down again and there were deep shadows under wide eyes that held a somewhat manic gleam. "It's wonderful. I have a baby. Isn't he just amazing?"

"I haven't even seen the baby yet," Archie said.

"Well, you just go right on upstairs," said Marvin.

"You're sure I won't be disturbing Caryn?"

"Here, Archibald, take her some tea as long as you're going up." Miriam handed him a mug.

Archie excused himself, not that anyone was listening, and went upstairs. The door to the guest bedroom was open but he knocked anyway.

From the bed where she sat sideways propped up on pillows Caryn said, "Archie, come on in."

"I brought you some tea. Your mom thought you could use it."

"Just put it there on the nightstand, if you can find room," Caryn said.

Archie negotiated a path around the antique white dresser, white brocade boudoir chair, crib, and dressing table.

"Mom's sweet but if I drink any more tea I'll have to pee again and that's something I'd like to avoid." She blushed. "Oh, too much information, I guess. I promised myself that when I became a mom I wouldn't bore everyone with minute to minute updates on the baby's poo, and yet I've already started."

"I brought you a little something," Archie said. "I dunno if it will help but ..." He handed her the tiny jar of lime-green salve and the tin of baby balm. "And this is for the little guy. It's supposed to help with diaper rash, stuff like that."

"Why, Archie, wherever did you find these?"

"I was running errands for your Mom in Rhinebeck. I'm sorry I haven't been up to see you before this. Everyone told me that you were resting."

Caryn sighed. "I wish I could rest. Here, help me up. I'm getting numb sitting and I'm really supposed to move around."

Archie stood alongside the bed. Caryn swung her legs over the edge, gathered up her nightgown hem, and leaned on him heavily. She giggled. "Oh, I can see what Debbie finds so attractive. You are a big strong one. How do you stay fit? I would think it would be tough with a sedentary job like yours."

"It is," he said. "I make it a point to do calisthenics whenever I've got the room, and I jog. Sometimes it's just around the truck but it's better than nothing."

"Well, let's jog over to the crib and let me show you my son."

Archie helped Caryn ease the few steps to the sturdy white crib outfitted in linens of white and blue and tied with white ribbons. Wrapped in coordinating blankets and wearing a knit cap that looked like something Miriam had whipped up in the hospital room, the little fellow lay on his back, soft pink lips slightly parted. At Archie's approach he cracked open his eyes and his lips turned up slightly.

"Oh, look, he's smiling," Archie said. It was hard not to smile back.

"Archie, meet Eli. Eli, this is your aunt Debbie's friend, Archie."

Someday maybe, to be your uncle, Archie thought but didn't say.

He rejoined Debbie downstairs.

"Archie, help me set the table," Debbie said. "Here, we need to pull this out and drop in a leaf."

At an ornate carved wood china hutch she pulled linens from a drawer.

"Don't forget the table pads," Miriam hollered from the kitchen.

"Got it, Mom." Debbie set aside the silver salt and pepper shakers and napkin rings, removed the tablecloth, and rearranged the protective pad custom-shaped in curved and rectangular sections to fit the long oval table. Archie helped her drape a fresh white-on-white patterned tablecloth on top of which Debbie spread a plastic cover.

"What's that for?"

"To protect the tablecloth."

Which itself protected the table pads which in turn protected the table. It seemed to Archie that the Stenowitz's dining table enjoyed a level of security a head of state would envy.

"The good china and the silver," Miriam called.

'Yes, Mom." Debbie moved spare dining chairs from where they stood alongside the china hutch. Stroking her chin she said, "Now let's see. Dad will be at the head of the table. We'd better put Leon at the opposite end. It'll cut down on arguments." She looked at Archie. "They don't get along. So if we put Isobel to his right and put Mom at Dad's right and Lilly next to Mom ..."

Even encased in its small blue velvet box and folded into a tiny blue paper bag, the rosy promise ring burned a hole in the pocket of Archie's jeans, but it didn't sound like there would be time tonight to present it.

Sitting at the Stenowitz dinner table, Archie felt like a noncombatant at the front lines. Frank and Edna battled Lilly and Isobel for the title of who had been most inconvenienced by the weather. Miriam and Debbie competed to see who could pop up the most often, Debbie to clear plates or Miriam to bring more food. Talking politics, Marvin and his brother sent volleys back and forth across the table. Leon opined as how President Bill Clinton's use of the Fleetwood Mac tune *Don't Stop* as his campaign theme song was inspired, while Marvin argued that it trivialized the very real issues of taxes and the economy.

"That's not the first time politics and popular culture have collided," piped up Rabbi Davis. "Why, take Hyde Park's own hometown hero, FDR. A lot of comic book readers at the time saw parallels between his programs and Superman."

Superman? Archie's ears perked up.

Davis continued. "Today, we see Superman sparing the world from colliding with asteroids and battling villains who are bent on world domination, but in the 1930s, what he did was much more about social justice. Superman fought crooked businessmen and corrupt politicians and shark landlords. His values were very similar to FDR's liberal idealism." Davis took a bite of brisket. "Then, with domestic issues being taken care of by FDR's New Deal, Superman turned his attention to global affairs. There was an old comic book episode where Superman flies to Germany, takes both Hitler and Stalin into custody, and brings them to the League of Nations for trial and punishment. Then there was also Captain America who promoted FDR's 'super soldier program.'"

"You don't say," Marvin murmured.

Davis grinned like a cat sucking canary bits from its back teeth. "Did you know the original *Superman* was created by two Jewish kids?"

"No," Leon said. "Really?"

Debbie leaned close to Archie and whispered, "Oh, here we go. Another round in the game of Find the Landsmen. That's where everyone gets all excited because some celebrity is Jewish, or half-Jewish, or his best friend is Jewish."

Debbie sounded peeved but she had only half of Archie's attention. Rabbi Davis had the rest.

"Two Ohio high-school boys, Jerry Siegel and Joe Shuster, sixty years ago. Actually Superman started out as a villain, a character that Siegel created and published in a fanzine."

"What's a fanzine?" Miriam asked.

"Basically a homemade publication put out by fans of a story or a character in someone else's work. Usually fanzines are free and not intended to make the publishers a lot of money. They're kind of just for fun, traded around like baseball cards," Davis explained between bites. "Then Siegel reimagined Superman as a hero. Siegel's buddy Shuster did the drawing. After a while, though, they got serious about the whole thing and tried to find a publisher. The Siegel-Shuster partnership broke up for a while but then they got back together. They ended up selling their work to comic-book publishers, but what they really wanted to do was sell it as a comic strip, for the papers."

"I had no idea," said Edna.

"OK, stop me if this is boring, but Superman isn't the only Jewish superhero. So was Batman. He got his start around the same time, late thirties. And Stan Lee? Creator of Captain American, Spiderman, X-men, all those guys? He's Jewish too, native New Yorker. Grew up during the Depression. I imagine all those young boys were escaping into the comic book world to get away from the harsh realities of the deprivation they were facing in real life."

"That's what made the Busby Berkeley musicals so popular, right?" Miriam said. "Escapism?"

"It's interesting what can arise from a stressor like that. Speaking of influences, one of Superman's creators had lost his father young. Siegel's dad was killed in an attempted robbery at the clothing store that he owned." Davis shrugged. "Could have been what inspired the boy to create a man who was bulletproof. And another thing that I find interesting: both boys were the children of immigrants. If you think about it, Superman's an immigrant. He's an alien, just trying to fit in. And he never really does. He 'passes' but he's always got to keep his true identity secret. Siegel and Shuster were probably fighting the same battle. A couple of kids who were different from their high school friends because they were Jewish, just trying to fit in to the larger culture."

Davis had everyone's attention now. "I can't imagine the two boys wouldn't have been influenced by politics. FDR had just launched the New Deal programs. Aid for the unemployed, the poor, minorities. It all would have been very much in the news."

"Makes sense," said Leon.

"If all that were happening today, I could see the presidential publicity department trying to recruit Superman to promote the administration's platform," Marvin said.

"Oh, Dad, you're such a cynic," Debbie said.

"So the Man of Steel was just a social activist," said Leon, looking very pleased.

"Possibly. Here's something else that could strengthen that argument." Rabbi Davis set his fork down. "Siegel and Shuster might have been motivated to invent Superman by a desire to escape the deprivations of the Depression, or by the painful experience of being ostracized teenagers. But their inspiration may have gone back a good many more years."

"How's that?"

The rabbi shifted in his chair as if settling in for a long haul. "Consciously, or maybe even subconsciously, they might have hearkened back to the story of Moses."

"We're still talking about Superman, right?" Elliot said.

"Yes. Remember what I said earlier about Superman being an alien? OK, think about the story of Moses. A people faces destruction. In order to insure the survival of the next generation, a couple puts their baby son in a capsule and sends him away. He's rescued by people who adopt him as their own, even though it's clear he's very different, and they try to keep his origins a secret. Later in life, his roots are revealed by way of a scrap of unusual cloth in which he was swaddled. The grown man confronts his foreign birth, his unique attributes, and commits himself to fight for justice."

Mouths hung open but no one spoke.

"I get it," Marvin said, pointing with his fork. "Moses in the basket in the Nile, Baby Superman sent from Krypton in a space pod. The Pharaoh adopts Moses, the Kents adopt Kal-El and name him Clark. Moses is revealed as a Hebrew by a scrap of cloth—"

"—that his mother, Jochebed, kept from the basket—"

"—and the Kents kept a scrap of Kal-El's blanket."

"Kal-El gets his mission from Jor-El as a hologram," Archie said.

"Like Moses and the burning bush?" Leon asked.

Rabbi Davis nodded. "That scene in Superman resonates with similar mysticism, don't you think? Now I'm not saying the Superman story is just the Moses story in modern clothing, but you see the similarities, don't you?"

Superman, Archie thought. An ancient Jewish hero in blue tights. It was an eye-opener.

"Is everyone ready for dessert and coffee?" Miriam asked.

"Unless you've really got your heart set on rugelach and *babka*, I can take you back to the truck and we can have dessert there," Debbie whispered.

Archie nodded vigorously.

With a wink, Debbie stood, gathered plates, and followed her mother into the kitchen.

CHAPTER EIGHT

HYDE PARK, NY, Sunday, February 14, 1993

Archie stepped outside into the icy air. He'd surprise Debbie with breakfast in bed—OK, a donut and coffee enjoyed in the sleeper berth. A jelly-filled or glazed might make her feel better about the bump she sustained when she knocked her head on the underside of the overhead bunk. More clearance needed there and he wondered if that should go in his review. *How would I word that?* "Those with amorous partners who are fond of the superior position should be advised." Maybe that wasn't appropriate for a review in *American Big Rigs* but prospective buyers needed to know these things, especially husband-and-wife team drivers.

In his sweats and boots, Archie trotted down the sidewalk headed for the lobby and nearly collided with a man on his way out. Looked to be the same guy as yesterday: ball cap, parka, munching a donut. The guy must have decided to check in after all, Archie figured. He didn't recall seeing the Riviera in the Manor parking lot last night, but then again he wasn't exactly paying attention to anything outside the truck. Maybe the man had arrived in the middle of the night. Archie noticed that this morning, the dark Riviera parked in virtually the same spot near the lobby entrance that it had been in the day before. *Seemed like if the guy had gotten a room he would have wanted to park closer to it.*

Archie tried to catch the man's eye but he dipped his head and pulled the brim of his cap lower. Before Archie could say "good morning," the fellow had ducked into his car, peeled out onto the highway, and turned left. It looked like the man was headed for the FDR Park again. *What could be the attraction?* The reporter Linc Haybens wasn't aware of any special exhibits. Even if the museum were open during the winter season, was it open on a Sunday? It all struck Archie as odd.

Speaking of getting a room, if he was going to be here for nearly a week, Archie didn't want to be taking spit baths in the Hyde Park Manor's restroom every day. He'd more than tested the functionality of the truck's sleeper berth. He grinned at the memory.

He stopped in at the reception desk and tapped the bell. Nisha stepped out from her office.

"Looks like I'm going to be here longer than I thought and I'm going to need a room after all."

"No problem," Nisha said. "You can take your pick. I think you're the only one here."

"Really? I've seen some guy hanging around, I thought for sure he was one of your guests."

Nisha shook her head. She offered Archie a photocopied sketch of the motel layout with the rooms numbered. Archie picked the one closest to where he'd been parking the truck. "I'll need it at least through Friday."

"You got it."

In the dining room, Archie found the continental breakfast already laid out. The room smelled of freshly-brewed coffee and the carafe was nearly full as was the donut box. It looked like the only one who had partaken of the offerings was the strange Buick owner. At least he had left a tip. Once again there was a dollar bill in the pickle jar. Archie added two of his own.

On his way out, Archie scanned the newspapers in their vending racks. There was a plentiful supply. Either none of the Manor guests were readers or Nisha was right and Archie was the only one on the premises. He bought one copy of every publication and hustled back to the truck in the freezing air.

"Oh, aren't you sweet," Debbie exclaimed. "What's Sunday without the color comics? Dad always goes out and fetches all the Sunday papers. I'd better call him and tell him I'll save him the trouble."

"You can try my cellular phone, or the payphone in the lobby. Then what say I buy you a proper breakfast?"

"Looking like this?" Debbie said.

"You look beautiful to me," Archie replied.

Debbie blew him a kiss. "You don't count."

"Oh, thank you."

She chuckled. "You know what I mean. Give me a few minutes in the motel's ladies room and let me see what I can do to freshen up."

"Spoken like a true road warrior."

Debbie chuckled. "That's what they're calling computer super-users who travel with a screw driver, alligator clips, and a wire stripper so that they can wire their Internet modem to a motel phone line when there aren't modem jacks. I'll call Dad and tell him he doesn't have to run out and get anything. Can you take the truck where we're going for breakfast and I'll follow you? I can take off from there."

"Sure. I'll pre-trip it while you get ready." He tugged on his jacket.

Archie was surprised to find that the T&C wasn't as busy on a Sunday morning as it had been the day before. Bonnie greeted him at the hostess station.

"Well, if it isn't my new friend the journalist," she said. "You know, I never did get your name."

"Archie," he replied. "Can we get a booth?"

"Doesn't look like that will be a problem," Bonnie said, waving an arm at the nearly-empty row of seats. "Take your pick."

Settling beside Archie in the booth, Debbie gave him a raised eyebrow.

"This is Bonnie," Archie said. "She waited on me yesterday." To Bonnie he said, "You're not working the counter today?"

"Working practically the whole room this morning. Cheryl won't be in until just before church lets out. That's when it'll get busy. So this must be your girl."

"Bonnie, this is Debbie Stenowitz. Debbie, this is—"

"Bonnie. So you said. Hi."

Archie didn't know whether to be delighted or dismayed by the hint of jealousy in Debbie's voice.

Bonnie handed out menus and asked about beverages.

"Coffee for me," said Debbie.

"Me too," said Archie.

"Yeah, you can handle it. Your aura's much rosier today," Bonnie said with a wink and went to get the pot.

Frowning, Debbie asked, "What was that all about?"

"Guess I was a little bummed yesterday morning. Not so much today."

"Gosh, I should hope not," Debbie said with a flirtatious grin.

Bonnie returned with coffee. "Know what you want or do you need a minute?"

"The waffle special," Archie said.

"And milk?" asked Bonnie.

Archie nodded. "And the lady will have—"

"Just coffee," Debbie said. She looked at Archie. "Mom's putting on an open house-slash-brunch. All kinds of people are going to be dropping in. More relatives, neighbors, friends, local customers of Dad's, people from Mom's painting classes." Debbie rattled off the names of people who would be coming for the impromptu brunch and how much food would be needed. "I told her I'd get bagels, lox, cold cuts. I'll have to go all the way to Poughkeepsie so I'd better hit the road."

"I can get that stuff and run any other errands you need," Archie said. "Stay. Have breakfast with me."

"You're a sweetheart. You got me that donut and I'd better leave room for all the food Mom's going to put out."

"OK, but don't eat too much. I was hoping we could have dinner together tonight, just the two of us. What do you think?" With any luck they'd be dining at the Beekman Arms.

"I think that would be lovely." Debbie gave him a kiss and slid from the booth.

"Drive carefully, OK?" The snow drifting down was light for now. Archie wondered if they were in for heavier flurries. He sighed, took the promise ring from his jacket pocket, and laid it on the table. He watched out the window and waved as Debbie backed out of her parking space. She idled at the driveway , turn signal flashing, waiting for a string of utility vehicles to pass. White on top and gray below, the vehicles bore horizontal black and orange stripes and were emblazoned with the letters NYNEX.

In her circuit among the diners, Bonnie paused at his table.

"What's NYNEX?" he asked.

"The telephone company. Why?"

Archie had noticed two more utility trucks headed south, all similar:

"There was a whole parade of their trucks out there just now." Archie said. "Isn't that kind of weird for a Sunday morning?"

"Maybe there's some big outage somewhere. Hey, sorry about your girl." She pointed to the gift. "Was that for her?"

Archie nodded. He hoped there'd be a quiet moment later in the day when he could present it. *Well, maybe tonight at dinner.* "You warned me. About the baby claiming everyone's attention."

"How are they, the baby and the new mom?"

"It wasn't an easy delivery and Caryn's still … 'uncomfortable' is the word everyone's using."

Bonnie rolled her eyes. "That's putting it mildly, I'm sure."

"The baby's cute, though. He's so tiny. It's hard to believe he could grow up to be as big as a basketball player."

Bonnie chuckled. "Your first time with a newborn? You don't have kids of your own?"

"Not yet." That was probably a good thing. The breakup of Archie's first marriage had been difficult enough without child custody issues to complicate matters. "You?"

"Not yet. So, does this baby have a name?"

"Eli." That was what was on the baby's birth certificate. Equally important, he learned, was the Hebrew name that had been given to the child in honor of a deceased uncle. "But mostly everyone just refers to him as The Baby." Kind of like The King, The Pope, or The President, all of whom who had first names that no one seemed to use much.

Bonnie winked, hefted the coffee carafe, and moved on.

The diner's lobby was filling with people waiting to be seated. Archie wanted to hang around for a bit in case Linc Haybens arrived with the promised copies of the digital pictures that he shot yesterday of the Kenworth. To free up a booth for larger parties,

Archie picked up his coffee cup and moved to the counter. Maybe he'd fetch his story and work on it while he waited.

He didn't have to wait long. The reporter paused in the foyer and spotting Archie, hastened to the counter. "Hey, man, saw your truck. I'm glad you're here. I got your pics. They came out great if I do say so myself." Haybens handed over a CD-ROM in a paper envelope. "Feel free to use them wherever you want. Just credit Linc Haybens, *Valley Voice*. All my contact info's right there if you have a problem."

From halfway down the counter, the waitress hollered, "Morning, Linc. The usual?"

"Thank you, Cheryl."

Sturdy, with salt-and-pepper hair, Cheryl looked old enough to be Bonnie's mother but that didn't keep her from tackling a counter now almost completely filled with customers.

"Say, uh, you still want to look at the story I'm working on?" Archie asked.

"Sure," Linc replied.

"I'll go get it. Be right back." Archie hustled out to the truck and grabbed the notebook into which he'd been transcribing his dictations. He flipped up the cover, tore out the first page on which he had doodled a globe encircled with the words "Daily Planet," and hurried back to the diner. Haybens had his work-in-progress spread out on the counter and was well into a gooey jelly-filled donut.

Archie took the counter stool beside him. "I feel a little like a school kid handing in homework hoping I'll get an A but pretty sure it's only worth a C."

Haybens chuckled and waggled his fingers. "Hand it over. If you're going to be a working writer you're going to have to get used to criticism and outright rejection. I promise I'll be gentle, which not every editor is. Like that guy there." Haybens tilted his head toward the man who had just seated his family at the booth Archie had vacated. "News desk editor for the *Herald*. I've applied for a job with him a couple of times. He keeps telling me my feature writing experience doesn't qualify me to cover news."

"Does he have a point?"

"I don't think so but I'm not the one doing the hiring, so ..." Haybens picked up his cup and turned his attention to Archie's story. While he read, Archie studied the diner's Sunday morning crowd.

"This isn't bad," said Haybens.

"Hey, don't get all slobbery on me there," Archie said. "I might get a swelled head."

Haybens chuckled. "Seriously. You got the who-what-where-when-how right up front."

Just as they'd taught in journalism school.

"If your target readers are other drivers, I think this works well. It's information that they can use from the perspective of someone who has to get performance out of the equipment."

"That's what I was trying to do."

"And I think you've got a little flair there too. It's fact and figures but with a personal touch. I don't know how your editor's gonna feel about it, but for me that adds credibility. You know, one trucker to another."

Archie tried not to grin. That's what he had intended. Let Kenworth's publicists write the puff pieces. Archie wanted to tell it like it is.

Linc wrote a big B+ at the top of the page. "I'll reserve my final grade for when I see the finished story. You need a memorable ending that pulls it all together and sums it up. Even better if you leave people wanting to read more of what you write."

"I'll keep that in mind. So what story are you working on today?"

Haybens shrugged. "Oh, something will come up. I hope."

"Well, something's going on somewhere, otherwise what are all those utility trucks for?" Archie described the line of NYNEX vehicles he saw from the booth.

Haybens swiveled on his counter stool and gazed out the diner's front window. "Hmph," he said. "Good question." He polished off his donut, gathered up his papers, laid some money on the counter, and slid from the stool.

Archie paid his tab and headed back toward to the Hyde Park Manor. He was about to turn into the motel parking lot and get settled into his room when movement up ahead caught his eye. The Riviera pulled out of the driveway of the FDR Park and onto the highway while a NYNEX truck pulled in. A lot of activity for a place that Archie hadn't even thought was open. *What was all that about?*

He drove into the site's entrance, a wide road bordered by a low fieldstone wall and numerous tall leafless trees. Snow covered the broad lawn but the asphalt drive had been cleared. He parked off to the side of the driveway curving in front of a three-story stone and stucco building: Franklin Delano Roosevelt's home. Even under a gloomy winter sky, its warm façade was bright with aqua shutters and scalloped white trim. A short flight of broad stone steps led to the piazza. Enclosed by a white stone balustrade, it ran the length of the building. A white-colonnaded portico shaded the arched front door giving it all a stately but not intimidating or ostentatious appearance.

Archie was surprised to find the facility open. A discreet National Park Service sign indicated that the historic site was open every day except for a few important holidays like Christmas. Taxpayer dollars hard at work, he thought.

The glossy white stone walls of the home's entrance hall were hung with paintings. He stood taking in the silence and the fact that this was the residence of a President.

A President had lived here.

FDR had overcome what some would allege was a disability to lead the Greatest Nation out of a depression and help to end a world war. It would seem that someone of that ilk should live in much more majestic surroundings. The FDR home was grand but it was in many ways still someone's house, a place where people slept, had breakfast, brushed their teeth. It felt odd to be wandering uninvited into what had been someone's private spaces.

Archie hadn't gotten far when a man approached him. "May I help you?" asked the man, a Park Ranger according to the badge pinned to his shirt.

"I, uh, just needed to see—"

"Are you with NYNEX? You want the Library. Back down the road and to your right."

"Thanks." Archie followed the fieldstone path to a low gray stone building with a dormered gabled roof. Shaped in a U around a courtyard, it was quite a bit more humble and utilitarian than the former president's home. A bust of FDR pegged the courtyard's center.

A shingle sign lettered in script kindly invited him to "Enter Here." Just inside the door he could see that one wing was dedicated to exhibits like the president's desk and car while the other was the repository of presidential books and materials, with worktables, chairs, and computers for researchers to use.

He heard voices down the hall, started towards them, then stopped when he picked up the conversation.

"I can't authorize that. That would be up to the Director."

Archie edged close enough to determine the speaker had been a man in uniform. The man had his back to Archie but from the utilitarian gray twill shirt and black trousers it was a pretty good bet he was an employee.

"Then let's ask him," said the other man. Turned slightly away from Archie, he wore work boots, jeans, a utility belt, and a white hard hat. Light reflected from the laminated plastic ID badge that the technician wore clipped to his work shirt. From where he stood Archie couldn't make out the writing but NYNEX in block letters ran across the top. Archie figured him for the tech that went with the truck parked outside.

"He's not here," said the park employee. "It's Sunday afternoon. He'll be in the office tomorrow morning. Why don't you come back then?"

"Why don't you call him and tell him there's an emergency and he's needed here?"

"Installing additional lines doesn't sound like an emergency to me. It sounds like something that can wait until Monday."

"Well, it can't."

"Why don't you call him yourself if it's that important?"

"It is that important and when you find out how important, you are going to feel like an idiot. But have it your way. Give me the number. I'll call him."

"Be my guest."

The staffer moved his arms to his front and Archie didn't have to be facing him to figure he'd crossed them over his chest. He stood at tense attention while the technician dialed the desk phone.

"Vernon Newton? Yes, I'm sorry to bother you at home, sir. I'm calling from the FDR Library." The technician introduced himself and reeled off his NYNEX employee number. "Feel free to call and check on me but—"

The staffer snatched the receiver from him. "I'm sorry, sir. I told him you would be in tomorrow, but he insisted on talking to you today."

The technician grabbed the phone back. "Mr. Newton, we need to install twenty additional phone lines in anticipation of a visit by the President of the United States on Friday, February 19."

The staffer dropped his arms. "What? The President? Here? Friday? This Friday?"

The technician held up a finger asking for silence but Archie had seen and heard enough. It didn't take years of journalistic experience to recognize a hot lead. *What Linc Haybens could do with this!* Careful not to make noise and draw attention to himself, Archie toe-heeled back out of the hallway and hustled out the door, and jogged down the path to his truck.

Archie could call Haybens from the cellular phone which he had left in the truck docked in its charger, drawing power from the Kenworth's electrical system. He scrambled into the cab, picked up the phone, and saw that he had missed a call. He dialed the number and reached the hostess from the Beekman Arms. "We haven't had any cancellations. I thought you'd want to know so you could make other arrangements. I know you had special plans for this evening." Archie could almost hear her wink.

Damn, Archie thought. He hadn't given any thought to Plan B.

He rustled up the CD that Linc Haybens had given him and dialed the phone number on the business card that the journalist had taped to the envelope.

The line rang three times and Archie expected a receptionist to answer "Valley Voice" or for Linc to answer "Haybens" but a man said, "the shop."

Archie looked at his cell phone wondering if he had misdialed or the phone had screwed up. He disconnected the call and tried again.

"The shop," came the response.

"I'm sorry, I must have the wrong number," Archie said. "I'm trying to reach Linc Haybens."

"Haybens? Hang on."

Archie heard the man yell "Haybens, call for you." Noise that sounded like music playing in the background came through the phone. The *Valley Voice* sounded like a fun place to work.

"Linc Haybens."

"It's Archie Harlanson. Hey, have I got some news for you."

"Oh, hey, man, I'm glad you called. I didn't know how to get a hold of you. Have I got news for you. Can you meet me? I'm at the shop."

"The newspaper? Where is it?"

Linc chuckled. "Oh, no, the shop."

Archie frowned. "Uh, OK. Tell me where it is."

"It's a bit off the beaten path."

"If there's a road leading to it, I can find it."

Archie half expected the *Valley Voice's* office to be something like Clark Kent's: an imposing multistoried masonry building with a ground floor pressroom and a bustling bullpen on an upper level boasting a panoramic view of the territory in the paper's coverage area. He assumed it would be located near the city center, but Linc's directions took him off the highway, down a side street, and into the parking lot of a windowless slump block rectangle. A neon sign over the door proclaimed it to be "The Shop."

Archie stepped inside and found not a newspaper office but a neighborhood bar. Even on a Sunday afternoon, men held down stools and a party of guys crowded a four-top. Parkas and feed caps were the uniform of the day. A juke box provided the music that Archie had heard playing in the background. The basketball game in progress on the TV mounted over the bar held the attention of a couple of barflies while two others smoked, drank, and had the occasional exchange of words.

Towards the rear of the room dimly lit by neon bar signs, a man played Mortal Kombat on a video game console and two other guys went at it in a fierce game of foosball.

Linc waved Archie over to where he sat at the end of the bar with his yellow lined tablet, camera, cigarette, and a beer.

"I thought when you told me to meet you at the shop, you meant the newspaper."

Linc chuckled. "The *Voice* doesn't have an office. I told you, we're freelancers. We just work out of our homes, or cars, whatever. This place is kind of centrally located for us. We make round-robin phone calls and say we'll meet at the shop but we're not the only ones who like the place because of its name. Those guys over there—" Linc nodded at the barflies—"there's times when they've had a killer day at work and need to unwind or just don't want to go home just yet. So they can call the wife and say, 'Hon, I'll be home late, I'm at the shop,' and you know, it's not a lie. Beer?" he asked Archie. "I'm drinking Rolling Rock."

"Sounds good."

Linc signaled to the bartender.

"OK, I get the freelance thing but what about the publisher? The editor? The photographers and stuff? Don't you have a press?"

"They're all freelance too. The publisher runs the whole thing out of his home office. The editor and the writers meet every week, here or the T&C or wherever, to go over assignments. We don't have a dedicated photo corps; the writers shoot whatever pics they need for their story."

"Thus your heavy-duty camera."

"Right. We put our stories and photos on CDs and give them to the editor who also does the layout."

"Don't you need like a bunch of serious hardware to do layout?"

Linc threw his head back and guffawed. "You're talking about hot type. Lead slugs, linotype machines. No one does it that way anymore, my friend. No, no, no, my man, all you need is a computer. Desktop publishing. I don't know how the editor does it. Waves some magic digital wand and makes a newspaper out of all the pieces that we hand in. It ends up getting run on a press in Albany and bam, we've got a paper."

"Cool," Archie said. Despite a certain cottage-industry appeal, he was disappointed. Editorial conferences held in a neighborhood bar definitely lacked the urgency and energy of a newsroom with cub reporters like Jimmy Olsen chomping at the bit and ambitious veterans like Lois Lane banging out late-breaking stories at the eleventh hour on clunky Underwoods that always jammed at the worst possible time. "So speaking of news, you said you had some."

Some joker set the jukebox to playing a hit from last year, *I'm Too Sexy,* a tune whose goofy lyrics and bouncy beat combined to make it a chart-topper.

"Oh yeah. You will not believe this. You know all those NYNEX guys you turned me on to? They've been the best source. One guy, he showed me his work order. It's all about putting in extra lines for voice and data at—you'll never guess."

"The FDR Park. For a visit from President Bill Clinton."

Hayben's mouth dropped open. He frowned. "You guessed. How'd you do that?"

"I followed one of their trucks to the FDR Library. Do you think The President is gonna be staying at the FDR Home?"

Linc shook his head. "I doubt it. The home is a historic monument, just for touring. It's not like it's some kind of B&B, not even for the current President. I'm guessing there's just going to be a speech there, but there'll be so many reporters trying to file their stories and staffers running the show that they're going to need extra phone lines."

"Why here of all places? It's not like Hyde Park is some Metropolis."

Linc took a thoughtful swig of beer. "The way I figure, Clinton's been trying to put over his economic plan. You know, making sacrifices in tough times so we can have a better future. He probably wants to make an association with Roosevelt's time, conjure up the thirties, all that patriotic fervor. Shower his own proposal with a little of that Roosevelt fairy dust, an implied endorsement from the man who pulled the country out of the Depression."

"Makes sense." Archie drank some beer. *What had Rabbi Davis said yesterday about recruiting Superman to shill for FDR's economic reforms?* Maybe Clinton was better served hitching his wagon behind the buoyantly optimistic Fleetwood Mac song than a Depression-era president. "Well, you've got a story now, don't you?"

"You bet I do. And I've got you to thank for it. That NYNEX lead, that was golden." Haybens tapped his temple. "I think you've got a bit of a journalist's instinct there, man."

"So where around here is a nice place to take a gal for dinner? I thought Debbie could use a break from the new-baby circus and besides, it's Valentine's Day. I wanted to take her to the Beekman Arms but they're all booked."

"Why didn't you say, man? I can maybe get you in. I did a story on them a while ago, they were pretty happy with me. I'll go give them a call." Pulling a small black book from his pocket, Linc crossed to the bar, leaned over, and grabbed the phone. A few minutes later he returned and said to Archie, "Sorry. I guess they didn't like me that much. They are booked solid."

"Damn," Archie said. "I was hoping to have a nice evening with Debbie. I've been here since Thursday and we've hardly seen each other. It's Valentine's Day. I don't want her to think that I don't care."

"Try an Italian restaurant. You ask me, those are always romantic. Candles in Chianti bottles and red-checkered tablecloths, and they always seem to have opera on the sound system. It's the thought that counts, isn't it?"

"Is it?"

Well, I do have a gift. And the ring. If Disney's cartoon dog Tramp could manage to romance Lady over a plate of spaghetti and meatballs, so can I.

CHAPTER NINE

HYDE PARK, NY, Sunday, February 14, 1993

Archie held the door open for Debbie. The stippled surface was clotted with several coats of green paint applied over the years and the dulled gloss suggested that a touch-up was once again due. "I'm sorry," he said. "Every restaurant in town was booked. It was either this or the Dairy Queen."

Giorgio's Honest Italian didn't have candlelit linen-covered tables. The laminate tables didn't have linens at all much less red-checkered ones, and the fluorescent overheads cast a bluish light that made everyone in the place look a little ghoulish. Instead of opera, the sound system treated diners to Top Forty pop music.

Archie wasn't even certain how Italian Giorgio's was, not with Nisha's husband Pacifico manning the kitchen.

"That's OK. I'm sorry too. I should have thought about it but the week just kind of got away from me," Debbie said. "But we're here together alone. Well, more or less." She gave him an apologetic smile.

A crowded pizza parlor didn't remotely resemble what Archie would call an intimate setting. "I'm glad you could break away."

"I told Mom that here you'd been in New York half a week, it was about time you had New York Pizza." Debbie sipped her soda.

At least the Solo cup's red color had a remote suggestion of Valentine's Day, Archie thought.

"I did get you a little something." Archie placed the toy truck with its chocolate candy cargo on the table.

"Oh, that's darling." Debbie stretched across the table and gave him a kiss. "I didn't get you anything, but maybe later I can give you something special." Her wink and her smile were devilish.

Archie had the promise ring in his pocket too, but now didn't seem to be the right moment to present it. Patty Smyth and Don Henley sang "Sometimes Love Just Ain't Enough," a group of teenagers at the table to his right tried to outdo each other in a farting contest, and to his left, a large woman grumbled, picked anchovies off her pizza, and flung them onto the plate of the equally large man seated opposite her.

"Number 16," called the counter clerk.

"That's us," Archie said. "I'll go get it."

He pushed his chair back and strode to the counter. A slim Asian man emerged from the kitchen behind it. "You Archie?" he asked.

"Yes," Archie replied, realizing that he didn't sound too sure.

"I thought that I recognized you. You're the trucker who's staying with us at the Manor. Nisha told me that you here visiting your girlfriend. You take her to Giorgio's for Valentine's Day. That's nice. I make your pizza special." He turned and pulled the aluminum pie pan away from the pass-through window and set it on the counter.

Archie was for the moment speechless. Pacifico had molded the entire pizza into a heart shape and little heart-shaped slices of pepperoni dotted the cheese.

"Enjoy."

Archie carried the pie, plates, and napkins to the table. Debbie nearly spewed her soda at the sight of the heart-shaped pizza.

"That is just the cutest thing I've seen," she said. "It's almost too special to eat." She gave him a penitent look. "You've just been so patient. I know this hasn't been much fun for you. What did you do all day, anyway?"

Archie chewed a mouthful of pizza. He was no aficionado but he had to admit it was pretty darn good. "I guess I can tell you. It's not like it's a secret. Or at least it probably won't be a secret for long."

Debbie's eyebrows went up. "What?"

Still not certain that he wasn't breaching some carefully guarded intelligence, Archie dipped his head and said in a half-whisper, "I learned that President Clinton is coming to Hyde Park."

For the second time, Debbie looked like she was about to spit. She blotted her mouth. "No. Why? How do you know?"

"Did you happen to notice all those NYNEX trucks that were on the road this morning?"

"Can't say that I did."

"Well, I did."

Debbie grinned. "You would."

Archie described how the fleet of utility vehicles had aroused his suspicions, leading him to explore the FDR Park.

"So my Super Man spent the day skulking around a historic home."

"I didn't skulk. I had a perfect right to be there. It's a federal park. I'm a taxpayer." He didn't mention how he had lurked just outside the administrator's office.

Debbie shrugged. "I dunno. Sounds farfetched to me. You've seen Hyde Park. It's not like it's a huge population center, there's nothing going on. So why here?"

"He's going to visit the FDR Library."

"They don't have books in D.C.?"

"Cute, Debbie. He'll be making an appearance, with the FDR Library as the background. Remember all that stuff your rabbi was saying about Roosevelt's new liberalism policies?"

"He's not 'my' rabbi, he's Mom's."

"OK, anyway, maybe Clinton wants to suggest he's made of the same stuff."

Debbie pursed her lips. "Makes sense. Still, it sounds like a nightmare to me. Think of his entourage. Security people, secretaries, photographers, publicists. Hoards of reporters following him. Paparazzi. He can't seriously be thinking of some kind of open-to-the-public gathering. Where's everyone going to fit? It's not like Hyde Park has a convention center. I'll bet if anything he's just passing through on the way to somewhere else, like Albany. No way he can plan on staying overnight. Where's he going to stay? The Hyde Park Manor?"

Archie chuckled. "There's plenty of room. Right now the only ones staying there are me and maybe this one other guy." His chuckle became a chortle. "I can picture it. The President stepping up to the front desk. Nisha would probably be cool. Running a motel, I'll bet she's seen just about everything. I can imagine her taking him down the hallway, showing him a room. Just think, Deb, I could be sharing a donut in the lobby with the President."

Debbie slid a trapezoidal piece of pizza from the pan onto her plate and grinned. "Well, we do know the president is fond of donuts. Pizza too, right?" She folded her slice nearly double and took a bite. "How is it for you? Honestly, it's not the world's greatest pizza. We'd have to go in the City for really good New York pizza."

"It's fine," Archie said, and it was. Frozen microwave pizza, Domino's, or a slice from the convenience store, it was all the same to him. Just something to eat. "How is Eli?"

"Eli's fine, it's the grown-ups who are having a hard time adjusting. Caryn's getting impatient to be up and moving around. Dad wants to get back to work. Mom's making us all a little crazy, bless her heart. I know she's been in a terrible tizzy and a little high strung—"

A little?

"—but it is her first grandchild." Debbie gave him an apologetic smile. "Elliot's just a champ. He wants to spend time with the baby but his law firm keeps sending him clients. He's reading depositions and writing briefs with one hand and cradling little Eli with the other. There's just so much he can do from the house, though. Clients and the other lawyers all want to meet. Poor Elliot's under a lot of stress. I guess it hasn't been much fun for you. You will stay, though, won't you? For the brit? It's really important."

"Oh, sure," Archie said. *The things we do for love.* "Is there anything that I can do?"

Debbie helped herself to another slice. "Other than shovel the driveway again?"

"I would."

"I know. I'm just kidding."

"Then you won't mind ... I'm taking on a load tomorrow."

Debbie laid her half-eaten slice on her plate. Her smile dimmed. "You are? You're going back to work? I thought you said that you were taking vacation."

Archie could tell from her expression that he was in trouble. Behind her polite smile she gritted her teeth. "I thought you said for the weekend. I didn't realize it was going to end up being a whole week."

Debbie looked down at her plate and muttered, "Well, if that's what you want to do."

"Look, I'm not talking about driving to California. I'll just do a short haul, a local run. You said you didn't need me to help with anything at the house." He reached across the table and covered one of her hands with his. "I'll be back by the end of the day. We can have dinner together. C'mon Deb, whaddaya say?"

She shrugged. "OK."

"I'll call you as soon as I'm done."

Debbie looked up and gave him a thin smile. "Sounds good," she said although it was clear to Archie it was anything but. She pushed away her plate, the pizza now cold, its cheese topping waxy with congealed oil.

"Done?" Archie asked.

She nodded. "I've had enough." She pushed her chair back before Archie could pull it out for her. He followed her out and hastened to get the driver's side car door before she could. She drove them to the Manor, pulled into the parking slot, and shifted into PARK with no sign of planning to get out. They exchanged lukewarm kisses and wishes for a "Happy Valentine's Day." He waved as she exited the parking lot and turned onto the highway. The evening hadn't at all gone the way he had planned, but there didn't seem to be much he could do about it. He went to his room and placed a call to his load broker.

CHAPTER TEN

HYDE PARK, NY, Monday, February 15, 1993

Archie spent a fitful night but he didn't blame the Hyde Park Manor. The blackout drapes in his room kept it plenty dark. Either the room was set far enough back from the highway or there hadn't been much traffic because road noise hadn't disturbed him. Nevertheless, he tossed and turned. Not that ending last night with Debbie on uneasy terms had anything to do with it. He figured that he owed his restlessness to getting accustomed to yet another unfamiliar bed. On more than one night spent in a strange city, he had stumbled to the bathroom in the dark to take a leak, forgotten where he was, and walked into a wall.

All the same, it beat trying to get comfortable on a flimsy cot in Miriam Stenowitz's painting studio and even in the Kenworth's sleeper berth, despite its roominess. He enjoyed having a bathroom all to himself so that he could take a real shower and get his entire body wet all at the same time. He left the courtesy soap that was no bigger than a soda cracker in its wrapper and lathered up with his own Irish Spring from his Dopp kit.

Despite the earliness of the hour there were coffee and donuts on the counter in the lobby. The donut box held a complete dozen and the coffee carafe was filled to the brim. Buick Man, as Archie had come to think of him, clearly hadn't been here yet. Archie grabbed an eye-opener and added a dollar to the lonely single in the tip jar. It didn't appear likely that anyone else had been around to make a contribution and Archie wondered if Nisha was seeding the jar in hopes of encouraging other donations.

Through the glass entry door he could see that the parking slots in front of the rooms next to his that had been empty last night now held vehicles. Apparently a few guests had checked into the Manor overnight.

By the truck's flood light he performed a pre-trip inspection. Circling around the rig, he spotted headlights on the highway and saw a vehicle turn into the Manor lot and park right outside the entry door. It looked to be the Buick. Sure enough, the man who stepped from the car wore a cap pulled low on his brow and a parka. *Yup, the Buick Man.* Archie watched as Buick Man ducked into the Manor lobby and reappeared, coffee cup in one hand and a donut clamped between his lips. He slid back into his car, left the Manor's parking lot, and turned into the FDR Park drive.

Archie shook his head. *Did the guy work at the Park maybe, and was scarfing a free breakfast from the Manor's lobby? You'd better leave a tip or I'm renaming you "Freeloader."*

Archie finished his inspection. As he merged onto the highway, he saw the Buick leave the FDR Park and head north. *If Buick Man did work there, it wasn't much of a job since it seemed to take mere minutes to complete.*

With an inward shrug, Archie continued to the Town and Country. Illuminated by exterior lights, the building's chrome sparkled in the early morning dark like a distant star.

In hopes that he'd hear from his broker, he pocketed his pager and collected the cell phone. He grabbed up his notebook thinking that he might work on his story and headed for the diner. He expected that on an early Monday morning he'd be about the only customer in the place, but a smattering of vehicles in the parking lot told him that a few eager beavers had beat him to it. *Well, Monday morning commuters.* Alongside well-worn pickup trucks and rusty vintage station wagons stood a couple of dark sedans. Aside from some recently acquired road dirt, their finishes gleamed as if polished yesterday and the vehicles bristled with antennas. Several of the license plates were white with an American flag in the background and the legends U.S. Government and For Official Use Only in navy blue letters.

Archie recalled Debbie's remarks about President Clinton's entourage and wondered if the cars belonged to some kind of advance team. Weekend mornings at the T&C had been raucous with dozens of conversations pitched loudly enough to be heard over the clatter of dishes. The weekday morning crowd was more subdued and the loudest noises came from the kitchen: the rattle of pots and pans and the cooks chattering over the radio.

Tradesmen in paint-spattered and grease-stained coveralls and farmers and ranchers in bleached-out overalls held down counter stools and filled some of the booths. In another booth, three clean-shaven men with butch haircuts hunched over cups of coffee, lined tablets, and a laptop computer. Black overcoats hung open revealing black suits and white shirts adorned with pocket protectors and laminated badges. To Archie the men looked like they could easily belong to the equally business-like government vehicles parked outside.

Another booth held a man that Archie recognized from Saturday, the *Herald* newspaper editor whose favor Linc Haybens courted. This morning, the editor was minus his family which was probably a good thing. There wasn't much room for them anyway, or at least not for their breakfast. The editor had several newspapers spread out on the tabletop.

In his plaid flannel shirt, puffy vest, and plaid wool cap, Leonard Peerman, the local farmer-turned-investor, held down the same counter stool he had occupied on Saturday. Coffee and cigarette at his elbow, he pored over his newspaper.

"Morning, Mr. Peerman," Archie said as he passed.

Peerman looked up and replied, "Good morning to you, Archie. And thank you. Your father-in-law was very helpful." Peerman held up a leathery hand. "I know. He's not your father-in-law yet. But let me say, I really enjoyed talking with him. Oh, I'm not in his league. Not yet anyway but he gave me some good ideas about how to get there." Leonard tapped his paper as if it held the key to his bright future and he fully expected to unlock it. *The Wall Street Journal* apparently had taken the *Daily Freeman's* place as Leonard Peerman's morning paper. "I'm headed to the library later to get some books that he recommended."

Archie clapped the man on his shoulder. "Good for you." He spied Linc Haybens and settled on a stool next to him. "What's happening with, you know, the *visit?*"

Haybens drew on his cigarette and let the smoke out in one exasperated puff. "I spent last night trying to parlay that lead into a writing assignment. OK, granted, I didn't share any details, just said I'm on to something big. Had a nice chat with the weekend desk editor from *The Poughkeepsie Journal.* Then I went to the *Herald*, then the *Daily Freeman.*" Haybens' glance slid over to the editor in the booth opposite who was patently ignoring him. "They all laughed me out of the office, so to speak. By the time I got to the *Freeman* I was starting to doubt myself. I ended up crying on the shoulder of a friend who works in production at WAMC, the National Public Radio station. He said he'd talk to their producer who does the local segments for their national newscasts. He figured that he could slip in a little story, you know, about the invasion of the NYNEX guys and what they're up to. Schedule it in the middle of the night when no one's listening. Quote me as the source. That way if someone does hear it and it turns out to be a groundless rumor, the egg will be on my face."

He seemed nonchalant about it but Archie figured Linc was pretty disappointed at losing his shot at the big time.

Bonnie emerged from the kitchen with a china cup and small metal pot which she set down in front of Archie. He smelled the steamy herbal aroma of her private tea blend. He looked up. "Something off about my aura?"

Bonnie cocked her head to one side and shrugged.

"Does it really show?"

"I'm afraid so. You seem a little down."

Linc elbowed him in the ribs. "Your Valentine's Day dinner didn't go so well?"

"The closest I could come to an Italian restaurant was a pizza parlor." *Lady didn't go for it and I'm just a tramp.*

"Hey, it wasn't for lack of trying."

"I'm telling you, Archie," said Bonnie. "It's tough to compete with a newborn."

The music on the kitchen's radio stopped mid-song and an announcer took over. Archie wouldn't have even noticed had the cooks' noisy patter not petered out while the radio's volume increased. Archie caught the tail end of the announcement that had interrupted Reba McEntire. Shouts of "hey" and "whoa" and "did you hear that?" were followed by one of the cooks bursting from the kitchen. "Bonnie," he yelled, "you won't believe what we just heard. President Clinton is coming to Hyde Park. It's all over the news. Some town hall thing."

Linc gave Archie a wink and a shit-eating grin.

"OK, so how did your NYNEX invasion story end up as breaking news on some country music station?" Archie asked.

Haybens buffed his fingernails on the lapel of his jacket. "I dunno. Maybe some night owl on their news desk heard the WAMC story. Or maybe WAMC put it out on the wire."

"The wire? Oh, you mean like the Associated Press?"

Haybens grinned. "That's the one."

The editor who had given Linc the bum's rush half-stood in his booth, mouth hanging open. He gathered up his papers and hustled toward the door leaving behind an unfinished omelet. Haybens and the editor locked glances as the man stood tapping his toe at the cash register, waiting to pay his tab. Haybens waved. The editor scowled, threw down some bills next to the cash register, and bolted from the diner.

Diners abandoned their booths and crowded around the counter. The men in suits turned in their seats and strained toward the kitchen, their expressions impassive but their posture tense. Archie could almost see their ears swiveling to home in on the radio. From the kitchen, shouts of "Will youse guys shuddup?" were followed by the radio getting louder. Archie couldn't make out everything that the announcer said and like everyone else he had to wait for the cook to emerge and bring them all up to speed.

"What I got was that something's scheduled for Friday," he said.

"This coming Friday?"

"What time?"

"What's happening?"

The cook gave a big shrug and hustled back to the kitchen. "Hey, Frankie, don't let that burn!"

The radio newscaster announced a return to regular programming and Billy Ray Cyrus commenced to wailing about his achy breaky heart. Diners retook their seats and rehashed what little they had heard. The men in suits settled back into their booth, hunched together in conference.

"OK, clearly we were on the right track. I gotta run, see what else I can find out," Linc Haybens said.

"Call me. You've got my pager and my cellular phone number, right?" Archie said. He patted the device at his elbow.

"Yeah, keep that charged up."

If Haybens's source was right, Friday was the big day. *As if with the ceremony for baby Eli it wasn't going to be big enough.*

Archie waved Bonnie over. "So, uh, do you think we could get the guys to settle down long enough to fix me a waffle?" he asked.

"You betcha. Milk too?"

"Yes, please."

"You got it." She passed his order to the cooks.

Archie lifted the tea cup to take a sip then set it down when his beeper went off. He recognized his broker's phone number. He was about to slide off the counter stool and head for the lobby payphone when he realized that he could return the call right where he sat. He picked up the cell phone and dialed.

"Funny that you called last night," said his load broker. "Turns out that I do have something for you. You know, I didn't think that there was a lot of industry or commerce in that area."

"There isn't. Not only is there not much, there isn't any. Further south around Poughkeepsie and north around Albany there is, but not right around here."

"Strange time and place for a wine festival then, I'd say."

"Huh?"

"The cargo," his broker replied. "It's cases of wine. Definitely LTL and this is PUD, not long haul by any means; the pickup's at a warehouse in New Paltz and there's three delivery points. But you said you were going to be there all week."

"I am and I've got some time on my hands so yeah, I'll take it," he said, suddenly jazzed about having something to do and somewhere to go, even if it was a less-than-truckload pick-up-and-delivery job.

"There's some urgency to it. The receivers all say they need the load today."

"Not a problem. Give me the details." Archie jotted down the particulars in his notebook. "Say, Mr. Peerman," he called down the counter. "Would you happen to know where around here I could rent a van trailer?"

Peerman rubbed his chin. "Ya know, I do. Well, not around here exactly. Poughkeepsie. Also, on the other side of the river near Newburgh there's a Ryder dealer. And a Penske dealer in Kingston."

Much as Archie would have liked an excuse to revisit Frieda's bakery in Kingston, it sounded like he was headed south. He could cross the river, pick up a trailer then head for the warehouse.

Bonnie slid his breakfast onto the counter and asked "More tea?"

"No, thanks, but I'd like some coffee after all. And if I could get that to go, that would be great."

"To where is it you're going, may I ask?"

"New Paltz, to start," Archie said over a mouthful of waffle, now in a hurry to finish his breakfast and be on the road. "Big wine wholesaler there, apparently. I'm picking up then making deliveries all over the valley. Not here, though."

"Well, no, we don't have a liquor license. Not even for beer and wine. We get a new customer now and then who wants a beer with lunch or wine with dinner but most of the time it's not a problem. New Paltz, huh? I don't know about wine but they've got great ice cream in the travel plaza on 84 around there. Carvel. Soft serve."

"Like Dairy Queen?"

"Oh, better. Much better. Nothing like it. If this were summer, I'd say you shouldn't pass it up."

"You steered me right with all those Rhinebeck shops. Debbie's sister liked the stuff that I got her." There was no saying how Debbie felt about the ring since he hadn't given it to her yet and now wondered if the time would ever be right.

"Glad to hear it. Seriously, if you're an ice cream fan, Carvel is not to be missed." She handed him his meal ticket and a tall lidded Styrofoam cup.

*****

Answering questions about what he did for a living sometimes earned sighs of envy. People would remark how much they too would enjoy spending all day driving around, seeing the sights, answering the call of the road. There was much that Archie liked about his work. He enjoyed the challenge of getting a load where it was supposed to go, on time and in perfect condition.

Sightseeing, however, wasn't always on the list. He had driven millions of highway miles and not all of them were something to write home about. Some interstates like 10 or 35 took him on long stretches of blacktop that ran past acres of endless monotonous scrubland. The main attraction on those routes was the occasional "easy-on/easy off" one-pump gas station-cum-convenience store featuring dusty bags of stale chips, dried up candy, and off-brand soda. The best that could be said for those miles was that traffic was often light. Other routes, like I-40, were often so congested with heavy vehicle traffic that it was like traveling in a convoy, truckers maintaining the barest minimum of following distance and struggling to make the best time.

Route 9 was more like it, carving a pleasantly picturesque path lined with snow-covered trees. As if the hum of the tires on the road were a mantra and the vibrations transmitted through the seat a therapeutic massage, Archie felt the knots of a restless night loosen. He smiled, pleased with the decision to take the load, and tuned in his road senses: sight, sound, spatial perception, and even smell. Like a gambler counting cards, he kept inventory of the other vehicles on the road. The four-wheeler that had been behind him hadn't exited and had to be in the "no-zone." Archie would have to keep it in mind should he have to make a turn or, heaven forbid, a sudden stop.

He crossed the river and found the trailer rental not precisely in Newburgh but a good dozen miles further west. A little miffed, he doubled back and got on I-87 headed north towards New Paltz. His personal radar reminded him that he now had a trailer in tow and needed to make lane changes with extra care.

He left the thruway, headed west to New Paltz, and received the second surprise of the day. He had expected a huge beverage warehouse with several trailer-height docks. Instead, the address he'd been given led him to what appeared to be a perfectly ordinary home with a detached wooden storage building. A placard with a grapevine graphic and the legend "Valley Wine Cellar" hung over the storage shed door. More barn than cellar, he thought, but the "wine" part suggested that he was in the right place. He pulled slightly past the driveway entrance and then backed partway down the drive.

He stepped from the cab and greeted the man who had come out to meet him: tall and slender with gray hair, dressed in a sleeveless burgundy quilted vest over a white shirt, brown corduroy pants, and boots. Around his neck he wore not only a dark red bow tie but also a heavy silver cable chain from which hung an engraved silver disk that looked like a tiny hub cap. He introduced himself as Warren Edelrath, the owner. "You've come for the wine?" He looked Archie's rig up and down. "I didn't expect such a large vehicle."

That made two men who didn't get what they had anticipated.

"I guess you thought you'd be loading from a big wine distributor," said Edelrath. "The Valley Wine Cellar is really a storage facility for local oenophiles. Folks who collect wines; wine clubs and their members, wine bars, restaurants. We have small lockers for customers with modest collections, actual storage rooms for larger ones, and we even have bulk storage capabilities. We've got more room here than your average aficionado has in his house and more than many commercial establishments. We also have ideal storage conditions. Let me show you."

Archie followed him into the shed. There was nothing cellar-like about it. The humble exterior belied the brightly lit interior's refinements: an epoxy-white polished concrete floor, white concrete walls, and ceiling finished out with a clean white knockdown texture. The huge room felt comfortably cool on his face. Cases filled with bottles covered part of the floor and tall wooden racks of bottles lined the walls. "But this is just the staging area for wine about to be put away or picked up." Edelrath explained. He led Archie to a hatchway in the floor and down a flight of stairs to "Our subterranean cellar. The wine here is stored at optimal temperature and humidity."

This was more like it. At the base of the stairs Archie found himself in a chilly corridor lined with many steel doors, each one striped in gold and fitted with an electronic security keypad and a spindle-wheel handle like he would expect to see on a bank vault. He'd never been to Fort Knox but he imagined it would look something like this.

"What have you got down here, gold?" Archie asked.

Edelrath smiled politely. "As good as. We've got customers who trust us to store a collection that's worth its weight in gold. Each one of these lockers is lined in French oak and backed by steel walls and doors. Some hold just a few cases, others can hold up to a hundred and sixty. We even have some walk-in lockers and others that hold casks. Each locker is individually secured as you can see and all are backed with a state-of-the-art alarm system, video cameras, and a fire sprinkler system. We take security very seriously. We've been entrusted with single bottles of wine that sell for five figures."

Archie let out a whistle. "One bottle of wine? You could buy the best truck on the market for that amount of money."

"Oh, that hasn't happened very often, I will admit. Most of our customers are wine bars and restaurants who simply don't have storage space on their premises that's large enough or that's properly climate controlled. We receive their shipments for them, store them until they're needed. Which for some reason is today. Every one of our restaurants, every bar. The phone's been ringing off the hook. They all want their inventory today. Now. Too many for us to deliver to and they're too busy to pick up. That's where you come in."

"Where's your loading dock? Around the back? How do I get to it?"

Edelstein's smile was apologetic. "We don't have a loading dock per se. We rarely ever deal in quantities that would necessitate one."

"I see," Archie said, although he didn't. "How about someone to help load?

Edelrath shrugged. "There's just you and me, and I can't help. Insurance. You understand."

He did. He often confronted situations in which employees were forbidden to go inside his van to help load. What Archie also understood was that he was going to have to tailgate the cargo: move it all to the rear of the trailer, lift it up somehow, and transfer it into the van. "You wouldn't happen to have a pallet jack?"

Edelstein nodded. "That I do."

Archie sighed with relief. That, at least, would ease the burden of getting the cases of wine near the truck. "And a forklift?"

"No, but I do have a walkie stacker. Would that work?"

God, I hope so, Archie thought.

To his credit, Edelrath did pitch in to move cases of wine at least up to the rear of Archie's truck with the pallet jack. Edelrath then used the walkie stacker to lift the pallet jack itself up to the trailer so Archie could distribute the cases throughout the van. He considered himself to be in fairly good shape, but by the time they were done he was winded. He'd worked up enough of a sweat to shed his sleeveless jacket. His legs, shoulders, and back complained about the unexpected workout.

Edelrath mopped his forehead with the sleeve of his white shirt. Despite the outside's cold temperatures and the shed's interior refrigeration, like Archie, the man had broken into a sweat. "I can't thank you enough," he said, panting. "Our customers will be in your debt. I think the least I can do is offer you a glass of wine. At the rear we have a climate-controlled tasting room. We're quite proud of it. It's a lovely relaxing space with comfortable leather chairs, leaded glass light fixtures, crystal goblets. Come sit, catch your breath before you take off."

"Can I have a glass of that five-figure wine you talked about?"

Edelrath laughed. "I wish. I would join you. No, but I could open a very nice New York State Riesling or if you'd rather a red, I've got a Cabernet Franc I think you'd like."

"Thanks. I'd better pass. I've got a lot of driving to do."

"Well, let me send you away with a bottle at least." He scanned the wall of racks and pulled out a bottle. "This one was very well received by one of the wine clubs that meets here."

Archie pointed to another case. "What's that one?" In addition to the name of the winery and a sketch of a vineyard, it had lettering similar to what Archie had seen on Debbie's childhood prayer book. *Hebrew?* "Is that imported?" *Like from Israel?*

"Not at all. It's a U.S. company, based in New York. That's quite a nice wine. A port, actually. It makes a good aperitif or after-dinner drink." Edelrath cocked his head. "It's kosher, too, if that's important to you."

It wasn't. Debbie had tried to explain kosher but Archie still didn't quite understand the concept. Pork products weren't kosher, but beef was. Except for filet mignon which wasn't. *Go figure.* Cod fish and salmon were kosher but catfish wasn't. *Confusing.* Debbie didn't follow the Jewish food rules but for all he knew her parents did and they might appreciate a kosher wine. "I've got an event coming up where that might be just the thing."

Edelrath handed him a bottle. "With my compliments, then."

Archie's remaining delivery destinations were all on the other side of the river. Typical, he thought. While he enjoyed getting views of the Hudson, the bridge tolls gave his bottom line a beating. *I should get me a barge and ferry myself back and forth.*

Barges had, he learned from a highway historic sign, been used to transport cargo on the river in its heyday as a commercial thoroughfare. Important to shipping, trading and industry, control of the Hudson was hotly contested during the American Revolution. Later, its banks became the address of wealthy families whose estates still lined the shores. Like the FDR home, many had been turned over to the state or federal government and now served as parks. As he traversed Route 9, he passed signs directing tourists to the mansions of wealthy families whose names he recalled from high school lessons about robber barons. Had they come by their money unethically? If so, perhaps it was poetic justice that now anyone could troop through their bedrooms for the price of a tour ticket.

Some of his cargo was needed at the Camellia Mansion in Staatsburg. If the double A in the town's name wasn't enough of a clue about the town's Dutch colonial roots, the quatrefoil cutouts in the gingerbread woodwork of houses and fences certainly was. The snow-covered pines crowding the roadway and the glimpses of quaint architecture made him feel like he could easily be traveling through a Hans Christian Andersen fairy tale.

With its stately white building, tall columns, wide balustraded terraces, and expansive grounds, the Camellia Mansion struck Archie as in some ways even grander than President Roosevelt's Hyde Park home. Its lofty hilltop location afforded a view of the nearby Catskill Mountains and the Hudson.

The harried manager of the Mansion's elegant Old-World-style bar greeted Archie with a sigh of relief and rustled up a couple of bar-backs and dishwashers from the kitchen to help offload the wine. That they stacked it in a hallway that was neither as carefully climate- or temperature controlled as the Valley Wine Cellar didn't concern the manager. "I doubt it's going to be here very long," he said. "We'll probably go through this in a night or two and need more."

The humble white clapboard exterior of Archie's second stop, the Portofino Ristorante, belied the elegant Italian food offered on their menu which Archie scanned while he waited for the manager. *Now this would have been the place to take Debbie for a Valentine dinner, if only I had known about it.* They were as proud of their wine list as their cuisine, the manager said, and it would be a grave embarrassment to be found wanting when the dinner crowd arrived.

"You're expecting that many people?" Archie said. Staatsburg was even less than a whistle-stop, hardly on the map, and didn't appear to be on the way to much of anywhere.

"While we are just about the best kept secret in Hudson Valley, we do have our devotees," the manager replied, holding his head high. "We have people come up from the City. But this week it's going to be crazy. You probably haven't heard. President Clinton is scheduled to visit Hyde Park on Friday."

"I did know that," Archie said, but what, he wondered, did that have to do with wine on Monday?

"You wouldn't believe how many hangers-on are going to descend on the area, days in advance. They're not going to want to eat at McDonald's every night and there just aren't that many places around here to get a decent meal." The manager folded his arms across his chest and nodded. "We expect we'll be making a lot of new friends."

Archie thought, Wow, Debbie had seen all that coming.

The manager scribbled his name on a business card and handed it to Archie. "Please, you come back. Tell your waiter that you are our new friend," he said with a smile. "Not tonight, though. We are completely booked and we already have reservations for tomorrow."

The manager at the Beekman Arms in Rhinebeck told the same tale. "You arrived just in time," she said. "We already had a larger-than-usual Monday lunch crowd and they put a hit on what we had on hand. We definitely need to restock for tonight." She looked skyward and shook her head. "This is going to be one crazy week." She took Archie's hands in both of hers. "Thank you for coming to our rescue. Please, anytime you want to be our guest, just give us a call and give the hostess my name."

Gee, Archie thought, where was all this hospitality yesterday when he really needed it? "Would tonight be alright? I've got a make-good on a Valentine's Day dinner that didn't go quite right."

"Absolutely."

He thanked the manager and from the cab of his truck, called Debbie from his cell phone.

"Hey, babe. Can you break away and meet me for dinner?"

"Let me see." Archie heard some discussion in the background and then Debbie came back on the line. "Yes, I can get away for a few hours. Where should I meet you?"

"Actually, I'm in Rhinebeck. The Beekman Arms."

"Really?" Debbie sounded intrigued and impressed. "All right. I'll meet you there."

Archie snagged a clean shirt and a sport coat and grabbed his duffle bag. He returned to the lobby, found the men's room, and did his best to freshen up. He'd been in and out of the cold all day, up and down stairs, and had hoisted more cases of cargo than he had in some time. A nice relaxing dinner with Debbie sounded like just the ticket.

He got a beer from the bar and sat in the lobby to wait for Debbie. He tried not to get so relaxed that he'd fall asleep. He was tired enough that he easily could. Instead, he concentrated on observing the steady stream of diners as they came through the door and were escorted into the restaurant's many different wainscoted dining areas, each equipped with a fireplace and furnished with linen-covered, wooden tables, and slat-back chairs. Before long, the softly lit rooms were filled, scented with tantalizing aromas, and hummed with the conversation of contented diners.

At last Debbie arrived and greeted Archie with a hug and a kiss. The hostess led them to their table and pulled out a chair for Debbie. "Your server will be right with you," she said.

"This is really nice, Archie."

"I've got to figure you've eaten here before."

"Oh, yeah, but it's still special. This is a kind of magical place. Just being here makes me feel more relaxed.

"Rough day?" Debbie did look a little weary.

"You wouldn't believe. Little Eli sleeps a lot, just not in long stretches. Every few hours he wakes up, day or night. Of course Caryn gets up with him, and then of course so does Elliot."

"Good evening. I'm Bonnie and I'll be your server ... hey, it's Archie!"

Archie looked over Debbie's shoulder to see Bonnie from the Town and Country Diner standing alongside their table. Gone was the pink uniform that she wore at the diner not to mention the numerous necklaces she usually draped around her neck. Only one pair of star-shaped earrings studded her lobes. She looked almost sophisticated in her white blouse and slim black skirt.

"You work here too?" he asked.

"Sometimes. They needed extra help last night, it being Valentine's Day and all, and tonight's just as busy. So, what can I get you two to drink? We've got some great New York wines on the list."

Quite a few of which Archie had personally delivered just a few hours ago.

"Or can I get you a cocktail?"

"Ya know, I'm in a celebratory mood." Archie said. Getting a table here had been something of an accomplishment. "I'm thinking champagne." He looked at Debbie. "Wanna split a split?"

Bonnie said, "We have some really nice sparkling wines produced right here in New York. May I suggest Chateau Frank Célèbre? Of course it can't be called Champagne since it's not made with grapes grown in France, but it is made by *methode champenoise*. Dr. Frank, I'll have you know, made an important contribution to the New York state wine industry."

Surprised by Bonnie's encyclopedic knowledge of viniculture, Archie was for a moment speechless, and Bonnie looked almost smug.

"Works for me." Archie finally said and Debbie nodded her assent.

Bonnie winked. "Coming right up and I'll bring you some water too."

Debbie sighed deeply and her shoulders lowered. "I'm taking shifts with the baby so Caryn and Elliot can close the door, relax, and get some serious shut-eye. Which doesn't always work if Eli needs to be fed. Which is also every few hours. Of course Caryn is taking care of that. You would think that breastfeeding would be a natural no-brainer but it turns out that it's not all that automatic.

Caryn did get a tutorial in the hospital but we've got a counselor coming to the house tomorrow to give her a refresher course.

"Then all that eating means lots of diaper changes. Elliot, what a guy, he's helping with that. Now I know why new moms seem obsessed with their baby's poop and pee. Caryn's supposed to keep a record of all that. Important information for the doctor. It all tells if the baby is developing properly or if there's a problem. Frequency, consistency, color ... Debbie gave him an apologetic smile. "Sorry. More than you wanted to know? Anyway, the little guy also needs a lot of cuddling.

"And Caryn needs so many things that we didn't anticipate. Oh, of course she had a baby shower and got just the cutest toys and clothes, very few of which are useful right now. I've had to run out to get, like, a nursing pillow. Who had ever heard of that? I didn't. Dad had to set up a changing table because the dresser in the guest room is too tall." Debbie accepted the glass of water before Bonnie could set it on the table, and drank half of it.

Bonnie placed two crystal flutes on the table, peeled the wrapper off the top of the little bottle of bubbly, and pried off the cap. "Pop," she said with a wink. "No cork on these little splits so I thought I'd improvise." She filled their glasses. Before Archie could even suggest a toast, Debbie had taken a long sip.

"Oh, that is refreshing," she said with a grateful sigh. She nodded at Bonnie. "Thank you, I feel better already." She looked around the room. "Maybe it's the subliminal suggestion of a simpler time when life was less hurried."

"You're quite welcome," Bonnie said. "Would you like something to start? An appetizer?"

Appetizer sounded good. His two breakfasts had been filling but Archie hadn't eaten since then. "The French onion soup." *No, not a bowlful of onions, not tonight.* "Make that the butternut squash soup. Debbie?"

She shook her head. "Not for me. It's been nonstop food all day at Mom's." She picked up the menu. "Maybe there's something light ..."

"I'll leave you two to enjoy and look over the menu. I should tell you that they have the prime rib only on the weekends. But everything here is good so you just can't go wrong."

"Archie," Debbie whispered when Bonnie had left, "you know this isn't the cheapest place in town."

"It's OK. It's a special occasion."

Bonnie delivered Archie's soup and a bread basket. "You will love the bread. It's from a local bakery across the river. They have this special oven. You could live on their bread alone but then you'd miss the rest of the stuff on the menu. Have you, uh, had a chance to decide about the food?"

"The trout sounds good to me." Debbie looked at Archie.

"The trout for the lady and I'll have the chicken."

"Oh, good choice. That's locally sourced, it's real good," said Bonnie. "More champagne?"

Debbie shook her head. "I've got to drive back and I'd better take it easy on the alcohol. It would make embarrassing headlines for Super Man's girl to get arrested for DWI."

"Much less Super Man himself. We'd better go with Pepsi."

"I'll put in your orders and get you those drinks."

"How is Caryn doing?" Archie asked.

Debbie shrugged and buttered a slice of bread. "Better, but still not one-hundred percent. Oh, Archie, your little friend was right. This bread is great."

"As good as Frieda's?"

Her mouth full, Debbie nodded.

"Does Caryn need to see a doctor?"

"I don't know. They told her at the hospital that it might take a while to heal. I guess if she's really unhappy we can have her looked at tomorrow. That cream you bought her?"

"Is it working?"

"I don't know if it's helping to heal the incision but it warmed her heart, that's for sure. What a nice thing for you to do. And the balm for the baby—"

"Any good?"

"Well, Eli hasn't said anything either way but it's sure making diaper changes more pleasant for the rest of us." She waggled her fingers. "We all have nice soft hands."

"And the baby's OK?"

"The baby is wonderful. He's so sweet. I just can't get enough of him."

Bonnie arrived with the entrees, sizzling and fragrant with thyme and rosemary, accompanied by fingerling potatoes glistening with butter, and green beans dotted with sliced almonds. "Guys, guys, I'm so excited," she said. "They've asked me to stay all week. It's the Clinton visit we heard about this morning at the T&C." To Debbie she said, "You heard about that?"

"Oh, yes, it's been all over the local news."

Bonnie said, "The management here thinks they're going to be mobbed." She shrugged. "Makes sense. Besides the T&C it's not like there's a whole lot of places in Hyde Park to eat, especially ones with liquor licenses. The boss is looking to see if maybe we can get a temporary permit, at least let people bring their own. Speaking of bringing, can I bring you two anything else?"

Archie looked a question at Debbie and she shook her head. "We're good," he said.

Bonnie nodded. "I'll be back to check on you later."

"Speaking of 'mobbed,' did you see who else is here?"

"No." He only had eyes for Debbie and would have said so if it didn't sound so corny.

Debbie leaned forward and whispered, not that she really needed to lower her voice so as not to be heard over the general racket of conversations and clattering cutlery. "It's the Town Supervisor. I recognized him from photos in the *Freeman*. Sitting with a whole table-full of suits. Looks pretty serious. A lot of talking, not much eating." She cocked her head.

Archie twisted and glanced behind him. Without staring, he caught just enough of a glimpse to make out that some of the people at the table were what he thought were the men from this morning at the T&C. The "G-men," as he came to think of them. Debbie was right about that group's focus. The diners had lined tablets directly in front of them while dinner plates sat neglected at their elbows.

He and Debbie had just tucked into their entrees when Archie's pager beeped. Debbie looked almost as startled as Archie who had forgotten that he still had it. He stole a peek at the message. It was from his load broker. "Uh, I think I'd better see what this is about," he said. "Excuse me a minute?"

He headed for the hallway where the restrooms were located and where he remembered seeing a payphone.

"I've got another short haul for you if you want it," his broker said. "A flatbed load of Jersey barriers for the highway department in Hyde Park. Tomorrow. You can get the trailer from the receiver but you'll need to go to north of Albany to get the cargo."

A flatbed. That figured, since I have a van. All in a day's work, though, and it gave him an excuse to avoid the Stenowitz home.

Archie returned to the table and Debbie looked up from her plate. "Everything OK?"

"I, uh, said I'd take on another load, tomorrow. I hope that's OK."

Debbie gave a noncommittal shrug.

"I just feel kinda in the way at your Mom's house. Not, you know, that I feel unwelcome or anything." Which he did but he certainly didn't want Debbie to know that.

Debbie tipped her head. "It has been chaotic there. Mom's taken going overboard to new heights. Or depths, I guess. But it's her first, so I'm not saying anything."

"Are you sure you won't need me?"

"Sweetie, of course I need you, but we'll be fine. Mom and I could manage easy if we didn't also have the brit to plan. I'll contact you if we need something. Meanwhile Elliot's swamped with work and Dad thinks he needs to get back on the ball too. I'm trying not to catch the crazies from Mom. I think I might even try to call and check in with the office which now seems like the sanest place on Earth."

Good, Archie thought. So he wasn't the only one abandoning ship. Still, the last remaining sip of champagne in Debbie's glass held more sparkle than she did. He was rehearsing strategies in his head to take some of the pressure off when Bonnie came by to check how their dinner was.

"I guess the empty plate can speak for itself," Archie replied.

"Done with yours?" Bonnie asked Debbie.

She nodded.

Bonnie leaned in to pick up the plates. "Hey, you guys, you won't believe what I heard over at that table." She cocked her head in the direction of the G-men. "That Town Hall Friday? It's two events. The President will be making a speech then stopping at the FDR Library."

That would explain some of the NYNEX work.

"The speech will be at Haviland Middle School. Since not everyone can get into the speech, they're going to broadcast it live on closed circuit in the school gym. Even though it's being held at a public school, it's not going to be open to the public. You have to have a ticket." She smirked. "The way people are trying to snag those, you'd think the Beatles were coming to town or something. You know who those tickets are going to go to, right? All the hoity-toity people. Oh well. I'll probably be working anyway. So, would you two like to see a dessert menu? There's killer chocolate cake."

"I'd better not," said Debbie.

Debbie passing up chocolate? Not a good sign.

To Archie she said, "There have been so many sweets at the house. People have sent gift baskets, Dad and Elliot pick up some treat every time they're out. Besides, it's getting late. I should be heading back. Caryn will need relieving."

"I guess I'll just take the check," Archie told Bonnie. *Just as well. I have a trailer to return.*

CHAPTER ELEVEN

HYDE PARK, NY, Tuesday, February 16, 1993

Eager to collect the highway department trailer and continue to Albany, Archie started his day well before light. He trotted towards the Hyde Park Manor lobby for a cup of coffee to drink in between showering and dressing. From the hallway, he spotted the Buick Man, now officially redubbed "the Freeloader," seated at one of the lobby's small round tables, a foam cup in one hand and a walkie-talkie in the other.

Archie's mother undoubtedly would have scolded him that it was rude to eavesdrop. Nevertheless, he stopped just short of the lobby to listen and heard the Freeloader say, "We gotta make a move."

Archie couldn't make out the scratchy response.

"I'm telling ya, he'll be here Friday. Meanwhile there's people all over the Park and it's only going to get worse. We need a plan and we need to act. We're running out of time."

The Freeloader spotted Archie. "Gotta go," he said into the walkie-talkie. He pushed back his chair, stood, and tossed his cup into the wastebasket. Glaring at Archie, he pulled his cap further down over his face and hustled out the front door.

Archie crossed the lobby just in time to see the Riviera peel out of the Manor's parking lot.

Something about the Freeloader made Archie uneasy. He couldn't quite put his finger on it. *Just what was the guy up to?* Whatever it was, from the snippet of conversation he overhead, the upcoming presidential visit would complicate it.

Archie turned back into the lobby and noticed that the newspaper vending machines weren't stuffed to the gills as usual. Apparently the Hyde Park Manor wasn't the only enterprise enjoying more business. As a result of the town's influx of visitors, the newspapers were selling more copies.

Daisy Donuts undoubtedly was also racking up more sales. Archie had gotten used to seeing the "daily dozen" short the single pastry snagged by the Freeloader. This morning the reverse was the case; only one donut remained, and the coffee carafe was nearly empty. The tip jar, however, held the usual lonely dollar bill. *Bunch of cheapskates.* Archie pocketed the single and replaced it with a fiver.

Archie went around the back to get the truck warmed up and inspected. The eaters of the donuts and drinkers of the coffee were all drivers of black Suburbans judging from the company the Kenworth was keeping.

Dressed and ready to roll, he headed for the Town and Country. The count of cars in the parking lot rivaled Saturday morning and he had to park a distance from the door. As he made his way to the entrance, he passed a number of black sedans and SUVs. Several vehicles bore federal license plates. Sedans with New York State plates had windshield decals for employee parking lots. All the Xs and Zs in the company names suggested telecom operations. Smaller models bore cards on the dashboard that read PRESS in big block letters.

Not many seats in the diner remained empty. A lot more suits and ties crowded into the booths than Archie had gotten used to seeing. Notepads and laptop computers competed with breakfast platters for tabletop space.

The counter at the T&C was nearly sold out. Archie spotted Linc Haybens but couldn't catch his eye. The reporter stood at the elbow of a man seated on a counter stool. Haybens had his yellow tablet in one hand, moved his pen furiously with the other. Working a story, Archie figured, although what would be newsworthy on a wintery Tuesday morning in Hyde Park?

Archie scanned the dining room for a free booth when a man at the counter collected his check and slid one leg from the stool. Archie made a beeline to grab the seat.

"Hey, Archie," the man said.

"Oh, Emmet."

The hospital security guard vacated his seat and Archie took possession. "Busy place."

"Tell me about it. And it's just going to get busier. Had to change my breakfast to a to-go order. Unscheduled meeting at the hospital about security measures for The Visit."

Archie could virtually see the quotation marks and capitals. "At the hospital? How's the hospital involved?"

"We hope it won't be but if heaven forbid something should happen to Pizza Boy—"

"Pizza Boy?"

Emmet leaned in to whisper his reply. "Our code name for the President."

Archie tried not to laugh. The nation's leader's well-publicized fondness for junk food would probably hound him throughout his administration and beyond.

"We'll be assessing our preparedness for any emergency."

Archie could hear the quotation marks around "preparedness."

"Not just whether we have on hand any medications or equipment we could possibly need, but also the ability to lock the place down. Vet anyone who wants or needs access. Someone with bad intent could use an emergency to slip through the cracks."

Cheryl handed over a white paper sack.

"Thanks, Cheryl. Be seeing ya, Archie."

"Hey, Emmet, hold up a minute. Let me ask you something. There's this guy at the Manor. He's not even staying there. Just cruises in every day to eat free donuts and drink free coffee. I'm calling him The Freeloader."

Emmet tsked and shook his head. "Some people."

"This morning I overheard him on a walkie-talkie." Archie described the conversation. "I dunno, just sounded suspicious to me. Security's your thing. What do you think?"

Emmet shrugged. "Could be nothing. Could be anything. Given this situation, all bets are off."

"You think I should tell someone? Besides you, I mean."

Emmet tugged on his ear. "Guess it wouldn't hurt."

"Like who?"

Emmet zipped up his blue parka, grabbed the sack, and his ticket. "The police, I guess. I suppose, like the hospital, they'll want to be prepared for any eventuality."

"Good idea. Thanks."

The security guard touched the brim of his cap and headed for the cashier.

Archie settled into the seat Emmet vacated.

"Coffee?" Cheryl asked.

"Milk," Bonnie hollered from across the room. "Hi, Archie. Did you enjoy dinner last night?"

Cheryl's head whipped in her direction then back to Archie. She looked him a question. "Really?"

"I took my girl to the Beekman Arms. Bonnie was our waitress."

Cheryl cleared her throat. "Oh, of course. I meant, do you really want milk and not coffee?"

"He's staying at the Manor," Bonnie announced.

Archie noticed that several of the diners looked up and gave him the once-over. *Did that guy just jot something down on a notepad?*

From the front of the diner someone yelled, "Hey who owns that big red truck?"

Archie gulped. *Am I parked illegally? Blocking someone?* When no one else owned up, he raised his hand. "I guess that would be me."

The man attached to the voice strode past the other diners, his unbuttoned tan overcoat flapping. At Archie's elbow, he held out a business card. "Mike Kelly. I'm with the *Post.*"

Archie had no comment and apparently one was expected because Mike Kelly said, "*The New York Post.*"

Ah, a New York City newspaper. Archie had made its acquaintance in journalism school. Sensationalized front-page photos, huge screaming headlines in big white block letters with thick black outlines, and an overheated approach to news coverage that often gave him a chuckle. Archie put out his hand. "Good to meet you. I'm a journalist myself."

Kelly frowned. "Are you? Who do you write for?"

"*American Big Rigs.*" *OK, it was a bit of an exaggeration. I don't quite write for them. Yet.*

Kelly breathed a relieved sigh. *Apparently a writer for* American Big Rigs *didn't pose much in the way of competition.* "So, you're not here to cover the upcoming presidential Town Hall meeting."

"No. Are you?"

"I am. I'm backgrounding the area." Kelly flipped back the cover of his spiral-bound notebook and clicked on his ballpoint. Holding the pen poised over a blank page he asked, "So, what can you tell me? How long have you lived here?"

"I don't live here at all."

Kelly again looked vexed.

"I'm just visiting."

Kelly's frown deepened. "But you said the truck was yours. That's just what you drive?" The reporter's eyebrows arched.

Yeah, a brand-spanking-new 80-ton personal vehicle would probably make a decent Post *story.*

"No, I'm a commercial driver."

Kelly leaned his back against the counter and shrugged in defeat. "Well, OK, tell me about that. Kind of every little boy's dream."

"Big boys, too. I've met doctors and college professors who ditched perfectly good careers to go out on the road. You want to see what it's like? Sit in the driver's seat. Blow the horn?" *Everyone wanted to operate the air horn.*

Kelly looked tempted. "Must be a helluva lot of fun just driving around all day," he said as he scribbled on his pad.

Here we go. "That's what everyone thinks until they try it. It's not for everyone. It's real work. First of all, it's not like driving a really big car. Especially these days now that commercial drivers have to get a special license."

Kelly looked up. "They do?"

Archie nodded and took a swallow of milk. "Law passed in 1986, went into effect last April. Anyone wanting a commercial driver's license has to take a bunch of tests. Written knowledge tests, driving tests. Under the old regulations, pretty much anyone licensed to drive a car could also legally drive a semi or a bus." Archie jerked a thumb toward the T&C parking lot. "You could jump in that thing and take it down the street."

Kelly chuckled. "Well, I couldn't. Can't drive. Lot of City folks don't. Hell, we got buses, subways, taxis. Who needs a car? Besides, there's no place to park one."

"But you get my point. Anyhow, that's gonna change. Oh, some drivers can be grandfathered in. If you have a good driving record, you won't have to take the skills tests. But you still will have to take the knowledge tests. I've been driving for years and I had to test to get my CDL."

"Hardly seems fair, making you prove you can do what you've clearly been doing."

Now it was Archie's turn to shrug. "Yeah, there's some resentment about it but really, only the bad gearjammers are going to try to get around it. The pros, well, we can see the upside. It's gonna weed out the ones who shouldn't be behind the wheel anyway. Hiding bad driving records behind duplicate licenses, stuff like that." Archie chewed some waffle. "I didn't mind having to take the test. I even studied up for it."

"There's books for that? For truck driving?"

"A book. Well, one that I found anyway. Just came out a few years ago. *Bumper to Bumper.* Five hundred pages. Everything anyone could possibly want to know."

"Five *hundred* pages?' Kelly whistled.

Archie grinned. "See. It's not an easy thing, truck driving today. Actually, it's never been. But now it won't be just anybody jumping into the cab and taking off."

Kelly nodded and closed his book. "This has all been very interesting but—"

"Not the story you came to get?"

Kelly shook his head.

"Ok, how about this? A popular landscape artist makes her home not far from here, in Salt Point."

Kelly shrugged.

"Not *Post* material?" *Probably not scandalous enough.* Archie swiveled back to his breakfast. "Don't let me hold you up."

"Thanks for your time." Kelly was already scanning the room for a new target.

Archie chuckled. *I wonder if I'll be seeing a big red Kenworth splattered across the* Posts's *front page. What would be the headline?* Truckers Grounded by New Law. Nation Grinds to a Halt.

The man seated to Archie's right angled toward him. "Pest."

"Excuse me?"

"That reporter. He's been nagging everyone, looking for some kind of story. Wasn't the least bit interested in hearing about my job."

"No? What do you do?"

"Run a Porta-Potties rental."

Archie tried not to snort milk all over the man.

The guy shrugged. "His loss. The stories I could tell."

"I'll bet."

Over the man's head, Archie spied Linc Haybens rounding the corner from the dining room and waved him over. When he reached Archie, Haybens stood at least an inch taller than yesterday and wore a smug smile. His parka unzipped, the clear plastic envelope clipped to his shirt pocket winked in the overhead light. Across the top, black capital letters pronounced PRESS. Smaller letters identified LINCOLN HAYBENS as a WRITER for the HERALD.

The image of a freckled young man with red hair and a sweater vest popped into Archie's head. "You're a regular Jimmy Olsen. You're working for the *Herald* now?"

"Freelance," Haybens replied. "Yup, they are now interested in talking to this humble unqualified 'feature' writer about covering hard news. 'Special to the *Herald*' but it's my byline. I'm still writing for the *Voice*. I've already filed a story for Thursday's paper. Basically a primer on Friday's visit. The POTUS—"

"The what?"

"POTUS. President of the United States. The POTUS is making a stop at the FDR Home and the Library. Photo op, pretty much." Haybens patted his press badge with his right hand and his camera with his left. "You can bet I'll be there. Lots of pics for the *Voice* and the *Herald*."

"Kind of upstages shots of a red truck in a diner parking lot."

Haybens smirked. "Oh, don't you worry. That's running this week in *The Voice*. We don't have much else for Thursday's paper except text, stock picks, and file photos."

"What about the speech at the school?"

"You know about that?" Haybens' eyes narrowed. "How?"

Archie squared his shoulders and tipped up his chin. "Hey, I got my finger on the pulse. Stick with me, Kid. I'll tip you to all the hot leads."

Haybens gave him a wry grin. "You have so far. In answer to your question, hell, yeah, I'm gonna be there. Press credentials are good for more than just preferred parking." He patted his shirt's breast pocket. "These tickets are rare as socks at a surfing competition." He leaned in conspiratorially like someone about to offer a fake Rolex. "Want one?"

"Actually, I have a prior commitment."

"Really? More important than this? And you call yourself a journalist." Hayben shrugged. "Suit yourself. OK, now that I'm a *news* reporter, I had better get going and dig some up. "

"I'd better get going too. Someone needs a whole load of concrete Jersey barriers picked up and brought to a central receiving warehouse."

But he had one stop to make first.

CHAPTER TWELVE

HYDE PARK, NY, Tuesday, February 16, 1993

A humble slump block building flanked by small yards hemmed in by chain-link fences housed a substation of the Hyde Park Police Department. Painted red with a white pitched roof and white-trimmed windows, the building could just as easily serve an independent insurance agent or Realtor, and before that might have even been a private residence. The white vinyl-sided storage building at the far end of the yard did not detract from that impression.

Archie stepped through an unimposing storm door into a tiny foyer too narrow even for a chair. Mounted on one wall, a large wooden shield displayed the department's insignia. With its red roses, white fleur de lis, golden helmet, blue scrollwork, and long-necked white swans, the grandiose emblem was worthy of some great monarchic European dynasty and struck Archie as serious overkill for a police force guarding the safety of a town of maybe ten thousand people.

An interior passage door led him into a small lobby. Four aluminum stack chairs lined the wall to Archie's right. Their faded beige molded plastic seats bore the scars of many years of sitting. Scuff marks marred the gray linoleum floor and thumbtack holes pocked the dingy white drywall. One bulb in the overhead fluorescent fixture was dark and the room smelled musty from steamy heat generated by a dusty radiator.

Ahead, a hallway led to the rest of the station which, based on the size of the building, couldn't house much of a force. Maybe, like Linc Haybens and his fellow *Valley Voice* journalists, the officers of the Hyde Park Police Department convened in bars and diners when not on duty.

Archie crossed to the tall wooden half wall facing the door. The officer manning the station was shaped like a snowman with a round head atop an even rounder body and was munching an equally rotund donut. "Help you?" he asked around a mouthful.

"I'm thinking I can maybe help you," Archie said.

"Great," replied the sergeant, Rademaker, according to his nameplate. "Cause we sure could use it, what with the President visiting and all. You do know about the visit, right?"

Archie nodded.

From down the hall came the sound of phones ringing. Archie hoped those weren't emergency calls because no one seemed to be picking up with any promptness. "'Scuse me," the sergeant said to Archie. "Everyone's in a briefing." Rademaker grabbed an extension at his desk, listened for a moment, and then barked, "Yes, we appreciate that you went to the Policeman's Ball fifteen years ago and we thank you for your support, Ma'am but no, we don't have tickets." Sergeant Rademaker hung up the phone with finality and rolled his eyes. "If I had a dollar for every ticket I've been asked for I could retire this afternoon. Like we don't have enough to do without answering every pesky question about the Presidential visit. Doesn't Clinton have some kind of publicity team to handle that kind of stuff? We've got more important stuff to do than answer questions about when he's arriving and where he's staying and whether he wears briefs or boxers. We've got public safety to take care of. You would think the White House woulda given us some kind of heads up but noooo. Now we're scrambling to get everything buttoned down in time." Rademaker took another call and informed the caller that just because her son belonged to the Police Explorer post, it didn't mean that he or his family were automatically eligible for tickets. "Now you're not here to ask me about tickets, or are you?"

"No, I—"

"Good. So what was it that you needed? 'Cause I'm trying to get to that briefing." Rademaker's expression went wistful and he gazed down the hall.

Archie felt a little sorry for the guy, missing out on what was probably the most action any HPPD officer had seen or would see for some years to come. "I'd like to report a crime," Archie said.

Rademaker's eyebrows went up and he scrabbled around on the top of the desk for some paper and pen. "Name?"

"Archie Harlanson. Well, Archibald, that's my legal name if you need that."

Rademaker jotted down the information. "Address?"

Archie gave him the Tampa address.

Rademaker looked up. "Florida? You're not from around here?"

"No."

"And you're here in the backwater in the middle of winter because? ... Hey, you with the Advance Team?"

"Advance Team?"

Rademaker leaned forward and narrowed his eyes. "For the POTUS."

"Me? No. Just a family visit."

"Hmmph." Rademaker jotted that down. "Phone number."

Archie recited his Florida phone number. "But I've got a cellular phone if you'd rather have that."

"Do you?" Rademaker's eyes got even squinty-er. "You sure you're not on official business?"

"I'm sure."

"Ok, well, give me that number too." He wrote that down and then asked, "Now, the nature of the crime. Robbery? Assault? When and where did this happen?" The man was practically frothing at the mouth.

"Nothing like that. It hasn't happened yet. More like a conspiracy to commit a crime."

Rademaker came down off his law enforcement high and his brow furrowed. "OK," he drawled.

"I think someone's plotting to harm the President."

Now Rademaker's mouth as well as his brow wrinkled. "You don't say." The sergeant seemed to pull back just a little bit.

"OK, maybe it does sound a little crazy. I guess you get conspiracy nuts all the time." Although what, Archie wondered, could people conspire to do in Hyde Park? Raid the church Halloween pumpkin patch? Egg the school principal's car? Toilet-paper the tree in the mayor's front yard. "Let me explain. Like I said, I'm in town for a family visit. I'm staying at the Hyde Park Manor."

"Who isn't?" Rademaker laid his pen down.

"When I first got there last weekend, there was nobody there. Of course, now, as you said, it's filling up."

"Uh huh."

"But last weekend when I arrived I noticed this guy skulking around."

"Skulking?" Rademaker picked up his donut.

"Yeah. I know he's not staying there because I asked. But I saw him every morning at the lobby coffee bar. Then I'd see him head across the street to the FDR Park. I thought maybe he was employed there, but he never stayed long enough to get any work done. He'd only be on the grounds for a few minutes and then he'd leave."

"And you observed this because you were spying on him?"

"No, not spying. It was just something that I noticed. Because there's not much else going on around here and I've got some time on my hands."

"I see." Rademaker held up a hand signaling Archie to pause while he took another phone call. The sergeant asked the caller to hold. "This one's kinda important," he said to Archie with an apologetic expression. "So if we're quite done here, I got work to do."

"I'm not finished," Archie said. "Go ahead, I'll wait."

Rademaker shrugged his rounded shoulders, put aside the paper on which he'd been writing, returned to the phone, and started note-taking afresh. While Rademaker listened and wrote, Archie perused the notices and memos tacked to the walls: faded posters for D.A.R.E and H.E.A.T programs to stop drug abuse and control auto theft, ragged and curling official U.S. government notices about minimum wage and the use of lie detectors on employees.

Rademaker finished the call and rose from behind the desk, his torso angled to head down the hallway. "Mr. Harlanson, the HPPD does appreciate your concern about loiterers but—"

"No, I'm serious. This is more than just about loitering. The guy's up to no good, I tell you."

"I'm sure." Rademaker stepped away from the desk into the corridor. "Well, thank you, Mr. Harlanson. We have your contact information. We know how to get in touch with you if anything develops. Thanks again and enjoy your stay in Hyde Park."

I tried, Archie thought, and headed on to the highway department. He picked up the trailer with no problems, but rain, fog, and ice made negotiating 9W to the precast concrete fabricator anything but a drive in the country. What should have been about a two-hour drive took a big chunk out of his morning. Enough four-wheelers ignored the sage advice of "Bridges May Ice" signs to have skidded off the road. The accidents, albeit minor, clogged 9W's two-lane segments.

While FDR was iconic for Hyde Park, there was plenty of Revolutionary War history in the area. Had he not been on a mission and if the weather was more pleasant, Archie might have tried to find a way to do a little touring. As it was, he found himself with "You're So Vain," an old Carly Simon tune stuck in his head and wondered why, until he realized that it was signs for nearby Saratoga Springs, mentioned in the song, that triggered the memory.

Despite the charming colonial homes, shuttered shops and boarded-up businesses lent the village a slightly downtrodden vibe. Archie figured the concrete fabricator had to be about the biggest employer in the area. At least picking up the load of J-barriers wasn't a hassle. Dropping them off was. The highway department dock foreman was busier than a traffic cop in a power outage.

Archie got the load dropped and all the paperwork signed. It had been a long and trying day of fighting weather and traffic. A short break before he hit the road for the return trip seemed to be in order. A place to take a leak, hit up a vending machine, grab a cup of coffee, bring his logbook up to date. Maybe find a phone to call Debbie. Sure, he had that cell phone but those calls were costly. He waited for a pause in the action then asked the foreman if there was anything resembling a drivers' lounge. Juggling a beeper, a clipboard, and a walkie-talkie, the man gestured in the vague direction of a hallway.

Archie wandered down one anonymous corridor after another. Floors tiled in identical grayish vinyl, walls painted a uniform eggshell, decorated with official memos, motivational posters, safety warnings, and mandatory employment law notices, windowless doors numbered and labeled with meaningless names and titles, they all looked the same. When he heard the hum of conversation, he figured he had finally found the lounge.

He stopped at an open doorway just short of striding into the room. From the looks of the people grouped around a Formica-topped steel table, this was not a drivers' lounge. Men and a couple of women, all in business attire, armed with yellow tablets, pens, and coffee cups, sat facing a man in a serviceable suit standing in front of a huge wall-hung map. Archie recognized the New York State highway system. Route 9 from Stewart International Airport to Hyde Park was highlighted in yellow and dotted along its length with red circles. The audience's attention riveted on the speaker, no one noticed Archie.

The speaker tapped the map with a pointer. "Now, in an effort to be proactive, we've identified some zones for special attention." He whapped one of the red circles. "Potential areas of congestion. Obviously the presidential cavalcade must proceed without interruption. Not only does the President need to arrive at his destination on time, but any bottlenecks leave the President vulnerable, which presents a security issue."

"And the nature of these bottlenecks?" asked one of the men ringing the table.

"Good question," said the speaker.

Read my mind, Archie thought.

The speaker moved his pointer. "Some of these segments are grades. They could be slick which would necessitate slower speeds. The forecast is for dry weather but we all know how reliable forecasts are."

At the conference table, a heavy-set man raised his pen. "We'll get road crews out there early. Clean, salt, sand. Whatever it takes."

The man at the head of the table said, "Good," and made a note on his tablet.

The speaker moved his pointer. "Some of these road segments are two-lane. Any accident, slow-moving vehicle, oversized load could cause a delay."

"We could deny oversized load permits for that day," suggested one of the women.

The leader said, "Good idea" and made another note.

"Put up temporary signage, reroute truck traffic."

The leader wrote that down.

Reroute truck traffic? Truckers gonna love that, Archie thought. At least come Friday he wouldn't be hauling freight. He'd be at the Stenowitzes for the big event.

The speaker moved to identify another portion of the map and spotted Archie. "May we help you?"

"I was looking for the drivers' lounge."

One of the men at the table turned in his seat. "Down the hall, take a left. Then another left."

Archie gave a thumb's up and redirected himself. He found the lounge, a closet of a room equally Spartan in its décor. At least it did have a vending machine although the sandwich was too cold to have any flavor. The coffee at least was drinkable. Between bites and sips, he used the payphone to call Debbie.

The weather hadn't done her any favors either. "We took Caryn to the doc in PK," she said.

"Gee, I would think all things considered, the doctor could come to her."

"Make a house call? Welcome to the twentieth century, fella." Even over the phone Debbie's laughter sounded a little manic. "I think we were almost hoping that they would find something wrong so that they could fix it but no, she's really doing as well as can be expected. It's just going to take time and rest. The body heals on its own schedule.

"Then Mom wanted to check out a caterer for Friday. Of course, by now Caryn was really hurting so we took her back to the house. Dad was doing some work from home so Mom and I left him in charge and went back out. Waste of time. The caterer said he was booked solid until after Friday. Asked if we could change the date to Saturday. Well, noooo. Has to be Friday, Mom says. Anyhow, we basically just got ... what's that, Mom?"

Archie heard some muffled conversation then Debbie got back on the line. "I'm sorry, honey, I've got to run. Mom needs some things for dinner and she doesn't want to drive in the weather so ..." Debbie sighed. "Wish she'd thought of it while we were out."

"By the time you've quit for the day, you'll have put in as many miles as I did."

"Nothing's near anything around here. I should start keeping a log book just for grins and we can have a contest."

"Well, you be careful out there. I know you're a safe driver but not everyone knows how to handle themselves in inclement weather." Archie thought of the cars he had passed on the side of the road. "You got to watch out for the other guy. Leave a—"

"Safe following distance. I know. I promise. I will."

"Hey, is there something I can pick up for you so you don't have to go out again?"

"You would do that?"

"It's been a while since I drove PUD but whatever the customer wants ..."

"Oh, you are a Super Man. Have you had dinner?"

Though the vending machine sandwich was still a lump in his stomach, he wouldn't call it "dinner." His options seemed to be pizza in his room at the Hyde Park Manor or dining with the Stenowitzes. At least he'd get to spend some time with Debbie. "What did you have in mind?"

CHAPTER THIRTEEN

SALT POINT, NY, Tuesday, February 16, 1993

Archie bobtailed it back to Hyde Park in the winter twilight gloom. After a day spent pulling a load of concrete behind him, the truck skimmed the slick road surface like a feather.

Miriam's dismay at having the truck parked in the driveway evaporated at the sight of the cartons Archie carried in. He'd been tempted by a barbeque place but didn't know if the meats would pass muster with Debbie's family. Ditto the Cajun-style seafood place. A helpful highway billboard advertising a Thai restaurant near Rhinebeck had solved the problem. Archie ordered up an assortment of vegetable-only take-out dishes.

While Miriam made up a plate for Caryn, Marvin invited Archie to join him in the den for a cocktail. "Name your poison," he said, and gestured toward a home bar bristling with bottles of liquors and liqueurs in every color of the rainbow.

Elliot strode in bringing with him the smell of cigarette smoke and cold air. He shrugged off his coat. "Did I hear someone say cocktails? How about a Manhattan?"

"I'm pretty much a beer drinker myself," Archie replied. Beer, at least, was readily available just about anywhere a tired trucker would find himself off duty.

"Really?" Elliot pulled out a cocktail shaker, bottles of golden whiskey, red vermouth, and maraschino cherries.

"Although in Florida we're kinda fond of Mojitos." The Cubans had introduced the drink to the Sunshine State, but for Archie the attraction was that the cocktail was alleged to be a favorite of Ernest Hemingway. He could picture the writer at some tropical bar unwinding from a long day of word-wrangling. "You've got everything you would need."

"Yeah? What's in it?"

"Rum, soda water, lime juice, and sugar. Oh, and mint. Gotta have mint."

"I'll bet Miriam's got some mint somewhere. I'll go see." Marvin took off for the kitchen. His eyes narrowed, Elliot handed Archie the cocktail shaker.

"Mmm, don't need that. You just fix these right in the glass." Archie dropped lime wedges into three tall glasses and measured out the sugar. He spied a muddler among the bar implements and crushed the fruit just enough to release some juice.

Marvin returned with a fist full of green mint leaves. Archie rubbed them around the glasses' rims and dropped them in. "Now, ice ... the rum, a splash of soda, and we got it." He handed Marvin and Elliot each a drink.

Marvin licked his lips. "This is right tasty," he said in an awful attempt at a Southern accent. "It does bring a little tropical summer to a New York winter."

"Hmmph," Elliot said. He set his glass down and proceeded to make a Manhattan.

Archie sipped slowly and sparingly. After a long day, he still had to drive the truck back to Hyde Park in the dark on slippery streets. "Say, would you mind? Could I use your computer, get on the Internet? Just something I gotta check on for work."

"Be my guest," Marvin said. "I was working earlier. It's still all booted up."

Archie put his glass on the bar and took a seat at the home office armoire. He logged onto some load boards to see if he could drum up work for the next day. Marvin and Elliot were deep in conversation about whether the economy was or was not recovering so Archie took another minute to stop in at the news forum. To alerts about road conditions and anticipated bad weather he added a warning about possible traffic tie-ups along 9G on Friday, especially in the areas that were red-circled on the highway department's planning map. Then he checked another forum for the next day's weather forecast. More of the same: rain, fog, ice. *Not the most pleasant day for playing tourist. Still, maybe he and Debbie could go drive up 9G, check out one of those historic mansions he had passed. That'd be indoors—*

"Are you gentlemen planning to join us?" Miriam called from the kitchen. "The food's getting cold."

"Gentlemen? Shall we?" Marvin said.

"The computer?" Archie asked.

"Just leave it," Marvin replied. "I'll shut it down later."

They all crowded around the breakfast bar and loaded up their plates with noodle- and rice dishes. "Careful," Archie said. "They told me that one's real spicy."

Debbie tapped one of the take-out containers, branded with the name and address of the restaurant. "You went out of your way."

Archie shrugged. "I would have had more options if I'd thought of it before I headed back." He gave a brief accounting of his trip to the fabricator and his unintentional tour of the state highway department. "You were right about this Clinton visit, Deb. It's got everybody working overtime putting plans together."

"You can say that again. I've spent half the day trying to find a caterer who can help out Friday. Everyone says they're busy." Miriam sighed. "Looks like I'm going to have to put it all together myself. Deborah, I'm going to need you all day tomorrow. We'll shop in the morning, get to work in the kitchen in the afternoon—"

"Mom ..." Debbie's voice was pleading.

She turned to Archie, her lower lip caught between her teeth. He answered with a sympathetic shrug. *Oh well. So much for touring historic mansions.*

"Oh, where will we put everything?"

"Call the neighbors," Debbie suggested. "See if they have room in their fridges. You're going to invite them anyway; I'm sure they'll be happy to help."

"Excuse me," Archie said in the tone that a guest who needed a bathroom break would use.

"Off the foyer, Archibald," Miriam said.

Before hitting the powder room, Archie ducked back into Marvin's home office. He pressed the keyboard's space bar and Marvin's bull-and-bear screen saver dissolved. Archie logged onto a trucker forum to see if he could find any work for tomorrow but found nothing. Whatever would he do with himself all day? he wondered. An idea hit him: he would call around to all the restaurateurs he had just met. Maybe one of them could be pressed into service to cater the Friday event. Archie returned to find his hosts discussing the new president's position regarding Israel's expansion in the West Bank.

"What do you think, Archie?" Elliot asked.

It wasn't anything to which Archie had given a moment's thought. *What was the right answer?* He made a show of not wanting to talk with his mouth full. "I don't know about that. I will tell ya what will be interesting is if Clinton will ratify NAFTA."

Miriam's puzzled expression called for an explanation.

"North American Free Trade Agreement. It'll replace the trade agreement we have now with Canada and will bring in Mexico. The Mexican president and Canadian prime minister signed it but Bush ran out of time to implement it so now that's up to Clinton."

"You sound like you don't think it's a good thing," said Marvin. "Eliminating tariffs should improve trade. I'm telling my clients to look for opportunities there."

Archie shrugged. "There's a lot of controversy about it among truckers. NAFTA's going to make it easier for Mexican trucking companies to get authority to carry freight in the U. S. Right now, Mexican trucks have to stop at the border and offload their cargo. Then U.S. drivers pick up the load in places like Laredo and take it the rest of the way. NAFTA would take those hauls away from American drivers."

Marvin's eyebrows rose.

"And there's concern about whether the Mexican drivers will meet U.S. safety standards. Not to mention their trucks. There's a lot of griping that their equipment isn't up to snuff. That it will ruin our roads, worsen air pollution, break down and cause accidents ..."

Debbie frowned. "That's tarring all Mexican drivers with the same feather. Sounds like there's a little bigotry going on there."

"Oh, no doubt about the bigotry. Some guys look for any legitimate way to excuse being assho— to be idiots. I dunno that I'd worry so much. At first it sounds like, yeah, we'd lose a lotta loads. We're talking about a zone of twenty miles. But the Mexican drivers can't transport shipments within the U.S. They can't take a load for the trip back. All that deadheading, that's gonna make it less attractive for the Mexicans. I guess we'll find out. Clinton says he supports it. He's said he thinks the whole thing means jobs in general. Everyone's expecting he'll ratify it. Unless the Teamsters can find a way to stop it ..."

Miriam looked past Archie's shoulder. "Caryn, baby. Are you sure you should be up?"

Archie turned to see Caryn standing in the hallway, the new baby in her arms.

"If you needed something you should have just called. Oh, I shouldn't have left you upstairs all by yourself."

"It's OK, Mom. I've been resting all day. I felt like I ought to give my blood a chance to circulate a little. Hi, Archie." She looked down at the bundle in her arms. "Say hi to Uncle Archie, Eli." She held the baby out to him.

Archie felt his face grow warm. He liked the sound of "Uncle Archie" but wasn't at all sure what to do with the baby. *Is this the right way to hold it?* "I, uh ..."

"Don't worry, he won't bite. Here, like this." Caryn put the baby in his arms. "Just put one hand under his neck and the other under his bottom."

Well, that wasn't so bad. The little thing looked up at Archie expectantly. *What to say? How to make a good impression on a newborn?* "So, um, how's life been treating you?"

Eli screwed up his face and let out a wail.

Oh my God, what did I do? Archie looked at Debbie for help. "I ... maybe he doesn't like me."

"What's not to like?" she said. "Anyhow, he's been a little colicky."

Caryn said. "I wouldn't call it colic."

"Caryn, he cries like every three hours."

Would someone please do something? Still cradling the baby, Archie held out his arms.

"I don't think I need to worry unless he's inconsolable. He'll stop after a while."

"Maybe he's getting a chill," Miriam said.

"Mom, it's plenty warm enough. He'll need to leave the bedroom eventually," Debbie said.

"He'll need to leave it by Friday at least. We're having the brit down here."

The baby continued to cry. *Somebody?* Archie looked a question at Elliot who seemed just as baffled.

"Well, maybe it's just too much excitement. Let's get him back to bed."

Good idea.

Elliot put an arm around his wife and helped her mount the stairs, Debbie, Miriam, and Marvin close behind.

Um, hello? Help!

From the stairs, Miriam looked over her shoulder. "Come on, Archibald."

As nervous as he was the first time he put a truck in gear, Archie carried the delicate cargo up the stairs.

It was late by the time he returned to the Hyde Park Manor but he still had work to do. He post-tripped the Kenworth before putting it away for the night. Then he scooped up the cell phone and his notebook. He'd pulled a van full of fragile cargo and now a flatbed loaded with concrete and needed to capture the experience for his story before he forgot the vivid details that would take his article from "report" to "story."

CHAPTER FOURTEEN

HYDE PARK, NY, Wednesday, February 17, 1993

With no particular plans for the day, Archie had set no alarm. The restaurateurs he planned to call weren't likely to be at their place of business until mid-morning at the earliest.

The guests in the room next to Archie's, however, were on a different schedule. The sudden blaring of their TV startled him awake.

He heard someone yell what sounded like, "Turn that damn thing off." The volume decreased and Archie heard voices raised to a level that was almost loud enough to be understandable. Annoyed, he crossed to the adjoining wall thinking a not so subtle rap or two would get his neighbors to tone it down so he could get back to sleep.

"Pisses me off," it sounded like. Archie made out "his fault" and "what do we do?"

He spied the two water glasses on the tray with the ice bucket. Chuckling, he peeled the protective paper cap off one of the glasses, placed the open end against the wall, and his ear to the bottom. He had seen this done in a movie once and wondered if it worked.

To his surprise it did and he found himself eavesdropping.

"Had to be him," one guy said. "He's ... trucker."

Could they be talking about me?

"... Shit ... everyone knows," came the voice of another man. "... boss will be pissed."

"President's route ... confidential ... how'd he find out?"

Oops. Maybe it wasn't such a good idea to get on that trucker bulletin board and let everyone know about the possible mid-Hudson Valley traffic delays they might encounter on Friday.

There'd be no getting back to sleep now. Archie pulled on sweats and boots and headed to the lobby for his customary eye-opening cup of coffee. Reaching the end of the hallway, he came to a standstill at the lobby entrance. Every chair in the little seating area was filled. Men with short hair wearing dark suits and white shirts clutched Styrofoam cups and cigarettes and radiated cold calculated menace, giving credence to the jibe "Men in Black." At Archie's arrival they all looked up and scowled at him. Tempted to shift into reverse and beat a quick retreat to his room, he took a step backward.

"It's you, isn't it?" asked one fellow, rising from his chair. With his black overcoat, the open top button revealing a white dress shirt, and buzz-cut hair, he was virtually indistinguishable from his tablemates.

"Uh, you talking to me?"

"Yeah, I'm talking to you." Long strides brought the man within inches. "You're the trucker right? Harlanson?"

"Yeah ..." *How did they know his name? They were federal agents; what didn't they know about him?*

"It was you who posted the details of the presidential cavalcade on the Internet, wasn't it?"

Archie swallowed. "I don't know—"

"We thought some reporter had gotten a hold of that intel and released it, but we traced the leak to the source. A truckers' billboard." The man all but grabbed Archie by the collar. "That was classified information. Now everyone knows. Including every terrorist who might intend to harm the President. Was that your plan?"

"Me?" Archie tried not to squeak. "Are you calling me a terrorist?"

The man pulled open his coat and Archie wondered if he was going for handcuffs or worse, a gun, but all he did was display the FBI ID clipped to his suit jacket's lapel.

"You've got it all wrong, Agent. I was just trying to help. Steer commercial traffic clear of the area, prevent traffic jams. And yeah, warn off other drivers so they could plan a different route."

The agent glared. "You say."

Three more men rose from their seats and came to stand alongside their fellow agent.

Archie squared his shoulders and stood his ground. "Look, I'm not the one you should be worried about. There is something going on around here that doesn't seem kosher to me." *Oh, brother, I've got kosher on the brain,* Archie thought, and suppressed a crazed laugh. "I told the Hyde Park police about it on Monday."

One of the agent's confederates jutted his chin forward. "Did you now? Believe me, we'll be following up on that. Just know that we've got eyes on you, Bud. We're right next door. You fart too loud, we'll be all over you like gravy on a biscuit."

Archie felt rising anger heat the back of his neck. "Sounds like I'd be better off staying somewhere else."

"Oh, no, Buddy, we like having you where we can keep tabs on you," said one of the other agents. "If you know what's good for you, you'll stay put until well after the president has left town."

"And if I've got business elsewhere?"

"Just sayin'. You've been ... cautioned."

So have you, Archie thought, but the feds didn't seem to be taking his warning any more seriously than had the Hyde Park Police.

He returned their glares with a scowl and edged toward the coffee cart. The carafe was empty and so were the two donut boxes on a folding table that had been set up next to the cart.

Well, so much for an eye opener. He crossed the small lobby and stepped outside to grab a newspaper. The vending machines were out of newspapers.

"Hey."

Archie looked up to face the Freeloader slouching against the front wall. He polished off the last bite of his donut. He apparently had managed to snag one before the G-men cleared them out. *Timing clearly was everything.*

"Hey," Archie replied, wondering why after a week of stealthy raids on the complimentary breakfast and furtive looks, the guy was now striking up an acquaintance.

"You the guy with the truck?" Freeloader asked.

"That's me." *No point denying it now. Apparently it was public knowledge.*

"Say, maybe you can help me out."

"OK ..."

"I'm in kind of a spot at work. I work over at the FDR Park." The guy nodded his head toward the opposite side of the street. "See, uh, I help with the landscaping. The grounds keeping, stuff like that, and uh, we gotta get it all ready for spring."

For spring? Yeah, sure. Along with serious redecorating and big-time rewiring for The Visit, the park grounds would need sprucing up too. No pun intended.

"I know that's hard to believe with all this snow on the ground, but that's how it works in this business. Lots of prep work to do even in winter."

"Uh huh." For someone who hadn't said a syllable to Archie all week, the Freeloader was suddenly pretty chatty.

"I got a bunch of new stuff I gotta get in, start getting it conditioned, you know?"

"Hardening off," Archie said. His dad had done that, taking seedlings that he'd nursed indoors over the winter outside so they could acclimatize to wind, sun, and rain.

"Yeah, that," said the Freeloader with a slight frown. "Hey, you know something about that, huh?"

"A little. My dad farmed."

"Yeah, well, so you know. Hardening off. Me and my, uh, partner, we got a trailer of stuff at the nursery in Tannersville. Gotta move it today."

So was that the conversation Archie had overheard yesterday morning? Not some nefarious plot. Just business. "Where's Tannersville?"

"Other side of the river, up in the mountains. North of here, about 45 minutes. Not far, but I got nothing to pull that trailer with. I had a guy but he bailed. Can't pull it with my car." He nodded towards the Riviera.

"No, I guess not."

"But, you know, you got that truck. It wouldn't be a lot of work. The trailer's all loaded up. All you gotta do is bring it down. For pay, of course."

"I get eleven cents a mile. And the cost of the fuel." Archie got eleven cents a mile if he was lucky, but he sure wasn't going to do this for nothing. There was fuel cost to consider, and a toll to cross the bridge. He'd have to cross the river soon to fuel up anyway though; he was running low. This haul didn't sound like a big money maker, but it would at least help to pay for the fuel run. Plus there would be mountain driving. It would give him a chance to report on how well the Kenworth pulled grades.

"Like, uh, today? See, I'm in a spot. I gotta get that trailer down to Hyde Park and back today 'cause they need it for other stuff tomorrow." Freeloader looked as beseeching as a guy could with the bill of his cap shading his eyes.

"Yeah, I can do that today." *What the heck.* He didn't have any other jobs to do today and after last night's awkwardness, he wasn't all that eager to head back to Salt Point.

"Bingo." Freeloader held out his hand and Archie took it. "That's my name. Bingo."

"Archie."

"Great to meet ya. OK, you got something to write on, take down the address?"

"Not on me. Hold on, they must have something at the front desk." Archie ducked back inside the lobby. The G-men had cleared out leaving nary a donut crumb or napkin behind. The coffee pot and donut box were still empty.

Looked like it would be the T&C for breakfast before he headed up to Tannersville, wherever that was.

Archie grabbed a pen and a Hyde Park Manor promotional postcard from the front desk counter, rejoined Bingo outside, and took down the nursery's address. "Sounds good. I've got a couple of things to do first, but I figure I'll get there around ten."

"I'll tell Yegor," Bingo said. "Thanks, Buddy." He touched the bill of his cap and headed for his car.

Archie got himself and the truck ready for a day's worth of driving. En route to the T&C, he edged around utility cherry-picker trucks lining the side of the highway nearly bumper to bumper, their buckets filled with technicians stringing more power and phone lines. The parking lot at the T&C was so crowded that Archie had to leave the truck at the neighboring roller rink. With any luck, no one was skating at this hour and wouldn't mind a bright red Kenworth taking up a couple of slots.

He mounted the steps to the entrance and glanced at the newspaper vending machines. They were empty but someone had taped a hand-lettered sign to the glass front. "More inside," it read. Sure enough, alongside the hostess station stood stacks of newspapers bundled with string and topped by a Mason jar sealed with a slotted cap and bearing a label that read "75¢." To Archie's way of thinking, there didn't seem to be quite enough quarters in the jar to account for the number of papers missing from the stacks.

So much for the honor system.

He made his contribution and took a copy of the *Post*. No big red Kenworths graced the front page. Perhaps he'd find Mike Kelly's expose of commercial trucking inside.

Men in business dress occupied tables in the dining room and filled the booths. Every counter seat looked taken.

A coffee carafe in each hand, one decaf, one regular, Bonnie paused in her circuit around the tables. "Hey, Archie, check out this crowd. All these suits, I'm hoping to go home with some change in my pocket."

"I dunno, Bonnie. I'm thinking lots of these guys are on per diems. That change is going to have to come out of their pockets."

Bonnie's mouth pursed in a pout. "Hmm. Now that you mention it, I do believe you're right. Oops, gotta hustle." She darted toward the dining room.

Archie spotted Cheryl at the far end. She waved him over.

He passed now familiar faces, including Leonard Peerman. Leonard had ditched his feed cap this morning; Archie could see that the man was thinning on top. Gone too was the early morning stubble, plaid shirt, and overalls. Under his puffy jacket Leonard wore a blue Oxford shirt, although the top button was undone, and black slacks. Standing next to him, a young man in a *Newsday Newspaper* varsity jacket jotted notes in a steno book. Leonard turned his head, nodded at Archie, rolled his eyes, and turned back to the reporter who was bending his ear.

Archie made his way toward the end of the counter noting the locals who all seemed to be, if not in their Sunday best, somewhat more formally attired than he would have expected for a midweek morning. Every one of them was paired up with someone holding a notepad or a camera.

Cheryl pointed at the last vacant stool. "We held it for you and it wasn't easy. This place is mobbed."

"I can see that. I guess that explains why you're here backing up Bonnie."

"And it's only Wednesday. If it's going to be like this tomorrow and Friday we're going to need more help. So, what can I get you?"

"Oh, let's just make it simple. Coffee and a Danish." Archie missed the caffeine and sugar rush he was used to getting at the Manor.

"You want that coffee to-go again this morning?"

"That would be great."

Cheryl worked her way down the line, topping up cups, picking up plates, and peeling tickets off her pad. She returned with a plate filled by a large iced flaky pastry ring surrounding a dollop of sweetened cream cheese and jam, and a lidded Styrofoam cup. "Where are you off to today?" she asked, handing him the bill.

"Tannersville."

"Ah, the Catskills. It's a pretty drive, but you be careful. It might be slick going. That's close to Hunter Mountain, ski country. Oh, but you'll be passing by Saugerties. You really must stop in Saugerties if you can and go to Krause's."

"A deli? Bakery?"

Cheryl shook her head. "Chocolates." She looked heavenward and sighed. When she returned to Earth she nodded at the pastry. "You sure that's going to hold you?"

"I'll grab some lunch when I get to Tannersville. There is a place to eat there, isn't there?"

"Yeah, there's a couple of cafes."

"Thanks." Archie wolfed down the Danish and emptied the coffee cup. He got his cup refilled on the way out the door.

His route was less direct than he would have liked. Truck stops and diesel depots were few and far between. He took 9G to Rhinebeck, paid the toll to cross the Hudson, and doubled back to Kingston. No time to stop at Frieda's Bakery, which was too bad. Cheryl had been right about the coffee and Danish. He should have had something more substantial. 9W took him a winding way north and easterly. Cheryl was also right about the traffic; he passed a number of cars with loaded rooftop ski racks, or rather they passed him. He left 9W briefly to go west and fuel up in Ruby, then returned to the highway headed north, looking for County Road 32. Before he got there, though, he passed signs for Saugerties. He thought of Cheryl's wistful sigh. Perhaps it would be worth the slight detour. If the chocolate was that good, it might get him out of the doghouse and back into favor with the Stenowitz women, older and younger.

Located shy of downtown, the confectionary shop didn't require that he go too much out of his way, and the generous parking lot made the stop even that much more convenient.

Housed in a mocha-colored clapboard building with peppermint-stick trim and a sign lettered in a quaint old-fashioned font, Krause's Home Made Candy shop was cheery with light-colored walls and floor and sunlight streaming in from white-pine trimmed windows. White-painted baker's racks held baskets and boxes and bins of hard candies while wooden bins held bagged chocolates. He expected to be knocked down by an overpowering smell of chocolate and wasn't, perhaps because nearly everything was wrapped.

Archie stepped up to the wood-and-glass counter displaying rows upon rows of milk and dark chocolates with scores of different fillings, from amaretto to vanilla and every fruit in between. *Where to begin?*

A young lady whose slim figure suggested that she did not take her pay in kind asked Archie if he would like a sample.

"No, thank you, I see what I want." Among the novelty chocolates he spied chocolate pops on a stick in an assortment of shapes, including a chocolate paint brush. It wasn't an artist's brush but he thought Miriam might appreciate the thought nonetheless. For Debbie he chose a filigreed heart and for Caryn, a tiny chocolate baby carriage.

"Milk or dark?" the clerk asked.

"Oh, gee, I don't know.

"Get one of each then you'll be on the safe side."

"Good idea. And I need one of those too." Among the pops was a chocolate truck. OK, it was a dump truck but it was a heavy truck nonetheless. "I'll take that in milk chocolate. That's for me."

The clerk looked out the window from which a glimpse of the Kenworth was just visible and turned back to Archie with a smile. "I could have guessed that."

A café next to the confectionary would have been convenient, but it looked like he'd have to head further down Partition Street to reach a commercial district. That would take him even further out of the way. He brought his log book current then continued north until he connected with 23A and headed west into Tannersville. He could feel gravity tug at the truck and the engine's response to the rise in elevation. In his review, he'd comment on that.

By now the coffee and Danish he had enjoyed at the T&C was but a distant memory. As he crept along the snowy street, Archie kept an eye out for somewhere to eat and somewhere to park. If the number of cars parked along the curb was any indication, the business of catering to skiers was good. Swiss chalet-type ornamentation aimed for quaint and was defeated by the many power lines strung overhead. One cafe and antique shop declared itself to be his Last Chance and that seemed as good a reason as any to stop. A tall white clapboard building, its picket fence and colorful shutters gave it frontier-saloon appeal. The multi-function establishment boasted a gift and cheese shop, a tavern, and café. The wood décor and Americana merchandise was a warm and welcome respite from the cold and snowy street. Candies and snacks filled wicker baskets, cheese, smoked meats, and pickles seasoned the air. The deli counter crammed with cheeses and meats promised a tasty and filling sandwich, and the café delivered on its promise. Tempted to wash it down with a lager, he settled instead for a Dr. Brown root beer, which, as sodas went, was really quite flavorful.

He returned to the street and wondered if he had somehow been beamed into 18th-century Europe. Across the road, two men in long black coats with long beards, long curling sideburns, and wide-brimmed black fedoras headed down the sidewalk. He recognized them as Chasids, Jewish people practicing their religion as it might have been done centuries ago in Eastern Europe, somewhat like the way the Amish kept traditional ways dating from pretty much the same time period. Debbie had explained it once in response to a news story they had seen on TV. What in the world were they doing here in Tannersville, a destination for ski aficionados? He'd have to ask Debbie, but that was one of the fun parts of his job: bringing home tales of unusual sights encountered on the road.

He continued toward the truck then stopped. *Chasids. Jewish people. Hmmm. Might they know of a caterer who could help with Friday's event? OK, wasn't that akin to racial profiling, to assume that they could or would?*

Still, he had planned to chase down caterers today. *Why not give it a shot? What could be the worst that could happen? He'd insult some strangers and embarrass himself with people he would likely never see again.*

Feeling a little bit like that bumbling fictional detective Dave Holman, a cheesy noir sleuth, or worse, a stalker, he fell into step behind the black-coated men, keeping enough distance so they wouldn't be aware of him until he had worked out the best way to approach them.

Talking among themselves, they strode down the street, slowed, and turned into a shop. Archie looked at the sign stenciled in the window: *Kosher Outpost.* The signage included a big white Star of David and alongside it another symbol, a block letter U inside a circle.

Kosher. That was the ticket. Whatever was inside the shop was kosher which was a beginning.

Archie followed the men into the store which proved to be a grocer's, one that had seen a lot of use. The faded vinyl floor and dingy walls were scuffed. Corrosion tinged the metal fixtures. Utility shelves of canned and dry goods crowded the center of the store leaving only narrow aisles. Mismatched glass-fronted refrigerators and freezers lined the walls. At his right, a lone cashier stood behind a single cash register just inside the door.

Didn't seem like they did a lot of business here.

Near the cashier's stand, a deli counter offered sandwiches and take-out entrees like stuffed cabbage and matzo-ball soup. A bakery case held cakes, cookies, pies, and pastries, bagels, and rye breads.

Any and all of which seem to Archie suitable for a home reception.

What would be wrong with platters of sandwiches, cookies, bite-sized pieces of cake? And knishes?

The warm, oniony aroma made his mouth water even though he had just eaten. He had to chuckle. The first time he heard the word, it sounded to him like something lovers did. *They knished all night long.*

Debbie explained it was a snack, dough rolled around a filling of seasoned mashed potato, a lot like the empanadas offered by Cuban restaurants in Florida.

Yeah, throw in some of those too.

OK, how to pull this off?

Still working on his approach, Archie trailed the men. At the end of the aisle, one man opened a small door labeled "Office" and Archie's quarry escaped inside before he could get a word out.

While he formed Plan B, he strolled around the store. It sure did carry some obscure items. Many of the items in the refrigerated dairy cases were "non-dairy," proudly proclaiming to be made of tofu or rice. Somehow, tofu ice cream lacked the same appeal of the Carvel that Bonnie raved about. Other items were labeled PAREVE, whatever that was. Things it never would have occurred to him to worry about were labeled kosher, like candy, gelatin dessert mixes, and baked beans, even soap, and candles for Shabbat, like the ones that Miriam had lit last Friday. *What could not be kosher about a candle?*

He was clearly in over his head. He would have to ask for help. He headed for the cashier's stand manned by a middle-aged woman in a long-sleeved top covered by a white apron. A flowered scarf covered her hair.

"May I help you? You seem a little lost," she said with a gentle smile. "Your first time here, I am guessing."

"Yes. I was really just passing through town. Just had lunch at the Last Chance."

"Ah. So a sandwich you do not need me to make you?"

The woman's strange phrasing had Archie thinking of Yoda in the *Star Wars* movie.

"No." *But a knish might make a nice snack for the return trip to Hyde Park.* Archie said he'd take one.

With tongs, the woman pulled one from the warming tray. As she wrapped it in white butcher paper, Archie said, "This is quite the specialty store for an out-of-the-way place like Tannersville."

The woman smiled. "Lumber mills and tanneries were what was here a century ago. Then, for a time, summer resorts. People got cars, planes, to go to other places for summer vacation but then many people came in the winter to ski Hunter Mountain."

"I noticed."

"But a hundred years ago our people came up from the city for the summer. Cooler. And stayed even through the winter. Over the years, more and more. Now there are enough for three *shuls*. Not open in the winter but if you are looking for a *minyan* ..."

"At the moment I'm wondering, do you do any catering?"

"Catering?"

"Let me explain. My in-laws—well, they're not my in-laws yet. But that's not important. Here's what I need, or well, what they need. That is—"

The cashier's eyebrows rose.

"OK, let me get to the point. They need food for a reception. Kosher food. On Friday. In Salt Point."

"Salt Point? You come all the way here for a caterer?"

"Everyone else is booked. It's for a ... I forget what it's called."

A patient smile on her face, the cashier tilted her head.

"A reception. For a new baby. Only it's more than just a party. There's a ceremony. You know. For the, um, circumcision."

The woman's smile broadened. "A *brit milah! Mazel!*" Her hands flew to her face. She came out from behind the counter and hugged Archie.

"Yes, that's it. The brit."

She narrowed her eyes at him. "You are not Jewish."

"Is it that obvious?"

"If you were, you would know very well what a brit is."

"Yeah, I guess I would. Anyhow, my girlfriend is the baby's aunt."

"So you are not Jewish but you would marry this woman?"

"Oh, it's not a problem."

"It is."

"No, see, Debbie—that's the baby's aunt—she doesn't ..." *How did Debbie put it?* "She isn't observant."

"Her parents are. Her sister is. A brit, a kosher seudah. Important to them, it is. To you, your girl, maybe it is not. Not today. But you marry. Children come. Now, important it is. Her parents, they want their grandchildren to be Jewish. Your son, what will he be?"

"Oh, he'll be circumcised." Most boy babies were, in the hospital as a matter of procedure. Archie didn't know too many guys who hadn't been.

"Yes, but a brit? That is different and you know it. Your son, will he be Jewish?"

Archie hadn't thought that far ahead. "We haven't discussed it."

The woman crossed her arms over her chest. "Discuss it you should. Now. Before you marry, or *tsouris* you will have."

That didn't sound good.

The woman patted his cheek. "A *mensch* you are, come all this way to help your girl and her family. Whom you wish to be your family. But ..." the woman threw up her hands and shrugged. She reached behind, grabbed the white knish sack, and thrust it into his hands. Turning her back to him she tsked her way to the register, shaking her head.

OK, this wasn't getting him closer to a caterer. In fact, it was making him uneasy. *Time to get back on the road.*

"Well, thanks for your time," he said, and turned for the door. He was about to make good his escape when a crowded community bulletin board caught his attention. Notices of various group meetings overlapped fliers about fundraising events. Posters announced movie night, a lecture, a concert. Ads for kosher bed-and-breakfasts, hotels, and restaurants. His eye fell on a homemade flier proclaiming CATERING. The bottom edge was fringed with tabs bearing a name and phone number. Archie tore one off and beat feet from the store.

He picked his way along the icy street, the gray sky as low as his spirits. Something had him feeling troubled; he couldn't put his finger on it. He shrugged it off.

When he neared the truck, he paused for a minute. The red finish glowed like a ruby in the bleak setting, bringing a smile to his face.

He climbed into the cab, fired up the engine, and got the heat going. He fingered the slip of paper he had torn from the flier. NOSH BY NAOMI it read, along with a phone number. He had enough of a signal on the cell phone to make a call.

CHAPTER FIFTEEN

TANNERSVILLE, NY, Wednesday, February 17, 1993

The phone rang and rang. He was about to give up when he connected.

"Hello?"

Archie had expected a greeting on the order of "Nosh by Naomi, how may we help you?" The responder sounded so uncertain.

"I'm trying to reach Nosh by Naomi."

"You got 'er. Well, Naomi anyway. I'm Naomi."

Archie introduced himself and explained about finding her contact information at Kosher Outpost.

"Oh, my. Is that flier still there? I should have taken that down ages ago. I haven't done catering since my second was born."

Archie's hopes cratered.

"And now I've got a third on the way. It's too bad. Not the baby, no. I'm delighted about that. I mean about not being able to keep up with the catering. It was a great source of income but with an infant and my first in the Terrible Twos ..."

Two little ones and a third on the way? When did the woman breathe, much less cook?

"I'm still trying to find another work-from-home job," Naomi continued.

Clearly breathing wasn't an issue. The woman hadn't stopped talking since her first "Hello" and Archie couldn't get a word in edgewise.

"Poor Yakov, it's so stressful for him, the struggle to make ends meet."

"Yakov's your husband?" *Maybe asking about her spouse wouldn't come across as too rude an interruption.*

"Yakov, yes, poor dear, saddled with such a useless wife."

From Debbie and from women truckers Archie had heard plenty about how hard it was to "have it all"—motherhood and a career. But Archie thought Naomi might be a little hard on herself and he said so. *Maybe this Yakov was having trouble holding up his end, might even be unemployed.* "What's your husband do, may I ask?"

"Why he studies, of course. He's just brilliant. I'm sure you've studied along with him at synagogue. Yakov Blumenberg?"

Archie's head throbbed. *Studying at a synagogue? Was the woman's husband a student? Maybe studying to be a rabbi? Wouldn't it have been wiser for them to postpone their family until after he graduated and got a job?* "I don't go—"

"Oh, you must go to the other synagogue."

Archie stopped short of saying he didn't attend at all. "Look, I, uh, I can tell you're busy. I'll let you go. I really need to get back on track getting a caterer. Would you be able to refer me to any? It's not for a big event like a wedding or anything. Just a home reception. A ... seudat. For a ... brit." Archie found himself grinning at how glibly the foreign words rolled off his tongue.

"A seudat brit milah? Why didn't you say so? Oh, how wonderful. Mazel tov. Your first? You must be ecstatic."

"It's not my son. My nephew. Well, I hope to be his uncle. And if I can find a caterer, it will really get me points with his grandparents."

"Aren't you a dear? OK, I'll do it."

Archie's hopes shifted into forward gear. "I should tell you it's for Friday. And in Salt Point."

Silence greeted the announcement and for a moment Archie wondered if Naomi had hung up on him.

"Sorry, didn't mean to leave you in the lurch there. Had to herd a toddler. Friday? Salt Point?"

"We're really in a spot. Everyone else is booked."

Again, there was no response but since Archie could hear crying in the background he knew at least Naomi hadn't disconnected. "Money's no object," he said. At least, he hoped it wasn't.

"It'll be a challenge. OK, I'll find a way to do it. I'll have to bring my babies with me."

Yakov couldn't squeeze some babysitting in while he studied? This had gotten way above Archie's pay grade. "How about I let you and Debbie work out the details?"

"That'll be fine. I'll look forward to talking with her. The sooner the better, though, OK?"

"I'll call her right now. Thanks, Naomi. You're ..." He was about to say "an angel" or "a Godsend" or "the answer to prayer" but would any of those be right? "A lifesaver." He hit END, then dialed the number at the Stenowitz home. The phone rang and rang then went to an answering machine. "You have reached Marvin and Miriam Stenowitz. We're sorry we missed your call and would like to return it. Please wait for the beep then leave your name, number, the time you called, and a brief message. Thank you and have a great day."

"This is Archie. I found a caterer. Her name is Naomi. Nosh by Naomi. She's going to call to arrange the details but meanwhile here's her—" Archie was about to leave Naomi's number when the cell phone signal disappeared.

He growled at the device. He hoped he wasn't too late. No one answering the phone meant either everyone was out buying supplies or had their hands full in the kitchen.

At least he'd made some progress. The sense of accomplishment helped dispel the unease that had plagued him since his conversation with the cashier at the Kosher Outpost. And it was high time he made tracks to meet Bingo's partner.

Archie drove out of town along Main Street and hadn't left the commercial district far behind before he spotted the nursery up ahead and slowed. A long, low timber building, it was flanked on one side by covered patios where in warmer weather potted plants were likely sold. On the inside, shoppers would likely find bagged goods like potting soil, fertilizer, and pesticides; seeds and pots, spades and shovels. Parking was not going to be a problem. The place was deserted, surprising even for a winter's day. The lot held only one car, a badly oxidized Ford Tempo. Archie's only challenge was that the lot hadn't been cleared recently. He steered the truck down the middle where the accumulated snow wasn't as deep.

He spotted a man in a parka standing in front of wide double doors painted an optimistic healthy green. The man trotted over to meet Archie. Archie rolled down the window. "Are you Yegor?"

"That's me. I don't have to ask who you are."

"The place doesn't even look open."

"It's not," Yegor said. "Not for retail business, anyway. That'll start up again next month. Until then, the employees come in part time, getting the place ready for spring. Receiving inventory, stocking stuff. Supplying businesses with plants for their landscapes. Like the FDR Park."

"Your partner said something about a trailer."

"Yeah, it's over there." Yegor pointed to the far end of the property where stacks of disposable black plastic pots, bags of mulch, pea gravel, and pavers in different shapes and sizes stood under blankets of snow. Beyond them stood a snow-dusted 28-foot pup trailer. Archie set the tractor's brakes and exited the cab.

"Hey, uh, don't you need to bring the truck up to the trailer?" Yegor asked.

"First I need to inspect the trailer," Archie replied.

"Inspect it?"

"Yeah. Make sure there aren't any problems with the tires or the wheels, the frame or the suspension, the kingpin. Stuff like that. We wouldn't want a breakdown halfway back to Hyde Park."

"Oh, right."

"If the outside passes, I'll hook it up and check the lights and the brakes. It's not locked or sealed, is it?"

"No, why?"

"I'm gonna want to take a look inside the cargo compartment."

Yegor looked perturbed. "Why you got to do that?"

"Stuff needs to be placed inside in the right way. So it doesn't shift around. That could damage the plants. Or worse, create steering problems for me. An improperly loaded truck can overturn, especially if I hit a slick spot. Of which there are quite a few out there today."

"Oh, I didn't know that."

"And I need to check the cargo against the bill of lading. Is that going to be a problem?"

"No, man. You go right ahead and inspect."

As he approached, Archie made a point of noting whether the trailer leaned to one side which would indicate a problem with the suspension. The van was just a plain old aluminum box. Dents and chipped paint spoke to years of wear but on first glance it appeared to be in acceptable shape for pulling down the highway. All the required lights and reflectors were in place, the reflective striping was worn but adequate, and even the mud flaps were securely mounted.

He opened the trailer doors and peered inside and saw a load that could only be called pathetic. The puny assortment of small potted trees was more than a pick-up could carry but definitely less than a truckload. It all could easily fit in a U-Haul and Archie wondered why Bingo hadn't just gone and rented one of those. He gave an inward shrug. It wasn't his stuff and it wasn't his business. The man was willing to pay and at this point Archie wasn't inclined to go back empty handed.

Archie held out his hand. "You got the bill of lading?"

"Well, uh, no. I didn't know I needed one."

Dimwit. Archie sighed. Had he really come all the way up for nothing? "Let me see, maybe I've got a blank you can fill in." He returned to the cab and rummaged around, not holding out much hope. Then he remembered where he had seen one. He retrieved the copy of the textbook that he had used to study for his license. He was long past studying but he liked taking the book with him on trips. He found that often enough he needed to consult it to refresh his memory. Sure enough, the chapter on cargo documentation had an illustration of a straight bill of lading. He carried the book to Yegor. "Here, fill this out. Put down today's date and where I'm taking the stuff. Come on, let's tally up what's in here and you can put down what I'm carrying." Archie clambered into the cargo compartment. The pots needed to be realigned and braced anyway so that they wouldn't fall over and become damaged in transit, although if they did become damaged it would be hard to tell. "These plants seem to be suffering."

"They've just been sitting in the trailer. Once they get in the greenhouse they'll perk up."

Archie wanted that noted on the documentation so that Yegor could sign off on it. Archie didn't want anyone accusing him of contributing to the cargo's shabby condition, much less penalizing him for spoilage.

Yegor called up from the ground. "Here under Description, do I need to put exactly what type of plant it is?"

"No, just potted saplings will do, and the note about the state they're in." As he rearranged the load, he took count and called the total out to Yegor.

Archie hopped out of the trailer and looked over Yegor's shoulder. "That'll work. Just put your name and address there under shipper, and sign your name. And you're gonna pay me when we're done, right? Check 'Collect on Delivery.'"

Yegor did as instructed. Archie decided that it was unlikely the man had earned high marks for penmanship in school.

"OK, Bingo will meet you at the Park."

Just to be on the safe side, Archie did a quick pre-trip, checked the brakes and the coupling. Confident that all was in order, he headed south.

He arrived at the FDR Park and parked in front of the historic home to find an impatient Bingo holed up in his car, the motor running.

"'Bout time you got here," he said. "I burned half a tank of gas just trying to stay warm."

"I didn't think you wanted me getting pulled over for speeding. Why didn't you wait inside?"

"I have been but I didn't think you knew where to find me. OK, you're here now, so follow me."

The Riviera steered down a winding asphalt drive past red-painted gabled buildings. Prim and functional, the largest of them bore the label "Coach House." At Archie's right, a neatly trimmed hedge enclosed a snow-covered courtyard of sorts. A break in the hedge gave Archie a glimpse of a structure at the yard's center: a long white cube austere in its simplicity. Mounted on a short pole, a small U.S. flag fluttered alongside it.

Bingo stopped in front of a long rectangular building made mostly of glass: a greenhouse. He waved Archie to a stop and signaled for him to roll down the window. "Back up to there." He pointed to a wooden door set into the stone fascia at the end of the greenhouse.

"Tight squeeze," Archie said, scanning the layout for a more convenient loading spot.

"Then I can do all the loading and unloading," Bingo said, his raised eyebrows making him look both hopeful and apologetic.

Archie gave the approach another look. A little work jockeying into position sounded like a fair trade for Bingo doing the lumping.

Archie opened the trailer doors then gently jacked and backed the rig into position. In the side mirror he saw Bingo open the greenhouse door. He retrieved a set of wooden steps and carried them to the rear of the trailer. Archie could feel the slight vibration when Bingo boarded the trailer and moved around. After Bingo's third trip, Archie tuned it out and focused on his *American Big Rig* story.

He had completed his latest installment, eaten his knish, and was catching a cat nap when a pounding on the driver-side door startled him awake. Bingo gave him a thumbs up.

"You're good to go. I'll meet you back at the nursery. Yegor will have your money for you."

Archie opened the cab's door and stepped onto the foothold.

"Hey, watcha doin'?"

"I was just going to inspect the load."

"Ah, you don't have to do that. I've got it all loaded nice and tight. Anyhow, you'd better hustle. Yegor won't wait there all day. You miss him, you'll have to wait until tomorrow to unload."

And either make more trips back and forth to Hyde Park or spend a night in the sleeper in Tannersville. Archie waved off Bingo, rolled up the window, and fired up the ignition, hoping to make quick work of returning to the landscaper, dropping the trailer, and connecting with Debbie.

He had no sooner pulled onto Route 9 than he felt something was wrong. Something about the trailer didn't feel right. *A tire going flat? Cracked axle? A problem developing in the suspension?* No, nothing that serious. It felt like maybe his load had shifted. Perhaps the uneven road surface or one of its many twists and turns had jarred something loose.

Damn. That dimwit Bingo. No, Archie thought, I'm the dimwit. I should have loaded the cargo myself instead of goofing off in the cab. To the uninitiated, cargo loading looked like a simple matter of shoving stuff in the boxy compartment of the van but it was more complicated than that and he knew it. Goods had to be stacked in such a way that they wouldn't damage each other, and for ease of unloading, placed into the van in a particular order, especially with mixed loads destined for multiple stops. Proper cargo securement called for blocks of wood, two-by-fours, or load locks to keep the stuff from working itself loose, which was likely what had happened. Heaven forbid something had broken. Even though Archie hadn't done the actual loading, it was his responsibility and he'd be liable for any damage. Handling the claim would make more work for his broker and he wouldn't like that.

Archie cursed himself for his lapse in vigilance. Served him right that he would have to leave the nice warm cab, climb into the cold van, and restack whatever was rattling around.

There wasn't much of a shoulder to park on so he drove a few yards until he came upon a single-story building housing a pest control operation. Its parking lot was just long enough for him to park the rig parallel to the road. Except for a couple of cars and pickup trucks close to the store entrance, the lot was empty.

He set the brakes and stepped from the cab just in time to spot Bingo's Riviera headed north. There was no way that Bingo wouldn't have noticed that Archie had pulled over. He would get to Tannersville long before Archie would, probably rat him out. Archie would have some explaining to do when he arrived with the trailer. Yegor would probably go over the cargo with a fine tooth comb and charge Archie for every crushed leaf and broken twig.

His breath fogging in the icy air, Archie tramped through crunchy snow to the rear of the trailer, pulled open the swinging doors, and stopped, stunned. It wasn't the sight of the greenery that filled the cargo space, he expected that. It was the odor. Bingo had told him that they were clearing out spruces and junipers left over from Christmas but there was nothing piney about the smell of these plants. They were pungently herbal. They smelled like—.

Archie peered more closely into the van's dark interior.

Weed.

He staggered backward and slammed the cargo doors closed.

The van's floor was covered in potted marijuana plants. Archie had been pulling a load of contraband down the road.

CHAPTER SIXTEEN

HYDE PARK, NY, Wednesday, February 17, 1993

Archie turned, leaned against the trailer, and tried to collect his thoughts. Out of the corner of his eye, he spotted Bingo's Riviera, now traveling southbound. As it passed the pest control's parking lot, it slowed. Archie caught Bingo's glare. Before Archie could wave him over, the Riviera accelerated and sped away.

Dazed, Archie stumbled back to the cab and sank into the seat.

What had gone on here? The load of plants that he had delivered to the FDR greenhouse seemed legitimate enough. Archie had thought that bringing plants to a legendary greenhouse was a bit like carrying coals to Newcastle or freezers to Eskimos but didn't question it. His father had to buy some seed and sprouts for the farm each year. Even a famous garden like the one at the FDR Park had to start somewhere.

Now it appeared that the point of the run wasn't to deliver plants to the park, it was to haul them away. Archie doubted that Yegor had been contracted to supply the FDR Park with plants or that Bingo actually worked for the National Park Service. It had all been a ruse, a sham.

They had been growing marijuana in the greenhouse. *Brilliant, really.* Apparently, the greenhouse wasn't secured; it wasn't even locked. Bingo and Yegor must have stumbled on the same realization and figured it would be a good place to store their crop. Protected from the elements, the plants would enjoy the retained warmth on cold days and the controlled humidity. For all Archie knew, scheduled irrigation was maintained throughout the winter, conveniently watering the pot plants.

Those daily trips of Bingo's to the park hadn't been to fulfill any groundskeeper duties; they had been to monitor the pot plants until it was time to harvest them. The two probably would have gotten away with it if President Clinton hadn't announced his intention to use the park for a public event.

In the Hyde Park Manor lobby, Archie had overheard Bingo saying into his walkie talkie, "we've got to move." He had meant that he and Yegor had to move the plants. NYNEX technicians had descended on the park as early as Sunday. Government security officials weren't far behind. They would go over every inch of the park looking for any possible threat to the President's safety. Even though the greenhouse wasn't included in the visit, they would check it just as a matter of procedure. As soon as the Hyde Park Town Hall meeting was announced, Bingo and Yegor must have realized that ready or not, their plants had to be relocated before the feds found them.

"Ohmigod," Archie breathed. *The scandal that would erupt if the dope had been discovered while Clinton was there, or even after he left. Even just a whiff of association ...*

Bad pun, Harlanson.

During Clinton's campaign, a TV reporter asked him if he had ever used marijuana. The candidate had answered that he had tried it a time or two when he was a Rhodes scholar in the late sixties but that he hadn't liked it. "I didn't inhale," Clinton had said and stated that he never tried it again. He had a hard time living that down as a candidate and even now, as an elected official, the subject still dogged his heels. Archie had found the whole thing ludicrous at the time. Who in the sixties and seventies didn't give pot a try? Even Archie had, although like Mr. Clinton, he found it didn't do much for him and it had been a short-lived experiment. It was for certain he wouldn't go near the stuff today. One failed drug test and Archie would lose his commercial license faster than you could say "Busted."

Archie was so stunned by his discovery that he was giddy. He needed to get a grip. *What to do?*

Well, he certainly wasn't going to deliver the load to Yegor. He shouldn't move another inch with it. That would just compound the crime of which he was already guilty. At least at this point he could say that he had stopped the minute he became aware of the nature of his cargo.

And whom would he be explaining that to? The cops? Should he call the cops? What were the chances that they would believe him when he told them that a man named Bingo, whose last name Archie didn't even know, had unbeknownst to him filled his van with marijuana plants?

Yeah, right, Buddy.

He could call his load broker. The man had been around the block a time or two, had handled all kinds of weird unforeseen mishaps that his drivers ran into.

And would Archie ever get another load? When word got out, and it would, would anybody ever hire him for anything again?

Get rid of it. That's what he should do.

There were plenty of wooded areas around. Archie could find one that he could back into, uncouple the trailer, and just leave it somewhere. Who would complain about the missing delivery? Certainly not Yegor or Bingo. What were they going to do if he didn't show up at the lot? Call the police and report that Archie had run off with their cash crop?

Yes, that's what he would do. He'd ditch the whole thing the first place he could spot. And he'd better get busy about it, too, before someone came out of the pest control shop and asked him what he was up to. Even now, some clerk or shopper had probably noticed his rig with the memorable bright red tractor.

Archie belted in, fired up the engine, and returned to the road, eyes flicking left and right, scanning for a place to ditch the load, trailer and all.

When the demanding "whoop" caught Archie's attention, he checked his side mirror to see what it was behind him that could have made that noise. The flashing red and blue of the light bar atop the white Chevy Caprice told him that he had been cruising down the road in ignorant bliss long enough that the police car following him had to turn on its siren to get his notice.

He was being pulled over? For what? He hadn't been speeding, hadn't run any lights. He had inspected the vehicle this morning and found everything in order. Perhaps, since he left the FDR Park, a turn signal light had blown a bulb. Even something as minor as a missing reflector was grounds for a traffic stop although he would likely be let off with a warning to get it repaired. He couldn't think of a single traffic violation he had committed, but there was the matter of the load of contraband. *What if the cops wanted to search the van? Was there anything that he had done to give them probable cause?* His pulse zoomed and goosebumps broke out across his shoulders. *Calm.* Remain calm, he told himself. Be polite and cooperative. Don't give the officer any excuse to go poking around.

He slowed, steered as far off the traveled part of the road as possible, and brought the vehicle to a stop on the shoulder. He had never in his entire driving life been pulled over and had no idea what to expect or how to respond. *Was this an emergency stop? Was he required to set out warning devices?* He racked his brain but couldn't remember what he had read. He wasn't broken down. It seemed like a police car with its flashing lights would be sufficient warning to other motorists about the parked vehicle.

The officer would want to see his license and registration. Archie fumbled to get the documents ready to present. Glancing at the side view mirror, he waited for the officer to appear alongside the truck.

The officer who appeared at Archie's driver-side door was more boy than man. Reedy and fair-haired, he looked lost in his puffy parka. "Good afternoon, sir," he said.

"And to you, Officer? ..."

"Haas."

"Officer Haas. I'm sorry, is there a problem?"

"We'll be finding that out, sir. There's a sizable dent in the rear of the trailer. I'll be calling for a DOT officer to come do a CMV safety inspection."

Archie sighed. *For a dent in the trailer?* It wasn't even his trailer, it was Yegor's. OK, technically a dent gave the officer reason to suspect that there might be other problems. Still, Archie figured it was probably a wonder that he hadn't been stopped before this, the Kenworth being a commercial vehicle in an area with little traffic. No doubt the officer hoped to find something defective for which he could issue a costly ticket. *Good luck with that.* Archie had pre-tripped the tractor this morning and knew everything was in order, and he'd inspected the trailer's tires, suspension, frame, wheels, coupling, and lights before leaving the nursery. He certainly didn't want to be out on slippery winter roads with underinflated tires or faulty brakes.

A safety inspection would turn up no problems, with of course the exception of the cargo which he hoped the officer wouldn't request to examine.

"Please remain at the controls," said Officer Haas. "Put the transmission in Neutral, release the brakes, and turn off the engine. I'll need to see your driver's license, your inspection report, shipping papers, and your independent contractor agreement."

Archie tried not to fidget while Officer Hass examined the documents.

"All seems to be in order, here, sir," said Officer Haas and Archie thought he might be able to breathe again. "Wait here, please, sir."

Haas returned to his patrol car where no doubt he placed the call to the DOT. *Just where were the state police barracks? Albany?* Archie wondered how long he was going to have to wait and could he keep his cool the whole time.

Officer Haas returned and said, "Sir, if you'd step outside of the cab for me, please." He himself moved a few steps back, a safety precaution to prevent a potential fleeing felon from smacking him with the door. The radio receiver clipped to his jacket collar barked and the young officer tilted his head to catch the transmission.

Archie had no sooner swung his legs over the side of the seat when he heard another noise. From behind, another car with flashing rooftop lights steered onto the shoulder and parked in front of Archie's truck. *That was quick,* Archie thought. Maybe he'd get out of here before nightfall. His heart sank when he saw big navy blue block letters running alongside the length of the car. The second car wasn't the highway patrol but a second officer of the Hyde Park Police Department.

Over the vehicle's public address speaker, the newly-arrived officer instructed Archie to turn off the engine and remove the keys from the ignition.

Well, he had already done that.

"Exit the vehicle with your hands showing," came a voice, its authority somewhat impaired by the scratchy PA speaker.

Exit the vehicle? With hands showing? This wasn't a simple roadside inspection, this sounded like a felony or high risk apprehension. Breathing deeply, trying to slow his pounding pulse, Archie told himself that if he was respectful and compliant this would all soon be cleared up and he would be on his way. He exited the vehicle as instructed, his hands not held high but at chest height, palms out.

"Walk to the right side of the truck, sir," came the disembodied voice over the loudspeaker. The door to the second patrol car opened, the driver emerged, and started toward the truck.

In his deep-blue uniform and peaked cap, the officer who approached was beefy enough to strain the buttons of his uniform, and his cap perched precariously atop a round head. Archie thought he looked familiar and as the man drew closer he could see that it was Rademaker, the officer he had met at the desk of the Hyde Park Police station. Rademaker's pale face bore a blank expression but Archie thought his eyes looked a little nervous. Rademaker had his hand on his weapon. Archie swiveled and saw that the young officer who had first pulled him over did also. Despite his resolve moments ago to remain calm and clear-headed, Archie too was now nervous. *OK, something was terribly, terribly wrong here. They couldn't possibly know about the contraband in the trailer.* They had the wrong guy, Archie thought. It was a case of mistaken identity. The second officer was probably following up on a warrant that owing to some silly typographical error had been issued for the Kenworth's license number. That had to be it. "Excuse me, Officer Haas, with all due respect, you have got the wrong guy."

"I don't think so. We got report from a call made to the Clinton Town Hall Tip Line. We've been on the lookout for a brand new, bright red Kenworth tractor. Not too many of those around here. Hands behind your head," he said. Archie noticed that the young officer no longer called him "sir."

"Oh, it's you," said Rademaker.

"Excuse me?"

"The troublemaker from yesterday. Conspiracy, huh? Looks like the only crime we've got to worry about is the one you've been up to."

"Me?"

"Transporting drugs. Now, over there. Lie down, face down, arms out at your side. Do as you're told and we won't have any further trouble."

Did the officer really expect him to lie down in the snow? Apparently he did. Grateful for his down vest, Archie followed the instructions, only to find himself patted down.

"No weapons," Officer Haas pronounced.

Rademaker applied handcuffs. "You can stand up now," he said.

Despite the fact that he knew he had done no wrong, Archie found it enormously humiliating to struggle to his feet with his hands behind his back, unable to brush the snow from his face.

"Officer, I honestly think this has gone far enough," he said, trying not to sound belligerent or intimidated. "I think I have a right to know what's going on." *He did, didn't he?*

"We'll decide how far it has to go," said Officer Haas. With one hand still on his sidearm, he gestured with the other for Archie to move toward the police car. Rademaker opened the rear door and handed Archie into the back seat.

"What about my truck?" Archie said, sounding more petulant than he would have liked.

"It'll be towed to impound," the second officer said. "It's evidence."

"Evidence of what?"

The police car pulled off the shoulder and merged into traffic. Archie twisted in his seat and kept the Kenworth in sight as long as he could.

*****

Archie tried not to wriggle on the stiff aluminum chair. He was used to spending long hours on his butt, but on a cushioned seat specifically designed for extended sitting. He didn't doubt that whoever came up with this chair meant the sitter to be uncomfortable.

No windows, not even in the small room's door. He had stared at the blank walls long enough to be tempted to count the acoustic ceiling tiles just to keep himself occupied. The door finally opened, but his elation quickly died when Officer Rademaker stepped into the room.

Archie rose from his seat. "At last," he said. "I'm happy to help in any way I can but I really have to get back on the road. I can come back tomorrow—"

"Sit, Mr. Harlanson," Rademaker said. "We're not quite done here." He set a tape recorder between them on the table, turned it on, and stated the date, time, and their names. "We're just having a little chat, Mr. Harlanson," he said.

Archie waved at the tape recorder. "Then why the formalities?"

"Just so there's no questions later about who said what. You're good with that, right, Mr. Harlanson? With this little interview?"

"I said I wanted to help," he replied, feeling less amenable by the second.

"Great. Not that we owe you an explanation, but we have strong reason to believe your vehicle contained a driver suspected of having committed a serious crime."

"What crime?"

Rademaker snorted. "You skells are all alike. Innocent as a newborn babe."

Newborn? Archie's mind flashed on the image of little Eli in his arms.

"Innocent until you're proven guilty. And we've got you dead to rights. What crime? Possession."

"Possession?" Archie squeaked, wishing he had instead sounded genuinely baffled.

Rademaker leaned into Archie's face. 'You gonna pretend you weren't hauling a trailer full of pot plants?"

"I'm telling you exactly that." Teetering on the flimsy aluminum chair with Rademaker towering over him made Archie feel about five years old. He scooted the chair back, planted his feet, and rose half out of his seat which only provoked Rademaker to lean in closer. "Where do you think you're going? I told you to sit," he bellowed, his nose practically touching Archie's.

"I'm leaving. Unless you're saying I can't."

Rademaker's reply was interrupted by a knock on the door. "Stay put." He stepped half out of the room and had a conversation with someone out of view. Archie stood and leaned to the side but couldn't get a glimpse of the other party.

Rademaker returned to the room closing the door behind him. "I thought I told you to stay put."

"This isn't what it looks like. I can explain everything."

"Oh, you'll get your chance. We're not the only ones interested in hearing it. There are some federal agents who got you on their radar too. So you just cool your heels until they get here."

Federal agents? The FBI guys from the Manor who were so angry with him for leaking the presidential cavalcade route? Archie wasn't eager for another confrontation.

"I'll tell them the same thing I told you. There's this guy who's been hanging around the Park. I knew he was up to no good. I told you that yesterday. I told you to look into it."

"Did you now?"

"Oh, come on. You remember. I stopped into the station and told you all about it. You were all busy with a big planning meeting."

"Might explain why there doesn't seem to be any record of your visit."

"You're saying I can't leave?"

"Not if you really want to help clear this up."

"I am. Why don't I come back tomorrow?"

His legs spread, his arms folded across his chest, Rademaker blocked the exit. "I don't think so."

"You can't keep me here. Not unless you're arresting me."

"Have it your way."

Another officer searched Archie and took his personal possessions—keys, the cell phone, wallet—and gave him a hastily-completed voucher in return. Throughout the fingerprinting and photographing process, Archie vacillated between humiliation and fury.

"We'll be checking to see if you're wanted for anything else," Rademaker said as he escorted Archie down a hallway. He waved Archie into a cell. "Make yourself comfortable."

The Hyde Park Police Department lock-up wasn't much bigger than the Kenworth's sleeper berth. Hung on the brick wall, the steel bedstead held a thin mattress with no more cushioning than the typical gym mat. A small barred window let in some natural light which somehow only made the interior more dismal. A welded steel one-piece sink/toilet combination was the only other furnishing.

Rademaker appeared at the cell. "We're still checking warrants."

"You won't find any," Archie said.

Rademaker shrugged. "So you say. Meanwhile, you get one call. Make it a good one." The hint of a smile twitched the corner of his lips and his eyes narrowed.

Whom to call?

CHAPTER SEVENTEEN

HYDE PARK, NY, Wednesday, February 17, 1993

At the jangle of keys, Archie looked up to see Officer Rademaker at the cell door. He unlocked it and said, "Lucky you, Harlanson. You've been sprung."

Behind him stood Debbie's brother-in-law, Elliot. Archie felt about seven years-old and freshly chastised for hitting a baseball through someone's plate glass window. There didn't seem to be anything he could do to stop the blood rushing to his cheeks.

Offered his one phone call, Archie had visualized his Rolodex. He could call Debbie or his broker or even Linc but in the end, he was going to need a lawyer. *Might as well just suck it up and make that call.*

Rademaker said, "You're free to go. For now. Your truck stays here but you can leave. Don't go too far, though. This isn't the last we'll be seeing of you."

Archie looked at Elliot. "The truck can't stay here. It's my only transportation. It's my means of earning a living," he said, trying not to whine.

"Damn right it's staying here," said Rademaker. "It's evidence. But don't you worry. It's nice and safe in our impound. The rest of your stuff you can reclaim from the property clerk."

Through the small cell window, Archie had done little but study the HPPD's so-called impound, the grassy lot adjoining the police station. A chain link fence and a padlock appeared to be all that came between the Kenworth and misadventure.

A hand at Archie's back, Elliot steered him towards the property office. "Let's just get out of here," he said in a whisper. "We'll sort it out later."

Suppressing a grumble, Archie let himself be guided to a counter where he signed a receipt for his belongings.

Elliot opened the passenger door to his burgundy Lincoln Town Car and waved Archie inside. He hustled around to the other side and got behind the wheel. "So, where would you like to go? Salt Point? Debbie's real worried about you. Or, the Manor?"

Archie wasn't quite ready to face Debbie yet, much less her parents. "I guess to the Manor ..." Archie opened the manila clasp envelope to find his wallet and cell phone. The police had returned his house, mailbox, and locker keys, even the key to his room at the Hyde Park Manor but "The truck's keys. They're not here. And my notebook?"

"No doubt they've got the truck keys in the stationhouse as part of the evidence. Your notebook too. Anything compromising in it that I should know about?"

Such as doodles of the *Daily Planet* logo? "Like the names and addresses of all my contacts in the drug world?"

"Don't even joke about that. I'm serious. Be thinking about what might be in the notebook that could incriminate you. I am not happy that they have it and I'm going to see what I can do to suppress that. You're lucky you got your cell phone back. I suspect some day in the not too distant future those will be seized too."

The phone rang and startled Archie nearly out of his skin. He looked at Elliot who waved "Answer it."

"Hello?"

"Hey, Harlanson." It was Linc Haybens. "So where are you, man? I heard that the police had a semi in custody. Sounded like yours. What's that all about?"

Elliot looked Archie a question.

Archie covered the microphone with his hand. "It's a friend of mine. A reporter."

"Oh, no. No talking to reporters."

"Oh, Linc's a buddy. I did him a favor." To Linc he said, "Uh, I'm uh, with Debbie's brother-in-law."

"Didn't you tell me he's an attorney? Hoo boy, are you in trouble?"

"I ... I guess I am."

"Anything I can do to help? Hey, can you meet me at The Shop?"

"I don't ... maybe. Yeah, sure." Archie couldn't imagine how Linc could possibly assist but a beer sounded like a real good idea. "Could we meet with him?" he asked Elliot. "He's a local guy. He knows everybody. And I ... I could use a little liquid courage before I face the music."

Elliot shrugged. "Sure, I guess. Where to?"

*****

Archie found Haybens holding down a four-top already furnished with a pitcher of beer and three mugs. As Archie and Elliot approached, he stood and held out his hand. "Linc Haybens, of the *Valley Voice* and special for the *Herald*."

"Elliot Jordan, J.D. Woodcuff and Terrowin."

They sat and Linc filled the mugs.

Archie took a long swallow. "You said you knew I was in trouble. How'd you find out?" Archie asked.

Linc shrugged. "I've got a scanner. I listen to the police channels. Great way to pick up a hot lead on a story. Or a case, eh, Counselor?"

Elliot frowned.

"Elliot's no ambulance chaser, Linc. He's a criminal attorney."

"My apologies." Linc lit a cigarette and offered one to Elliot, who accepted. "You?" he asked Archie. "Oh, right. You don't smoke. Anyhow I heard something about a code 420. That's a drug bust. And something about a semi on Route 9. I thought, you're plugged in to the trucker network, you might know something about it. I didn't think it was you. So what the hell happened?"

"Anything he says is off the record, Mr. Haybens," Elliot said.

Linc took a puff. "Let me clue you in, Mr. Jordan. There's no such thing as 'off the record.' Not really. Maybe we can't use something in print but we remember everything." He tapped his temple. "Nothing goes to waste. But this guy?" He jerked a thumb at Archie. "I'm on his side. You got nothing to worry about." To Archie he said, "So?"

Elliot pushed his untouched beer mug aside, laid a lined yellow tablet on the table, and flipped to a clean page. "Yes, tell me exactly what happened. In as much detail as possible."

"I pulled over—"

"Back up, back up. Let's start with where were you."

"I was on 9, headed north."

"Because you were? ..." Elliot circled his pen in the air.

"I had taken this load from a landscaper in Tannersville named Yegor. He had me haul some new plants to the FDR greenhouse and for a backhaul, I was supposed to be carrying plants that they no longer needed. I met a lumper—"

"That's the guy who's going to do the loading and unloading?"

"Yeah," Archie said. "I met him at the Park, this guy Bingo."

"Bingo?" Haybens asked. "That's the only name you've got?"

Archie shrugged. "Hey, we don't always get the life story of every dock worker. If it's a regular run we do but ..."

Haybens rolled his eyes.

"So Bingo did the unloading of the delivery and loaded the backhaul?" Elliot asked.

"Right. I offered to help and he said he didn't need it." Archie sighed. "Of course he didn't. He wanted to fill that trailer with weed all by himself."

"And you didn't think to supervise the loading?" Elliot asked.

"Mea culpa, Counselor," Archie replied. "In hindsight, sure, I wish that I had. It was cold. It was, I thought, a bunch of dead and dying plants. What could go wrong? I did check the loading of the original plants at the nursery. Got Yegor's signature on a BOL, too."

"Great. That will help."

"Except, the paperwork is in the truck cab."

Elliot closed his eyes and sighed. "OK. Next?"

"I left the park and headed for the nursery. And before you ask, yes, I knew that was a city street and I swear I was doing the posted speed limit and not a minute faster."

"OK, good to know. "

"Really, in a big bright red truck? Would I want to do anything to attract any more attention? No. I didn't run any yellow lights, I didn't coast through any stops. But there he was, this Officer Haas, flashing his lights at me."

"So why did he flag you down?"

Archie took a swig of his beer. "He said there was a dent in the trailer. And there was. But seriously, when isn't there? These things take a beating. And I checked before I left the nursery yard. There weren't any safety defects, nothing that warranted noting on my DVIR."

"DVIR. That's Driver Vehicle Inspection Report."

"Yeah," Archie said, impressed that Elliot knew the lingo.

Elliot scribbled on his pad. "OK, it wasn't a safety violation but it did give him cause to stop you."

Haybens snorted. "I'll bet he was hoping that your license was expired or something so he could write you a big ticket. It's like *Mayberry R.F.D.* around here most of the time."

"Maybe so. He couldn't find anything wrong with my paperwork so he went back to his car. I thought he was calling for a CMV inspector to come do a roadside safety inspection."

Elliot shrugged. "Not unreasonable."

"But who shows up? The other town cop, Rademaker. Before I know it, I'm lying down in the snow, getting frisked and handcuffed.
"

Haybens chuckled. "Like I said, not much happens around here. They do tend to go a little overboard when it does. Not exactly *Keystone Kops,* but ..." He shrugged. "Well, this whole business with Clinton visiting is about the biggest thing to hit Hyde Park since I've been on the beat. Everyone wants a piece of the action."

"Including you?" said Elliot.

Haybens smiled good naturedly. "Guilty as charged. Oh, sorry, Archie," he said. "But ya know, this could be my ticket outa here."

"Speaking of tickets," said Elliot. "So about Sergeant Rademaker?"

"He told me they got a call into the Town Hall tip line that someone driving a red Kenworth was trying to move drugs through Hyde Park."

Elliot laid down his pen. "He told you that? Those were his exact words?"

"More or less."

"No, this is important. He specifically mentioned the Kenworth, and drugs?"

Archie took a smaller sip of beer. "Yeah. He specifically mentioned a red Kenworth, and he specifically mentioned transporting drugs."

Elliot tapped his pen on his tablet. "Who could have called that in? Who could have known what was in the trailer besides Yegor and this Bingo?"

"Who even knew about your run?" Haybens asked.

"Nobody."

"Not even Debbie?" Elliot asked.

"No," Archie replied. "I told her I was taking a load but I didn't say what or where." He took another swallow of beer. "OK, I left the Park. Then I made a stop at the pest control shop. I thought something about the load had come unbalanced and I wanted to check it out. I went around the back and opened the trailer and that's when I discovered what was really in there. Someone passing by on the street could have seen it too but I doubt it. The only one I saw on the road was Bingo. He had been a little behind me. I guess when I pulled into the pest control lot he wondered why I was stopping.

"I dunno, maybe somebody in the shop saw something. I only had the doors open for a few minutes and it would have been hard to see anything unless you were right behind me." Archie spread his hands out, palms up. "Honestly, I can't think of anyone who knew what was in there besides those two guys. I guess someone could have just made up the whole thing to get me in trouble, but who would want to get me arrested?"

Elliot and Haybens exchanged glances and looked at Archie. "Bingo," they said in unison.

"Huh? Why?"

"Here's how I see it," Haybens said. "You stopped to check the load. Bingo saw you and realized that now you knew what it was."

"He may have thought you might keep it for yourself, sell it," said Elliot.

"OK, I can see that. But how does getting me arrested help him?"

"Cause now the load is safe," said Haybens.

"In the trailer," said Elliot.

"Nice and secure in the HPPD impound."

Archie was for a moment speechless. "OK. Let's go with that for a minute. How are they going to get it out?"

Haybens tipped his chin up and blew a puff of smoke into the air. "You've seen that lot. How hard would it be to break in?"

"Oh, hey, it doesn't look like much. A chain link fence, a padlock. Yeah, maybe they think they could break in to the lot but there's a big old street lamp right there. Unless they have a lot of help, it will take them a while to get all the plants unloaded. Someone's sure to catch them in the act."

"Unless they just take it trailer and all. By the time anyone one notices, Bingo and Yegor will have recovered the money crop."

Archie drummed the table top with his fingers. "There's just one little problem."

"What's that?" Elliot asked.

"The trailer's still coupled to the tractor. They'd have to uncouple it, assuming they can figure out how."

"Or steal the whole rig."

They sipped beer in silence. Haybens' dreamy unfocused look made Archie wonder if the man's creative writer mind wasn't crafting other larcenous scenarios.

Elliot capped his pen, stubbed out his cigarette, and jogged his papers. "I'd better get to work on this. I've got some research to do and forms to fill out. Archie, can I take you to the house or? ..."

Archie licked the suds from his lip. "Neither. A car rental agency. I'm going to need wheels."

"I suppose you do. You could borrow Marvin's or Miriam's."

"No, there's something I need to do and I don't want to involve them."

Elliot frowned. "Wait a minute. I think you need to tell me. As your legal counsel, I need to know you're not going to do anything to aggravate the situation."

"I'm not going to 'do' anything, but I can't just leave the truck there. That so-called impound lot? The security there is barely good enough to keep honest people honest. And here you've been talking about crooks making off with the rig."

"And? ..."

"I just want to make sure nothing happens to the truck."

"Like what? Just what do you think is going to happen?"

"I don't know. Local kids sneaking in to climb around in it, work the horn. Hell, for all I know one of the cops might want to see what it's like behind the wheel. I'm serious. You'd think no one ever saw a truck before. The whole time I've been here it's been like the circus came to town. Look, all I want to do is park across the road, keep an eye on it."

"A stakeout," Linc said, his lips pressed together and eyes big.

Elliot shook his head. "You don't need to do that. There will be officers there all night long."

"Reduced staff. Am I right?" His hands spread in appeal, Archie turned to Linc.

Linc looked at Elliot and nodded. "He's right. It's a skeleton crew. Around here most of the graveyard shift officers are on patrol, answering domestics or break-ins, refereeing bar fights. I should know; I listen to the scanner. About the only people at the station are the desk sergeant and the dispatcher."

"I just want to keep watch. I've got my cell phone. That way if anyone makes any kind of move, I can call for help. Anonymously, even. I don't even have to leave the car."

Elliot drummed his fingers. "Assuming you're telling me the truth—"

Archie held up his hand, palm out. "I swear."

"Then why not borrow one of the Stenowitzes' cars?"

"And tell Miriam, Marvin, and Debbie why I need it? Put yourself in my shoes. Could you tell Caryn and her parents?"

Elliot shuddered. "I see your point."

Linc blew out cigarette smoke. "You still don't need a rental. We'll take my car."

"We?"

"It'll make a great story. I'm not passing this up." He hollered to the bartender. "Steve, we're going to need a growler."

"Not a word to the Stenowitzes," Archie said to Elliot.

"Not even Debbie?"

"I'll call her. Tell her I got hung up on a run."

"Which is basically the truth," Linc said.

"And thus isn't a lie." Archie grinned.

Elliot narrowed his eyes. "You sure it was the CDL test you took and not the bar exam? You prevaricate like a lawyer."

CHAPTER EIGHTEEN

HYDE PARK, NY, Wednesday, February 17, 1993

Elliot sighed. "All right. Make the call. I'll think of something to tell Caryn."

"You're coming with? You don't have to do that."

"You want to keep an eye on your truck. I want to keep an eye on you."

Archie thought of the warning the FBI agents had given him and frowned. *Join the club.* "You don't trust me."

Poker-faced, Elliot said, "Hand me that cell phone."

In the dark of night, the route from The Shop to the HPPD boasted little traffic and less light. Between a blanket of snow and a starless sky and forbiddingly black thickets of trees lining the road, the scene was more Ichabod Crane than Currier and Ives, but Linc piloted his Civic vehicle with a local's quiet confidence. In the passenger seat, Archie mentally drafted various ways of explaining the day's events to Debbie. Behind him, Elliot quietly swigged from the growler of Rolling Rock.

"What did you tell Caryn?"

Elliot lowered the growler. "That today's new client turned out to be a bigger problem than I expected."

"I had to ask," Archie muttered.

"It's happened before. Not a lot but ..."

Linc slowed as the HPPD came into view.

"There." Archie pointed. "Can we park there?"

"Not much in the way of shoulder but I'll see what I can do to get us off the road." As Linc edged off the pavement, his vehicle's headlights swept the so-called impound lot, dimly lit by two feeble floodlights. To all appearances, the Kenworth seemed OK. Linc slowed and stopped. Archie opened the door and got one leg out before Elliot said, "Where do you think you're going?"

"I just want to get a closer look."

"Oh, no, you don't. There's closed circuit cameras trained on that lot, see?' Elliot pointed to the roof's gutter overlooking the lot. "So you can rest easy. If anyone makes a move on your truck, they'll see it on camera. Probably record it. No one's going to get away with anything. And I sure don't want the cops catching you poking around."

Archie settled back in his seat and turned to face Elliot. "Seeing it happening doesn't stop it from happening. Recording who did it doesn't stop it from happening. Video cameras may capture who stole the vehicle, but by then it will be gone." Archie folded his arms. "We're staying put."

"For how long?"

"Until the day shift arrives. Look, there's nobody manning the station. There's hardly any cars in the staff parking area."

"Fine. Guess I'll get comfortable." Elliot leaned back and stretched his legs out across the seat.

Linc fiddled with the radio's knob, raising the volume.

"Better shut that off."

"Really?"

"How many stakeout scenes have you seen where the cops are playing the radio?"

"Well, I don't see the harm but OK, you're calling the shots."

"Better turn off your lights and the ignition too."

"The lights? Wouldn't it help for someone coming down the road to see that there's a vehicle parked on the shoulder?"

"It actually works the opposite way. When there's poor visibility drivers tend to follow other lights. So if you'll pulled off to the side you want to turn your lights off."

"If he turns off the engine, it's going to get cold," Elliot said.

"You didn't have to come."

Elliot harrumphed and sank back into the cushions.

Linc said, "Hey, Archie. Under the seat. Wanna grab me that notebook?"

Archie reached between his feet and fished out Linc's yellow tablet, and passed it over. "You're going to write?"

"You betcha. I got a deadline; this story's due Thursday." Linc looked at his watch. Technically, today."

"How can you see to write?"

"I've got a little penlight. Unless that's too much light for this cloak-and-dagger. I can write in the dark if I have to. I do that when I cover rock concerts." Linc nodded toward the police headquarters. "There's about as much light coming from there as there is in a club." He clicked on his pen and flipped to a clean page.

Archie propped his elbow on the door's armrest and stared out the window. *What a mess.*

On the largely deserted road, the occasional rustle of the pines in intermittent wind gusts were the only sounds, and in between, the scrabbling of Linc's pen and Elliot's muffled snores. Archie stole a peek at the rear seat. Elliot lay across the back seat sound asleep, his knees drawn up in a fetal position.

Then even Linc's pen stopped scratching. Archie looked over to see the man slumped forward, his forehead resting on the steering wheel. Archie pulled his collar closer against the frosty air and returned to his vigil.

The next thing he knew, he jerked awake to the shattering of glass. He bolted upright to find his lap littered with shards of tempered glass and a gun pointed through the empty space where the passenger door window had been.

"Great," said the man holding the gun. "Glad I got your attention."

The passenger door yanked open with a squeal; a hand reached in, grabbed a fistful of Archie's collar; pulled him closer.

"Yegor?"

The Tannersville landscaper said, "Just the man I need. You're gonna make this so much easier."

"Make what?" Archie stammered, still not fully awake and not certain he wasn't dreaming.

"The job of transporting our load. You're gonna finish the job we hired you to do. We were gonna do it ourselves but as long as you're here ... what are you doing here, anyway?"

At Archie's left, Linc's "Hey, what's going on?" was cut short by more breaking glass. Archie struggled to turn in Linc's direction but Yegor held him fast.

"Making sure no one messes with the truck." *This had to be a dream.* He couldn't be standing on a snow-covered New York road in mid-winter having a perfectly normal conversation with a man holding him at gunpoint. In front of a police station.

A police station! Why was there never a cop around when you needed one?

Linc or Elliot could run and fetch the law. *Why didn't they?* Archie peeled his eyes off the gunman to look over his shoulder and caught a glimpse of the driver's side door standing open, the busted window gaping like a blackened eye, and Linc's seat empty.

"This is your lucky day," said Yegor. "We were gonna mess— as you put it—with your truck for sure. But now that you're here, our plans have changed. You're going to move it for us."

Archie shuddered, from the cold he told himself, although that didn't explain the hollow sensation in his belly. "Why would I do that?"

"Because you don't want your buddy here to die," came a familiar voice.

A movement at the corner of Archie's eye drew his attention away from the gun in his face. From around the car's driver's side, one figure, then another, came into view: Linc, and behind him, Bingo, also armed, the gun in Linc's back. Linc's face was a sickly ashen color in the feeble light from the police station across the road.

The police. How were they missing all this happening mere yards away?

"Now here's what you're going to do, Mr. Trucker."

"Archie. My name is Archie." *Maybe, if he reminded Yegor that he was more than some anonymous truck jockey, the man would be less likely to kill him. Wasn't that how it worked in all the crime-show hostage situations?*

Hostage situation. He was a hostage. Archie's legs trembled uncontrollably. "I ... I can't," Archie realized, his panic mounting. "I don't have the key. The cops have the key. I'd have to go inside the station." He could give the cops the high sign—

Bingo snorted. "Like that's gonna happen. Just hot-wire it."

Hot wire a semi? Was that even possible?

Archie's brain scrambled around the truck's innards. He knew a bit about the electrical system, even more since studying for his license. The license test didn't demand detailed knowledge. Mostly the questions were about battery maintenance, short circuits, what constituted a normal ammeter reading, the vital importance of having spare fuses. But his textbook had a whole chapter about the truck's electrical system, the idea being that the more a trucker knew about what made the vehicle work, the better he'd be able to cope when it didn't. Made sense, so Archie read the whole chapter, even got acquainted with his vehicle's wiring diagram.

Hot-wiring a semi ought to be a matter of bypassing the ignition switch itself. He could see the illustration in his mind's eye: the ignition switch with wires leading to the battery, the regulator, the alternator. He would just need to find the right wires.

"Like you're never hot-wired a car before?" Yegor said it as if that was part of everyone's experience, like using an ATM or programming a VCR. "C'mon, let's get moving." He poked Archie in the ribs with the gun. Archie took a stumbling step forward, Bingo and Linc a few paces behind.

Archie stopped. Yegor almost collided with him. "Are you nuts?"

Archie cast a glance backward to the car. *What about Elliot? Had he slept through all the glass breaking? Was he? ...* Archie was about to ask when it occurred to him that Elliot might be laying low, playing possum. Fingers crossed, Bingo and Yegor didn't know he was there in the back seat.

Archie scanned the impound lot's chain-link fence. The one gate in the front expanse was doubly-secured, the latch padlocked and the gate chained to one of the posts. "How am I supposed to get in there?"

"Climb it. You telling me you never climbed a fence before?"

"What if it's electrified?"

"You'll be the first to know. Get going," Yegor said. "I'll be right behind you and don't get creative. Bingo can pick you off and take out your friend."

Archie gave the fence another once-over and headed for a spot he hoped would be scanned by the closed-circuit cameras. Two men scaling the fence would certainly get some officer's attention.

"Not there," Yegor said and marched Archie around the back to a darkened section in the eave's shadow. "I told you not to get creative."

Archie sighed and addressed the fence. Sure he'd climbed plenty of fences—in his youth. Then it had been a quick scramble, up, and over, and jump down. Not so easy as a grown-up, despite his motel-room push-ups and parking lot jogging sessions. He pushed, and pulled, and hoisted his way to the top, got one leg over, then the other and climbed halfway down before launching himself the rest of the way to the ground. The landing reverberated all the way up his legs. The exertion left him breathless, and despite the frigid air, sweating. He caught a glimpse of Linc standing alongside the fence, his face pinched. Archie shivered and it wasn't from sweat drying in the cold air.

As promised, Yegor completed the assault on the fence and escorted Archie toward the truck. As they neared the vehicle, Archie's steps slowed.

"Now what?" Yegor growled.

"The truck. It'll be locked. I'll need the key, the same one I'll need to start it. The one the cops have. And don't ask me if I never broke into a vehicle before because I haven't. But I'll bet you have, plenty of times. What have you got, a Slim Jim?"

"Better," Yegor said. He jumped up onto the passenger door foothold, clutched the grab bar, and with his other hand, thwacked the window with the gun butt. Archie wailed as glass shattered onto the ground.

Yegor yanked open the door and swept broken glass from the passenger seat with his jacketed forearm. "Get in."

Archie boosted himself in, inched across the passenger seat, threaded himself behind the steering wheel and into the driver's seat, and glared at the starter switch on the dash.

"What are you waiting for? The cops? Get busy," Yegor said.

That was exactly what he had been stalling for. Archie glanced at the rear view mirror, praying to see someone emerge from the stationhouse side door that gave access to the yard. "I'm going to need more light. I've got a flashlight in my toolkit in the sleeper." Archie swung around and made to step behind the seat.

"Flashlight. That's all. Don't you be grabbing no gun."

"I don't have a gun." He knew plenty of truckers who did, for protection on those occasions when they had to stay in less-than-five-star truck stops or worse, park alongside the highway. If he survived this, Archie planned to get himself armed.

Archie pulled his toolkit out from under the driver's seat and fished out a flashlight. He found a small Swiss army knife, swag from some truck show, and took that, too.

"What you got there?" Yegor said as Archie shoved the toolkit back under the seat.

"A little knife. I'll need to strip insulation from the wires."

"Gimme that," Yegor said, punctuating his command with the gun.

Archie handed it over. "How am I going to? —"

"Use your teeth like everyone else."

Archie slid back into the driver's seat and stole another hopeful look in the rearview mirror. *Did he see a figure darting across the road toward the stationhouse, or was that just wishful thinking?* Despite the cab's freezing temperature, he shed his padded vest, the better to squeeze under the dashboard. He checked to make sure the truck was in neutral and wriggled into the tight space.

"Could you shine the light down here?" he asked.

In answer, Yegor handed him the flashlight.

"I'll need both hands for the wires," Archie said.

"And I'm holding the gun, or did you forget?"

Archie sighed. The flashlight was too bulky to clamp between his teeth so he tucked it into his armpit.

"When you get this thing started, you'll drive through the gate, then stop and pick up Bingo and your friend."

"I'm not allowed to take on unauthorized passengers," Archie replied.

The muzzle of the gun appeared under the dash. "This is your authorization."

"How's your buddy going to get that gate open?" Archie replied. "Does he have bolt cutters or something?"

"Who needs bolt cutters when you've got a machine like this? You're just going to ram it."

Archie straightened so abruptly he cracked his head on the underside of the dash. "Ram it? You can't ram a chain-link fence."

"I've seen it done all the time."

"In the movies. Those scenes are rigged. The fences have a weak spot where the vehicle's going to make contact. Chain-link fences are meant to stop a vehicle. They use them at racetracks to keep runaway race cars from plowing into the grandstands."

"Well this ain't no race car, so just power this up and get us out of here."

A broken window. Some stripped wires. Archie figure he could get that fixed. *But a front end flattened like an accordion? And who knew what a crash like that could do to the radiator, the engine? The truck might not be drivable. Ever.*

"The damage—"

Yegor pressed the gun's muzzle against Archie's forehead. "You wanna see damage? I'll give you damage, you and your friend. Now get this fired up and out of the yard."

And then what? Surely a semi crashing into the fence would bring out the cops. If Archie could manage to keep himself and Linc from being shot—it might be their best chance out of this mess.

Archie squirmed back under the dash, his forehead throbbing where he'd clonked it, and lightheaded from flashing hot with anger and cold with fear.

In the wavering illumination of the wobbling flashlight, he poked around in the spaghetti bowl of wires until he isolated the ones leading to the starter switch.

Careful to bite through just the covering and not the metal, Archie stripped some of the insulation from the wires, which left the sharp taste of plastic and copper on his tongue. Wishing he had three or even four hands, he tentatively wangled the bared wires into one combination after another, some of which produced an alarming spark, until he had differentiated the battery wire and the ignition wires from the starter wire. The radio sputtering to life told him he had the right combination. He twisted the battery and ignition wires together.

"I'm losing patience," Yegor grumbled.

"You wanna try?" Archie fired back. "You're the one with experience."

"I'm the one with the gun," Yegor replied. "I got experience with that too."

Archie touched the starter wire to the others and any further discussion was halted by the promising rumble of the diesel engine. He pushed the wires to where they wouldn't contact any conductive surfaces and short circuit. Then he wriggled out from under the dash. He plucked his vest from the seat back. As he shrugged into his vest and retook the driver's seat, Yegor said, "Kill those lights. No lights until we're on the road."

"No lights? How am I supposed to read the gauges?" Archie needed to know if he had fuel, the proper water temperature, oil pressure, a half dozen other important measurements, and perhaps most importantly, air pressure to work the brakes.

"Then get us on the road," Yegor roared.

Archie's eyes strained to study the fencing, looking for the most vulnerable spot. The street side gate with its reinforcements, probably not. But the expanse along the side of the lot—in the middle, one span seemed longer between the posts than the others, as if the installer had used a different width of material. *That might give the least resistance, might stretch, even yield.*

He'd have to run into it with some speed, 30, 40 mph at least. The most lurching of takeoffs, exactly what a license applicant would be docked for on the driving test. *Talk about a jackrabbit start, this would be a jackrabbit on steroids. Jackrabbit, hell, a jackelope. God only knew what the stress would do to the transmission, the drivetrain.*

Archie got ready to gun it when white lights dotted the yard like overgrown fireflies. He glanced at the rearview mirror. The stationhouse door to the lot swung open. One, two, three dark shapes, each studded with a light, drew near. *Men, with flashlights. Cops.* At least he hoped they were cops. *Halle-freakin'-lujah.*

"Stop. Police," one of the men shouted. "By order of the Hyde Park Police Department, we order you to stop."

Yegor leaned out the window. "Stay back. I've got a hostage." He fired off a shot for emphasis.

In the mirror, Archie saw the advancing men halt, retreat a few steps. "Stop where you are. You're under arrest," came a distant shout.

"Screw that. Open the gate or the hostage dies." Yegor got off another shot. Archie saw a small dark spot sprout in the snow near the cops.

The three figures drew together. The impromptu conference involved finger pointing, hand gestures, and arm flapping.

"I'm getting tired of waiting," Yegor hollered. "You can open that gate or I can take out this hostage and mow it down myself. Either way, I'm leaving with this truck. Your choice."

One of the cops—Archie hoped they were cops and not night janitors—ran toward the stationhouse. The other two took ready stances, legs spread, side arms drawn. "Now don't do anything hasty," one called. They advanced.

Yegor leaned out the truck window and waved the gun. "Don't come any closer. All I need to see is that gate opening. If it's not in five minutes I'm making my own exit."

It sounded to Archie that one way or another the truck was going to be moving. He flipped on the lights and the dashboard came to life.

Yegor's head swiveled towards him and he scowled.

"Hey, the jig's up. I might as well see what I'm doing. You got an objection to that?"

Yegor made no reply but returned his attention to the cops.

Archie scanned his gauges. Of all the things that had gone wrong today, at least the equipment wasn't presenting any problems.

He glanced in the rear view and side mirrors. The armed cops held their position. Archie wondered just what they thought they could accomplish. The stationhouse was now brightly lit as though it had finally come to life. He spotted activity at the gate. A figure stood alongside it. Archie heard metal clank and clatter as the cop worked the padlock and wrestled the chains.

Two figures emerged from the shadows and approached the cop at the gate who took a step back. He brandished a weapon, then lowered it slightly as Bingo shouted that he, too, had a hostage, and the cop should stay back.

"Get ready to get this tub rolling," Yegor said.

Tub? Archie gritted his teeth. At least this operation wouldn't require a jackrabbit start, ridiculously rapid acceleration, a short stop, and major damage. He released the brakes.

More armed men emerged from the station and ran into the yard.

From a distance, the sound of sirens heralded the arrival of a vehicle sweeping down the street from the east, rooftop light-bar flashing. It screeched to a stop parallel with the fence. Its headlights washed over Linc and Bingo. The cop who left off working the padlock pulled out his weapon. Two cops sprang from the car and fanned out around Linc and Bingo. Bingo kept a gun trained on Linc but now faced three armed men.

Yegor flung open the passenger door and stood sideways on the foothold. His back braced against the inside of the door, one outstretched arm held the door open, his other kept the gun trained on Archie. "Bingo! Get in here."

Bingo's head swiveled toward the truck then back to the cops holding him at bay. They made compelling arguments for him to give up now. His body angled as first one man then another urged him to surrender before any real damage was done.

Archie saw his chance. He threw the truck into motion.

Yegor wobbled and fought to regain his balance, but his left foot lost its grip on the slick metal step. He struggled to straighten and get back into the cab. "You shit," he screamed and fired.

CHAPTER NINETEEN

HYDE PARK, NY, Thursday, February 18, 1993

Fluffy white stuffing erupted from Archie's padded vest and he felt something sock his midriff hard, which really stung when he grabbed the shift lever and threw the truck into reverse.

Yegor stumbled forward and collided with the door frame. The door swung to and slammed him in the rear. Another shot rang out. Archie heard the bullet punch the headliner and clang against the truck's roof.

Practically in one motion, Archie shifted into neutral, set the brakes, and threw a flying tackle at Yegor. They tumbled down the steps and landed in a heap on the ground. Still gripping the gun, Yegor fought to get out from under Archie, but by now the cops in the yard had converged on them.

"Release your weapon," yelled one.

Yegor writhed, angled his hand to aim the gun at Archie, but a black-booted foot came down and pinned Yegor's arm to the ground.

For the second time in less than twenty-four hours, Archie heard, "Face down, on the ground, arms at your side. Both of you."

He eased off Yegor, staggered several paces away, and complied with the command. He turned his head to see two cops wrestling Yegor's arms behind his back and cuffing his wrists.

From above, someone grabbed Archie's wrists and pulled his arms back which made him aware that there was definitely something wrong with his side. "Hey, I'm the hostage," he said.

"Are ya now?" The cop who helped him to his feet was neither Officer Haas nor Rademaker.

"I am. Just ask my attorney. Elliot?"

From where he stood, backlit in the open stationhouse access door, Elliot edged behind the line of cops. "Officers, I suggest that you release my client."

"And, uh, a little help here," Archie said as dizziness and a pervasive chill overtook him.

*****

Archie struggled to raise eyelids that were as heavy and creaky as roll-up trailer doors. His eyes opened to a brightness that wasn't glaring. Above him, translucent light panels checkerboarded an acoustic-tile ceiling.

He tried lifting a head that had taken on the weight of a bowling ball, struggled to prop himself up on his elbows; and realized that his midsection throbbed. He settled for turning his head left and right. Neutral-colored drapes hanging from a U-shaped metal rod blocked most of his view to either side. Railing hemmed in both sides of the bed on which he lay. He looked past one shoulder and caught a glimpse of a white-painted utility stand that held various pieces of electronic equipment. He looked down the length of his body which was covered by a lightweight white thermal blanket. Straight ahead, beyond a stretch of empty space, stood a pale wall against which stood a cabinet, a rolling metal cart, and a stack chair.

Sounds impressed themselves on him: machines beeping and humming, people talking.

A hospital room. That's right, he was in the hospital. He'd been shot. The cops had rushed to his aid, brought blankets which was good because he remembered shivering so uncontrollably hard—

"Great. You're awake."

Archie blinked and brought the white-coated man at his right into focus.

"I'm Doctor Rinquettes."

Archie lifted his arm to offer a handshake and found the movement made his side ache.

"You're in a ward at Mid-Hudson Regional."

"Have I been out long?"

"You were pretty out of it when you got here. We sedated you while we operated."

Archie tried again to rise from the pillow. Its crisp cotton cover was cool against the nape of his neck. The emergency room doctor patted Archie on his left shoulder. "Relax, you're not going anywhere for a while. Although I will tell you that you were lucky."

"Lucky?"

The doctor gave him a rueful smile. "You started to go into shock at the scene. The cops did a great job of keeping you conscious, administering first aid—"

After they cuffed me?

"—and getting you here in record time. An ambulance couldn't have done better."

Archie could remember feeling suddenly woozy and chilled to the bone, someone shouting, "Hey, this man's been shot." Like slides in a balky carousel, he pictured handcuffs coming off, being rolled over. A flurry of activity, blankets tucked around him. Several men bundling him into a squad car. Lights and sirens and the sensation of speed. A blurry memory of the vehicle in which he rode coming to a stop and his being transferred onto a gurney, wheeled up a ramp, and into a brightly-lit lobby with a sharp antiseptic smell.

"You have what the cheap thrillers call a flesh wound. I'm pleased to say that I haven't had to treat that many gunshot wounds but I have had enough experience to figure that the shooter had poor aim. Must have, because from what I can tell he was close enough that he could have done you some major damage. As it is, he missed any major arteries, organs, bone, or nerve."

"It was kind of a wild shot." *Had Yegor not been fighting to stay upright ...*

"Your vest took out some of the punch. Small caliber weapon, too. A thirty-eight."

A rock song popped into Archie's head and the chorus to *Hold On Loosely* hummed in his brain. *Oh, of course, made perfect sense.* That was a hit by an eighties Southern Rock group that Archie liked: 38 Special. "Can I see it?"

"See what?"

"The bullet," Archie replied, surprised at his own morbid fascination.

"Sorry, no. The police wanted it. It's—"

"Evidence."

"Right."

"So this 'flesh wound.' In those cheap thrillers, the injured party just walks away. Am I good to go?"

"Not so fast. You've got some torn muscle. We debrided the damaged tissue—"

So that's what they called all that digging around.

"—stitched you up. It doesn't hurt now because of the anesthetic and the local we gave you but when all that wears off, this is going to be sore. We'll be giving you a prescription for painkillers. Antibiotics too. We've administered some but after we release you, you're going to have to keep this clean.

"And you're going to need to keep that braced, stabilize the whole area so it can heal. You're conscious, you're talking, you're lucid. That's good but your body took a pounding. You've lost a lot of blood. Your electrolytes are out of balance. We're going to keep you for a bit, give you more time to stabilize, make sure there's no leaking at the sutures. Watch for elevation of temperature that could be a sign of infection."

"When can I go back to work?"

"That kind of depends on you and what you do. Not for a few days at the earliest. Weeks maybe. What do you do, anyway?"

"Drive a truck."

The doctor tsked. "You're going to have to take a break. Your range of motion will be limited and you can't drive with the painkillers we're giving you."

Archie sighed. He couldn't drive anyway, not with his vehicle all busted up the way it was. He sure would like to get it in for repair, though. Where was the nearest shop? he wondered. *Poughkeepsie? Kingston? Albany?* His fingers should be doing some walking through the Yellow Pages.

"I'll be checking in on you, but I'm not anticipating any problems. So long as you take it easy, give healing the attention it deserves. You hear me?"

Archie nodded.

"Good." The doctor nodded. "And hey, what you did, that was really something."

Archie frowned. *Break into a police impound lot? Hot-wire a semi? Get shot for his troubles?* "All in a night's work," Archie replied for lack of anything else to say.

The doctor gave Archie's shoulder a pat and stepped away.

The nurse who had been quietly bustling around the room approached. "Hey, Champ. There's a few folks who'd like to see you. Feeling up to it? Say, one at a time?"

"Sure," Archie replied.

"OK. Don't overdo it. Don't hesitate to let me know when you tire. You do need to rest. Your body's been through a lot."

Archie nodded. The nurse stepped back a couple of paces and beckoned to the left.

Debbie came into view, rushed toward the bedside then slowed and approached more cautiously. "Archie, I don't know whether to kill you or kiss you. One minute you're hauling traffic cones, the next minute you're in the Emergency Room with a bullet in your breadbasket."

"I guess I'm not that easy to kill." Archie patted the bandage over his wound.

Debbie sucked in her lower lip and blinked eyes bright with tears. She leaned over and planted a kiss on his lips.

"Good choice," he said.

"How are you?"

"I'm told I'll mend."

She sat on the edge of the bed and frowned. "What were you thinking?"

He shrugged. "Honestly, this all started out Wednesday with just a simple little job. I didn't know these guys were up to no good."

"OK, but when you realized what you were hauling, why didn't you just go to the cops?"

"I was pretty certain they wouldn't believe me. An out-of-towner. A trucker?" *Who had raised a fuss at the station earlier in the week and incited the wrath of federal agents.*

"And what were you doing on Cardinal Road in the middle of the night?" Her tone wasn't accusatory and her expression was one of simple bewilderment, for which Archie was grateful.

"I ... I just felt like I needed to keep an eye on the truck. For all the good that did me." He felt sapped as the extent of the damage sunk in.

Debbie took his left hand. "Don't you worry about the truck. It can be fixed. You just worry about you. I'm going to."

"I'll be OK. I might need to hang here for a while." *The brit Friday. The caterer, Naomi.* "You wouldn't have happened to get a call from a gal named Naomi, would you?"

"We did. Archie, you ..." Debbie chuckled and shook her head. "You totally went way beyond the call."

"No, I didn't. I only went to Tannersville. So, will that get the job done?"

"Oh, yes. It's way more than we needed."

Archie bit his lip. "I'm sorry. I can pay for it. It just sounded like she needed the job. She's got little kids and her husband, he's a student. He doesn't have a job."

"Being a student, that is his job." Debbie's smile was sweet. "It takes a little explaining. Anyhow, I gave her the go-ahead." Debbie picked up his hand and kissed his palm. "You're a sweetheart to have thought of helping us, helping her. You are my Super Man." She stroked his cheek which he was certain was bristly. "Ok, I'd better go. There's other folks lined up to see you and we don't want to wear you out. I'll check in on you later." She gave him another kiss, somewhat on the chaste side but good enough given the circumstances.

Archie's next visitor was Elliot. The man wore more than a five o'clock shadow and yesterday's suit.

"So you didn't get hurt?" Archie asked.

"No, thank God. I'm sorry you did but ..." He lifted his chin, rolled his eyes, and shook his head. "Clients," he said with a sigh. "Can't tell 'em a damn thing."

"Is Linc OK?"

"Oh, he's fine. Not injured at all. Making a pest of himself, trying to convince the head nurse to let him use their fax machine so he can file an update to his story. Big news, as you can imagine."

What Archie could imagine was how this was going to look in the papers. *What would Marvin and Miriam think? What would their relatives and friends think?*

"Caryn and the baby?"

"Oh, they're doing fine. She's starting to feel like herself. Well enough to be angry with me."

"I'm sorry I got you into it."

"Well, that really was my choice. As it turned out, I'm glad I was there."

"How did you? ..."

Elliot plucked a stack chair away from the opposite wall, pulled it alongside the bed, and sat. "I was catching some zees there in the back seat when I heard the first window break. I no sooner got my eyes open when I saw the gun and the guy at the passenger side. I was so stunned I almost couldn't believe it. I thought I was dreaming. Too much beer."

"I hear ya. I didn't believe it myself."

"I was still trying to wake up when that second guy—Bingo?—nabbed Linc. I realized the crooks didn't know I was there."

Good thing Linc had told me to kill the lights, Archie thought.

"I figured I'd try to keep it that way so I slid down to the floor. I stayed there, didn't make a peep until I heard that Yegor fellow leading you away, and then that other guy, Bingo, with Linc," Elliot said. "It felt like forever and I had no idea how things were going for you two. Finally it got quiet and I let it stay quiet for as long as I could stand it. Then I chanced a peek. I saw two guys across the road standing near the fence. They were in a shadow, and it was so dark I really couldn't make them out but I figured it was either you and that Yegor, or Linc and Bingo. I decided to take the chance, found your cell phone, but the damn thing's battery was flat. Then your truck's courtesy light went on. I figured time was running out so I made a run for the police station."

"I thought I saw someone crossing the road. If the crooks had seen you, you could have been shot."

Elliot pressed his lips together and nodded. "I was scared as shit. I don't think I'd ever run so fast in my life. I made it into the station and there was hardly anyone there."

"So, like Linc said, a desk sergeant and a dispatcher."

"More or less, and I made that crack but that wasn't the case at all. Sure they were short-staffed. A lot of the officers were at a briefing with the Feds and the Staties about the President's visit. Looks like it's going to be all hands on deck, everyone's going to be working double and triple shifts. Other officers were out on calls.

When I raised the alarm, the ones that were left put out an all-points to rally the troops, call back every man that could be spared. I've never seen people move so fast, throwing on vests, grabbing weapons, planning strategy on the fly the whole time."

"They had a strategy?"

"Given that they really didn't know what the situation was. I told them about the two guys with guns but ... well, they were reserving judgement until they could get on the scene and evaluate it for themselves."

"Thanks, Elliot. If you hadn't called in the cavalry ..."

Elliot shrugged. "Sounds like you had it under control."

Not really. "So, am I still under arrest?"

"You're released under your own recognizance."

"Released?" Archie jerked up abruptly. Too abruptly. He collapsed back into the pillow. "Released from what?"

Elliot drummed fingers on a trousered knee. "Trespassing. Tampering with evidence—"

"Evidence? My truck? That was my truck. I broke into my own truck. How can that be a crime? I didn't even do the breaking, Yegor did."

"Take it easy. I'm getting it worked out. I keep reminding them that you were instrumental in exposing a significant drug operation. Which, by the way, you did. Turns out that Yegor is the tip of some Russian criminal iceberg. Not to mention saved the President from what at the very least would have been an embarrassment, if not a PR nightmare."

Archie snorted. He would imagine what the political cartoonists, Op Ed columnists, and *Saturday Night Live* writers would do with the story. The revelation that Clinton had held his Town Hall surrounded by cannabis plants surely would have reignited last year's scandal.

"Leave it to me." Elliot patted his chest. "This is what I do. I'm going to see that not only are criminal charges filed against those two, but also civil charges. You should be compensated for the damages to your vehicle."

Archie sighed, suddenly exhausted. "Oh, yeah. My truck. I need to get it fixed, now. Not after some lawsuit's been filed."

Elliot lowered his eyes. "Uh. About your truck. I'm afraid you won't be getting that back any time soon. It is evidence. In a whole laundry list of crimes. Don't worry about it. It's safe."

"In the police impound lot? We've seen how well that works." Despite the painkillers he felt anger spark.

Elliot fluttered his hands. "Simmer down. That's a factor in your favor. Speaking of which, I've got work to do and you're supposed to rest. So you try to do that and leave the legal stuff in my hands, OK?"

Archie sighed.

Elliot stood and replaced the chair against the wall. As he turned to leave, Archie said, "Elliot. Thanks."

Elliot gave him a thumbs-up and headed toward the door, waving to an unseen visitor who proved to be Linc, a bundle tucked under his arm. He grabbed the chair Elliot had just stowed, planted it next to Archie's bed, dropped into it, and laid the bundle—a yellow tablet and newspapers—on his knee. Linc hadn't had a chance to change clothes either.

"Look at you," Linc said. "None the worse for wear."

"Really?"

"No. You look like hell. The nurse said you need rest and I can see that you do, so I won't stay long. I just needed to know you're OK."

"I will be. You're not hurt?"

"Oh, hell, no. Takes more than some idiot with a peashooter to keep Linc Haybens from meeting a deadline." From the pile of paper in his lap, he pulled out a newspaper and held it up for Archie to see. "I'll leave this for you. But you had to see this. Look, above the fold, man." He slapped the paper.

Even from where he lay with his head on the pillow, Archie could read the headline which stretched from margin to margin. "HYDE PARK HERO FOILS DRUG PLOT." There was a subhead but Archie's weary eyes couldn't bring it into focus. His chest fluttered with a chuckle. Not only had Linc gotten a front page headline story in a major daily, he'd gotten himself named a hero. *Next thing, they'd be giving him the keys to the city. Good on Linc.*

"You're OK. How about your car?"

Linc scowled. "Not one but two broken windows. I'll bet that won't even meet the deductible and I'll be paying for the repairs myself. But it's drivable and I'm grateful for that. I have been doing some driving." Linc laid the paper at the foot of the bed. "You can read this later, Buddy. I can see you're tired. I've got follow-up to do and more stories to write and file, but I'll be back, and not just to interview you for your side of it. Which, by the way, I'm hoping you'll give me an exclusive."

"Why would I talk to anyone else?" Archie asked. Even to his own ears, his voice sounded feeble.

Linc patted the blanket over Archie's shin and gave him the second thumbs-up of the day.

Out of sight but within hearing range, a woman said, "We've been waiting. Everyone else has seen him. Can't we go in now, just for a minute?"

Oh, no. Miriam Stenowitz. No way could he face Marvin and Miriam, Archie thought.

CHAPTER TWENTY

POUGHKEEPSIE, NY, Thursday, February 18, 1993

"He should get some rest," replied another woman. "I'm going to have to ask you to come back later to visit, Mrs. Stenowitz. But I can assure you, he'll be fine."

Thank you, Archie thought. He let his eyelids fall closed.

Despite everyone's insistence that Archie rest, he got little. He had no sooner fallen asleep than a new nurse arrived and introduced herself, a bit like a waitress in a restaurant ("Hi, I'm Stacy and I'll be your server this evening."), and briefed him on the care he would be receiving. And while Archie would have liked to have gotten some uninterrupted sleep, he could hardly complain about the service. Everyone from the orderlies to the doctors treated him like some kind of celebrity. *Nothing like a little notoriety to get attention.*

All of which got explained when a food service worker brought him lunch and wheeled over the rolling table on which lay the newspaper Linc had left behind. Archie picked it up, eager to see how the journalist had handled the drama played out in the police impound lot. *Was it accepted journalistic practice to write a story when one figured in it? Shouldn't Linc have recused himself, or whatever the journalism equivalent of that was?* Archie shrugged. A reporter putting himself in the middle of the action had worked for George Plimpton.

A couple of sentences into the story, Archie stopped, stunned. That "Hyde Park Hero" turned out not to be Linc, but Archie. Sure,

Linc had pointed out in the story, Archie Harlanson— originally from Swadell, Iowa; graduate of Eastern Iowa's Community College's journalism program; Navy veteran, and now a resident of Tampa—just happened to be in Hyde Park to attend a family event—

Family. I should be that lucky, Archie thought.

Linc had couched the story to make Archie look less like a fool who had stumbled onto a conspiracy that had escaped everyone else's notice, and more like a sharp-eyed patriot who took action to ensure the President's safety the minute he heard about the upcoming visit.

There was even a photo of the "hero," posed with his truck. *The photo Linc took in the T&C parking lot Monday.*

Follow-ups were promised, including an exclusive interview with the hero himself, once he had recovered from the wounds that his courage had earned him.

Deliveries interrupted subsequent attempts to nap: flowers from Debbie, from Bonnie and Cheryl at the T&C, a big card from Patricio and Nisha at the Manor, all with hospital-logo'd Post-It notes reading "Tried to visit but you were sleeping. I'll be back."

True to his word, Elliot returned, in a fresh suit with de-whiskered cheeks. Archie rubbed a hand over his own stubbly face and passed his tongue across furry teeth. "I see you made it back to Salt Point."

"I did. You know, Marvin and Miriam are concerned about you."

I'll bet they are. Their daughter's would-be fiancé, now the notorious would-be fiancé.

"They did come by to try to see you this morning."

And check out the damage for themselves?

"They were hoping to make it back but with the brit tomorrow, things are getting really crazy." Elliot sank into the guest chair alongside Archie's hospital bed.

The brit. "About that. I don't know how long they mean to keep me but I'm really going to try to be there. I'm gonna need some things, though. Clothes. Where are my clothes?"

"Some are in the closet." Elliot nodded to a cupboard on the opposite wall. "Your vest and shirt, though, the cops have those. Evidence. You wouldn't want them anyway. They're—"

"Bloodstained?"

Elliot nodded and shuddered.

"Speaking of evidence. If I can't have my truck, I'm going to need a car. A ride to a rental agency?"

"About your truck." Elliot sat a little taller and squared his shoulders. "I've worked that out with the P. D. They're keeping the trailer of course."

"Of course."

"But they've been all over the tractor. Took photos, dusted it for prints, collected fibers. It took some doing but I convinced them to release it to you."

Archie sat up straight, only to feel the sudden movement as a twinge in his trunk. "That's great—"

Elliot held up his hand. "Hold on, there's some conditions."

Of course there would be.

"Neither you nor the truck are to leave the area, not yet."

"I wasn't planning to go far. Just to get the truck fixed. The stripped wires and the window at least." The punctured headliner might have to wait. In his uneasy slumber, Archie could hear the truck whimpering like a hurt and abandoned hound dog.

"I think that should be all right, so long as you don't make any modifications to it. OK, here's what you need to do when they release you. You must keep me advised of your movements. I want to know where you are at all times, and when you're planning to change your location, I want to know about it in advance. The cops could still lobby to press charges, so we don't want to do anything to piss them off. Got it?"

"Yes, sir."

Elliot heaved a sigh and stood. "OK, back to work."

"Clients," Archie heard him mutter as he left the room.

Energized by the encouraging news, Archie wished he had tasked Elliot with bringing him fresh clothes and personal care items. Now he had no interest in trying to sleep. The need to know where he could get the truck repaired nagged him. He wanted to form a plan.

He swung his legs over the side of the bed. The small dresser next to it held a phone. *What were the chances of a phone book?* The drawers were empty. He stood, unmoving for a moment, to make certain he was steady on his feet. He padded over to the cupboard.

His envelope of "personal items" from the police station was nowhere to be found. *Must still be in Linc's car.* His jeans, socks, and skivvies lay folded on a shelf along with extra blankets and pillow, his boots stood on the floor, but no phone book.

He stepped into the corridor and snagged a passing nurse hugging a stack of folders. "I'm sorry to trouble you but could I possibly get a phone book? With a Yellow Pages?"

She nodded toward the nurses' station at the end of the corridor.

He barefooted down the hallway, gauging his strength with every step and feeling surprisingly sturdy. He reached the nurses' station, repeated his request, and was rewarded for his efforts. He ambled over to a hallway chair, flipped to the Truck Repair section, and was relieved to find he would have several options. *Now to get out of here.* He would need clothes, a ride ...

He brought the directory back to the station. "Excuse me. How do I get out of here?"

One of the nurses looked up. "Get out of here?"

"You know. Get discharged?"

She frowned. "You just got here."

Archie gave her a smile. "You have all done such a good job that I'm ready to leave."

The nurse's frown softened a degree. "Thanks. But the doctor will be the judge of that."

"Ok, where can I find him?"

"My, aren't we impatient?" She rolled her eyes. "Go on back to your room, I'll have Doctor stop in to see you."

Archie climbed back into bed and switched on the wall-mounted television. Afternoon TV was all game shows albeit studded with crawls and flashes from local news stations with warnings and updates about preparations for Friday.

He zoned out, making a mental inventory of whom he could bum a ride from. It sounded like Elliot was busy keeping him a free man; Archie didn't want to get in the way of that. Linc was running around a snowy mid-Hudson valley in a windowless car making hay of his fifteen minutes of fame. Debbie was helping orchestrate tomorrow's brit ...

"Hey."

Archie cracked open an eye. "Oh, come on in."

"You looked like you were sleeping," Linc said. He had one arm wrapped around a big, cellophane-wrapped wicker basket. "I was in the area and I thought I'd check up on you, drop this off. It's from Bonnie and Cheryl. They wanted to come see you but things are crazy at the T&C. Everyone's working overtime. They had to bring in extra cooks, dishwashers, bus boys, a hostess."

"I can imagine. I'm surprised they had a minute to even think about me. Your car, then. It's drivable?"

"More or less. It's a really cool car now, with two broken windows. Two-sixty air conditioning. I haven't had a chance to get it fixed."

"Could you give me a ride?"

"You're ready to leave?"

"Ah, it's just a flesh wound," Archie said with all the nonchalance he could muster. "I just need to get discharged, and get dressed. Hmmm, speaking of dressed ..."

"What?"

"Elliot told me that the cops kept my shirt and vest. I could just tough it out until I get to the Manor but ..."

"Might be a chilly ride in the middle of February. It's below freezing out." Linc frowned. "OK, let me take care of that little problem. Getting checked out is a whole lot harder than checking in. You get yourself discharged and I'll meet you in the lobby."

Archie was pawing through the gift basket which contained fruit, packets of nuts and candies, and a small stuffed teddy bear with a bandage on its tummy, but no spare shirts, when Doctor Rinquettes arrived.

"I understand you feel you have overstayed our hospitality," said the doctor. "We would really like to keep you at least overnight, just to make sure that an infection doesn't flare up. Gunshot wounds are septic because material and debris can get pulled into the wound with the bullet."

"I'll admit I'm sore, but I really feel fine."

"You'd be surprised. Being shot can really take it out of you. You might not be cognizant of it now, but later, when you least expect it ... and you really need to rest."

"I'm not having much luck with that."

"Oh, I know. Everyone complains that a hospital is a busy place. But it'll settle down tonight."

"No, it's not that. I've got some things I've really got to attend to. I can't stop thinking about it."

"We can give you a sedative to help you sleep."

Archie shook his head. "Or I could just go, get them taken care of, and put my mind at ease. I promise, I'll rest tonight."

Doctor Rinquettes scowled. "You can't get someone else to take care of these things for you?"

Not unless they have a CDL. Archie shook his head.

Doctor Rinquettes snorted then shrugged. "All right, it's not as if we've got an abundance of spare beds. But give me a few more minutes of your attention."

Archie nodded.

The doctor stretched his neck, loosened his shoulders, and cleared his throat. Sounding out a beat by patting his thigh, he said,

> "This wound needs care
> so you beware
> to keep the dressing clean.
> When you change the bandage
> don't apply
> ointments or cleansers. Keep it dry.
> You can take a shower,
> just don't get
> the bandage wet.
> If your skin itches,
> don't pull the stitches.
> They'll dissolve on their own.
> No creams or lotions
> or herbal potions
> to speed the healing.
> You'll get pills for the pain
> but you'll have to refrain
> from driving or operating machinery."

Dr. Rinquettes grinned. "Any questions?"

Too stunned for words, Archie simply gaped.

"I know, it's a lot to remember. You'll get a handout. In very boring prose." The doctor rolled his eyes. "And one more thing, Mr. Harlanson. Being shot by a gun is a shock to the body. You may feel shock, paranoia, depression, or anger. You may have nightmares or trouble sleeping. You may feel unusually fatigued.

These are completely normal feelings for someone who has been through something like this. This isn't a sign of weakness and don't feel ashamed about it or push it aside."

"Sounds like post-traumatic stress disorder."

"Well, it's how a body reacts to an injury and regardless of how you rationalize it, you have been through a trauma. If the feelings become overwhelming or last beyond a couple of weeks, we want to see you. We can help. We also want to see you if your pain gets worse or doesn't respond to the pain relievers. If that wound starts to bleed again, apply a bandage and keep gentle, direct pressure on it but if that doesn't stop the bleeding within about ten minutes, you need to get medical attention. Same thing if you notice draining from the wound, run a fever above 100 degrees Fahrenheit for more than four hours, and definitely if you see red streaks radiating from the wound. OK, I guess you're good to go."

Archie used the restroom sink, soap, and paper towels to clean up as best he could, taking care to work around the bandage. He found that getting dressed was not a simple matter as bending triggered painful twinges.

He needn't have rushed. The discharge process took ages and required a visit from a nurse, a case management official, the discharge planner, and yet another nurse, all of whom reiterated much of the doctor's instructions, before at last an orderly arrived with a wheelchair to escort Archie out. Before Archie could protest, the man explained. "I know. You can walk. They all say that. It's hospital policy." They neared the lobby and Linc rose from a chair to meet them.

The orderly wheeled Archie toward the door. "Little brisk out there," he said, eyeing the flimsy hospital gown that Archie wore over his jeans.

"Got that covered," Linc said, hoisting a plastic Walmart bag. "No pun intended. Hang on."

Linc rummaged in the bag and pulled out a plaid flannel shirt. He removed the tags, undid the shirt buttons, and helped Archie out of the gown and into the new garment one arm at a time.

The orderly wheeled Archie to the curb and let down the foot rests. "He's all yours," he said to Linc and turned the chair back toward the lobby.

Linc held open a car door that had a sheet of thick brown paper taped where the window had been. He helped Archie ease into the passenger seat. "Sit tight, I've got a blanket in the trunk."

The car's heater running full blast and the blanket tucked under Archie's chin and around his shoulders helped offset the cold air thwapping against the paper windows, but Archie was grateful that they didn't have too far to travel.

"So, back to the Manor?" Linc said.

"No, the police department."

Linc took his eyes off the road long enough to look Archie a question.

"I'm getting the truck back."

"Oh, good deal. OK, next stop, the HPPD. Red lights and sirens?"

"I think I've had enough of that for a while, thank you." As Linc drove, Archie brooded about the work that lay ahead, beginning with sorting out the bill for the emergency room visit with his insurance company. Then there was the matter of contacting his vehicle insurance agent. He was a reasonable guy but Archie had to admit his was a wild story. Maybe Debbie could help him. She was an expert at those types of negotiations.

Debbie! He needed to let her know he was out of the hospital. He could call her from the cell phone. *The cell phone. Where was it?* Archie felt under the passenger seat and found the manila envelope of personal items that the police had returned to him right where he'd left it. He dug out the cell phone. *Bummer.* Job Number One when he got the truck back would be to charge the phone's battery.

He glanced out the windshield at the passing scenery. A roadside sign caught his attention and almost immediately set his stomach rumbling. "Say, could we stop at the next fast food place? The hospital gave me lunch but it was the only meal I've had since—"

"Gotcha," Linc replied. He found them a Wendy's and was about to turn into the drive-through when Archie said, "Might as well park it. I'm going to see if they have a phone."

They placed orders for burgers and fries and while Linc waited to collect the food, Archie called the Stenowitz home, only to get the answering machine.

"Oh, hi, Mr. and Mrs. Stenowitz. It's Archie Harlanson. I hope everything's going OK there. Please let Debbie know I've checked out of the hospital and I'm headed back to the Hyde Park Manor. I'll try to catch up with her again when I get there."

He joined Linc at a booth, they polished off the burgers and fries, and got back on the road.

*****

Officer Rademaker led Archie out into the impound yard. "Sorry about the rough handling last night ... this morning," he said. "Your attorney told us you were being held hostage, but we couldn't take his word for that. We didn't know him from Adam. It was a situation that we had to evaluate for ourselves. You understand?"

Archie grunted in begrudging acknowledgement. He stood and regarded the truck. Someone had covered the space left by the broken passenger door window with thick translucent plastic sheeting.

"We did what we could to keep out the weather," Rademaker said.

"I appreciate it," Archie replied and he did. He sighed. *Could be worse. Could have been the windshield.* That would have made the vehicle essentially inoperative; he could be put out-of-service for an equipment safety violation. He walked around the truck making a cursory examination. He'd give it a thorough pre-trip before hitting the road but so far, so good. The side mirrors, the lights and reflectors, the tires, were to all appearances undamaged.

"Where ya headed next?" Rademaker asked.

Archie frowned. "I was told not to leave town."

Rademaker caught his lower lip between his teeth. "It's an active investigation. You're a key witness."

"OK, it's not like I'm going to take a cross-country haul." Archie sighed. "The Hyde Park Manor tonight. Tomorrow I need to be in Salt Point."

"You feeling OK to drive? You want an escort?"

Archie turned his attention from the truck to the officer. The man's expression was almost beseeching. *Maybe he was sincere.* "No, thanks. I'm good. I'm not going that far." He looked at the rig and back at Rademaker. "I could use assistance uncoupling the trailer."

"Hey, not a problem. Just tell me what to do." At Archie's direction, Rademaker cranked down the landing gear to support the trailer and released the fifth wheel lock. While Archie disconnected the electrical and air lines, he reflected on how much heavy lifting his job required. He had the ignition key now, but was too tired to repair the switch, so Archie hot-wired the engine to life.

Though it was just a short ride, by the time Archie neared the Hyde Park Manor, the burst of energy that getting the truck back had given him had fizzled and his injury was making itself known. He had one more challenge to meet before he could give in to his exhaustion and pain: finding a place to park the truck. He sighed with relief when he pulled into the Manor parking lot. Unlike Wednesday morning it was nearly empty. The Manor's guests must be at last minute briefings, he thought, or supper or happy hour. The image of a bunch of G-men bellying up to the bar struck him funny.

Well, first come, first served. He pulled the truck into the space nearest his room. It would probably piss someone off but he didn't care. He didn't have the strength to park in some remote corner and hike across the lot. Anyhow, he was paying for his room; he was entitled to a nearby parking slot. *OK, maybe not the slot-and-a-half the truck needed but screw it.*

He buttoned up the truck and bundled up his personal items then regarded the plastic sheeting stretched across the space where the passenger window had been. It kept out the weather all right but it wouldn't keep out thieves. He should pack up everything valuable and take it into the room with him. Better yet, he should sleep in the truck. He'd have to run the APU to keep warm but ...

Then he laughed. Tonight, this would be possibly the most secure parking lot in the state of New York. In a matter of hours, his truck would be surrounded by the vehicles of DPS troopers, state highway officials, National Park Service rangers, Secret Service, and FBI special agents.

He collected the cell phone charger, his log book, and trudged to his room. He tore the paper cover off one of the drinking glasses and bolted down a pain pill. The bed beckoned but in the last remaining minutes of the business day he wanted to nail down an appointment to get the truck fixed. He fished a phone directory from the bedside table, propped himself up in bed, and dug into the phone book as if it were the latest bestselling novel.

He called the first mechanic listed, A Automotive Repair, but the earliest they could get him in would be next Tuesday. The next, AA

Automotive Solutions, didn't have an opening until Monday. He worked his way through AAA Truck Repair, ABC Truck Service, and Ace Truck Repair, but the answers were the same: no appointments available until next week.

CHAPTER TWENTY-ONE

HYDE PARK, NY, Friday, February 19, 1993

His heart sinking, his brain racing ahead planning how he would manage the next few days, Archie called Amazon Truck Service.

A receptionist answered. Readying himself for a negative response, Archie asked if he could get the broken window and the stripped wires repaired Friday. Despite the late hour, she chirped, "Sure, we can do that."

"Friday? As in tomorrow Friday?"

"You betcha," she replied. "Especially if you get here first thing in the morning. We've got a window in our schedule. Get it? A window in our schedule?" The receptionist laughed.

Archie mustered up a chuckle. "About how long would it take?" Archie had a brit to attend.

"Shouldn't take long. An hour or so.

"Great." Archie promised to be there the minute the bay doors opened.

Then he called the Stenowitz home only to get the answering machine again.

He eased out of his new shirt and yesterday's pants and stepped into the shower, adjusting the spray head so as not to get the dressing wet. The hot water running down even just his head and neck drove out the chill and helped loosen tight muscles. He climbed into bed and picked up the phone to try reaching Debbie one more time.

An alarm sounded and he jolted awake to find that he had fallen asleep with the light on, the phone receiver in hand. Beside him, the phone bleeped.

Archie had slept for nine hours but didn't feel refreshed. Groggy, he eased to a sitting position. The doc was right about the pain. It wasn't unbearable, but this morning there was no mistaking a bullet had burrowed into his midsection. There'd be no taking of prescription pain pills, though, not for a while. He had some driving to do. He'd make do with a Tylenol from his Dopp kit and take the painkillers with him for later when the day was done.

Coffee. Coffee would be good. At this early hour, he'd no doubt have his choice of donuts.

He cleaned up as best he could, his body so stiff it almost creaked. Sweatpants and the flannel shirt would do for sitting in the truck repair shop, but little Eli's brit no doubt called for more formal wear. *What did one wear to a brit anyway?* Archie hadn't packed a suit. He did have a white shirt and trousers in the truck's clothes closet, that sport coat. He could change in the truck. With any luck he'd find he'd stowed a tie in there too.

Debbie. Way too early to call the Stenowitz home. He would call from the service shop.

Archie stepped from his room. At the end of the semi-dark hallway, a figure stood silhouetted in the glow from the brightly-lit lobby. A uniformed man, a police officer, Archie discovered as he drew closer. He peered over the man's shoulder but couldn't see beyond the people jammed into the small space. Dressed in parkas and stadium jackets, it was clear they weren't officials but townspeople. They crowded just inside the glass entry doors.

The motorcade. They were hoping to catch a glimpse of the motorcade even from this distance. The scene reminded Archie of his childhood, arriving hours in advance of a parade just to nail down the best viewing spot.

"Going somewhere, sir?" asked the hallway officer. A star-shaped badge identified him as a Special Officer of the U.S. Secret Service.

"Just the lobby."

"Might as well stay right where you are, sir. I'll bet the view's better from your window."

"I'm not restricted to my room, am I? I'm not under house arrest."

"No, sir. Not at all." The officer stepped aside to let Archie pass. "Just don't try to leave the motel. Officers everywhere are trying to control crowd movement."

Archie edged toward the coffee pot only to find both the pot and the donut box empty. *So much for that idea.* He would grab breakfast at the T&C before heading off to Poughkeepsie.

Two officers with star-shaped badges guarded the doors against any comings or goings.

Archie squirmed through the throng with full intentions of leaving the motel although he hadn't figured out how. No way could he sneak a huge red truck out the driveway. Maybe he could convince the officers that he had a critical run.

"Something I can help you with, sir?" asked one of the officers at the door.

"I need to get to my truck, Officer."

"Can't it wait? We don't want people milling around outside unnecessarily."

"It's necessary. To tell you the truth, I have to make an emergency run."

"I can't think of too many things that would qualify as an emergency today."

"It is, sort of."

The officer narrowed his eyes. "Hey, wait. You're that guy."

"What guy?" Uh, oh. Archie thought. *Did this officer know about the arrest yesterday? Was the communication between agencies that good?* Probably so, considering the extra effort everyone was making for the Presidential visit. Surely the officer also knew it was all a misunderstanding and that Archie had been released.

"The guy. The truck you're talking about, it's the Kenworth. You're the trucker."

"I am," Archie replied, although it came out more like a question than a confirmation. "How do you know?"

"The picture. In the paper."

Oh, right. The photo in The Herald, *the "hero" and his truck.*

"Excuse me, ma'am, would you please get a little further back," the officer said to an older woman who was getting a little too pushy.

Grumbling, she stepped back into the crowd.

The officer crossed to where a second officer guarded the other side of the entrance. The noise of the impatient crowd kept Archie from hearing the conversation and he didn't like the puzzled expression on the face of the other officer or the piercing glance he sent Archie's way. The first officer rejoined him and said, "You sure you want to leave? You won't be able to get back in until it's all over."

"Not a problem. I won't be coming back until then."

The officer still hesitated.

"Look, if I move the truck that will open up two more spaces.

The officer nodded. "Good point. OK, suit yourself." The officer opened the door.

Archie stepped out into the pre-dawn dark to find the lot jam-packed with vehicles, some double- and triple-parked. His truck was hemmed in by an FBI Suburban and a sedan with New York State government plates. It would take every bit of skill he had to get the truck out without hitting anything else. He turned back to the officer. "What would be the chances of getting a little help with spotting?"

The officer tilted his head. "Yeah, I can see you're gonna need it. Well, it's early. I think I can break away. Just a sec'." He had a quick conversation with the other officer then returned to Archie and said, "OK, let's go."

Not wanting to try the officer's patience, he gave the truck a cursory inspection then climbed in and got it warmed up. He was going only a few miles, he told himself. He'd give it a thorough once-over when he made it to the diner.

Archie was thankful that this wasn't his license-application skills test because it took pull-up after pull-up to maneuver the truck to where he could pry it from the lot.

Road crews must have worked all night, he thought as he threaded his way past orange cones and Jersey barriers. The road was lit up like Main Street through Winter Wonderland with the flashing blue and yellow lights of utility trucks, the blue and red of cop cars, and the amber of road cones.

Archie could hardly believe it. The sun was barely up on a weekday morning, but the Town and Country's parking lot was so full he couldn't find a space for his truck. He tried the Italian restaurant and the Dairy Queen but both places had traffic cones and ropes and sandwich board signs reading "Parking for Customers Only." He ended up parking on a side street and walking, feeling every step reverberate in his midsection.

The crowd thronging the diner's entrance steps was a bad sign. Every time he tried to squeeze through just to make it to the front door someone grumbled "Wait your turn" or "They're full up, Bud." He tried saying, "Look, I got a delivery to make. I just have to find out where I can park my truck" and showing his commercial driver's license as if he were flashing a detective's badge.

Finally, a man said, "Hey, you're that guy, aren't you?"

"What guy?" Archie asked, a little less anxiously than when the officer at the Manor had made that remark.

"The one in the paper."

Linc should be very proud. That story of his had its fair share of readers. And he and Linc were certainly getting a lot of mileage out of shots taken for a photo essay about an out-of-towner with a shiny red truck.

"Good on you," the man said, and clapped Archie on his shoulder. "You go right on in."

Just inside the door, the entrance was packed. A line of people with expectant looks crowded near the cash register where Cheryl stood with a strained expression and a clipboard. Another line formed by the payphone.

Not only was every seat taken in the diner and at the counter but behind him, the dining room had been pressed into service to handle the overload.

"Archie," Cheryl cried. "It's so great to see you. Bonnie and I wanted to come visit you in the hospital but we've been putting in double shifts—"

"Oh, don't worry. Linc told me. Thanks for the gift basket."

"I can't believe you're out already."

Archie shrugged with one shoulder. "They needed the bed for someone who was really sick."

Cheryl shook her head. "Tough guy. Linc wasn't kidding when he said you were a hero."

"Aw shucks. 'Tweren't nothin', Ma'am," Archie replied in his best John Wayne imitation.

"I'm sorry, but there's just no place to sit. Maybe I could get you something to go?"

"You know, you've got enough on your hands. I'll find a place to stop on the way. Tell Bonnie I'll be back after all the excitement has died down, OK?" He grabbed several newspapers from the tall stacks just inside the door and handed Cheryl some bills. She leaned forward and bussed him on the cheek.

Getting out was only slightly easier than getting in. Recognizing that Archie's departure had freed up a space, the crowd edged forward.

As Archie hiked back to the truck, he mentally traveled Rte. 9, trying to recall where along the way he could stop for coffee and something to eat which he now desperately needed. He really wanted to take a painkiller despite the warning against "driving or operating machinery." In the light of a rising sun, he pre-tripped the truck then headed south along a route lined with traffic control devices and official vehicles.

At least he didn't have a long drive ahead of him. Southbound Route 9 was smooth sailing with little traffic, although signs at the exits warned of detours to come later in the day. The opposing northbound lane was another story. Archie pitied anyone with a load to fetch or deliver who didn't know what he was getting into, and felt not one bit of regret for having sounded the alarm to the commercial driving community.

He found Amazon Truck Service easily enough. Archie chuckled at the logo prominently displayed on their sign and company vehicles. It was "mudflap girl," the iconic silhouette of a curvaceous woman seated with bent knees, leaning back on her hands, her hair blown back by the wind, except Amazon Truck Service's lady held a wrench in her hand and wore a ballcap. He had arrived early enough at the service shop that he had some minutes to wait for the place to open. He considered updating his story but the task of recounting everything that had happened in the last twenty-four hours, much less put it in the context of a product review, was daunting. Maybe he could pitch "How to Hot-Wire a Semi at Gunpoint" to *True Detective* magazine. Time to do what he usually did when stuck with downtime waiting to unload: catch up on his reading. Usually he had a stack of trade magazines and after-market catalogs to pore over. He didn't have those but he did have the newspapers he bought at the T&C: *Newsday, The New York Post, The Poughkeepsie Journal, The Herald,* and Linc's paper, *The Valley Voice.*

Newsday and *The Post's* reporters had cobbled up stories about the uproar at the Hyde Park Police station using Linc as the primary source. Though it captured the event's drama, *Newsday's* coverage was cool-headed whereas *The Post* story could have been written by Raymond Chandler.

It hit him. *Hyde Park Hero.* Archie leaned back in the truck seat, agog. No wonder everyone was giving him special treatment. *Hyde Park Hero.*

Somewhat overshadowed by the other papers' coverage of a dramatic drug bust and a President's impending visit was a *Valley Voice* story that Linc had clearly written earlier in the week: a profile of local artist Miriam Stenowitz. It was a flattering portrait. Archie chuckled at his own pun then found himself intrigued by details Linc revealed that Debbie had never mentioned.

At eight on the dot, Amazon Truck Service opened for business. Archie strode into the office area. The smell of coffee brewing competed with something sweet and floral. *Perfume?* Behind the counter, a middle-aged blond woman wearing an Amazon Truck Service cap, crisp teal coveralls, and bright red lipstick took notes as she listened to messages on the shop's answering machine.

"Hi, uh, Greta," he said, reading her name badge. "I'm Archie Harlanson. I called yesterday afternoon."

"You're an early bird, aren't you?" She checked her clipboard. "Oh, yeah. The guy with the window. Or without the window."

"That's me."

"OK, let's see what we can do for you." Greta lifted a hatch and stepped out from behind the counter.

"Oh, don't let me take you from your work. Just point me to the service manager."

"I am the service manager," she said with a rosy-lipsticked smile. "Follow me."

As she led him out of the office to the adjoining service bays, another teal-overalled woman passed them on the way into the office. "Morning, Val," Greta said. "Our first customer of the day is here, so you can check that one off the schedule."

"Good deal." Val smiled back with lips painted the same shade of red. "Gonna be a busy day."

"We're gonna try our damnedest to get everyone back on the road before the day is out," Greta said.

The service area doors opened to four bays. The cavernous space smelled of petroleum, rubber, and that same floral scent he had picked up in the office. Mechanics bustled around draining Styrofoam cups of coffee or cans of soda and readying their tools. Every one of them wore an Amazon cap, teal coveralls, and red lipstick because every one of them was female.

I get it, Archie thought and chuckled. *Amazon* Truck Service.

"Andrea," Greta called. "This is the guy with the busted window."

A woman whose cap kept dark curls off her face turned to Archie and waved a hand. "Hand over the keys. I'll just drive that K-Whomper right on in here, we'll get you fixed up." Lips painted the same color as the service manager's turned up in a smile.

As she climbed into the cab, Archie pointed out the stripped wires and asked about getting those fixed too.

Andrea said, "Sure, that's easy enough." She frowned. "If I didn't know better, I'd say someone tried hot-wiring this truck."

"Right you are. I did. It was kind of an emergency."

Her frown deepened then her eyes opened wide. "Oh, it's you. You're that guy."

Even here, in Poughkeepsie, the Hyde Park Hero's fame had spread?

She bowed. "I am honored to help you, sir. Now you just go on back to the office, customer lounge, make yourself comfortable, and we will get you taken care of and on your way pronto."

Archie gave the mechanic a thumb's up and left. In the office, he poured himself a Styrofoam cup of coffee from a glass carafe. The nearly-full pot looked and smelled freshly made, promising a more drinkable beverage than one that had sat for hours on the warming plate, but at this point Archie would have swilled gas station coffee.

Behind the counter, Val caught him eyeing the donut box. "Help yourself. Early birds get the worms, err, the donuts."

Archie tried not to wolf down the pastry which he chased with a swig of coffee. "Amazon Truck Service, it's all women?" Archie asked.

Greta, the service manager, looked up from her clipboard. "You got a problem with that?"

"Oh, heck no. My girl's in the industry."

Greta smiled. "Is she? Mechanic? Driver?"

"Customer service rep for a carrier's claims department."

Greta snorted. "Good on her. I wouldn't do that job for any amount of money. I would so much rather work with machines than people. I think you could say that for all the women here. We prefer tinkering around with trucks than secretary-ing in some office. We're good at it, too. Look at us, we're made for the job." The service manager held up her hands and wiggled them. "We're compact. We can get into some tight spaces."

Archie had to admit, crawling under the dash had been a squeeze for him. More nimble fingers would have made faster work of manipulating the wires.

"Yeah, there's some heavy lifting involved but there's power tools for that. Even the guys use those."

Archie raised his hands in surrender. "Hey, no argument from me. You, uh, all wear the same lipstick?"

Greta laughed. "We do here at least. It started out as a joke one day but then it kind of stuck and now it's part of the uniform. We call it Trailer Air Supply Red although of course that's not what's on the tube."

"The same perfume too?"

"No, that's an air freshener. You like?"

Why not? No reason the workplace had to stink. Or be dark and dirty. The pale-blue painted walls were hung with the required licenses, payment polices, and workplace advisories but also colorful posters of Brad Pitt, George Clooney, Kevin Costner, and Harrison Ford. At Archie's knees, a low table held the usual service-station reading material: the day's newspapers, current editions of *Time* and *Newsweek,* trade magazines, and after-market catalogs, plus *Family Circle, Cosmopolitan, Cooking Light,* and *Women's World.*

Archie chuckled. *Debbie would get a kick out of this place.*

He settled in a guest chair. *Speaking of Debbie* ... He opened his cell phone, and was glad to see that he had both a full charge and a strong signal. He dialed the Stenowitz's home number and prayed that someone would answer. The phone rang once, twice, three times. He'd gotten the answering machine enough times now to know that after the fourth ring, if someone didn't answer, the machine would.

He was preparing his message when he heard Debbie say, "Hello, Stenowitz residence."

"Debbie, thank God, It's Archie. I've been trying to reach you but all I could do was leave a message."

"Archie! I tried to call you back but I never got an answer. I called the hospital but they said you'd been discharged. I tried to reach you at the Manor but the line's always busy."

"That place is a madhouse. Every room is filled."

"What are you doing there? Why aren't you in the hospital? I can't believe they discharged you. Are you really OK?"

"I'm fine, Deb. It was just a flesh wound," Archie said. *He wasn't going to tire of saying that any time soon.*

"So are you getting any rest there? Do you need anything?"

"I'm fine, Deb, really. I was going to ask you the same thing."

Debbie's deep sigh was audible even over the ringing of the shop's phone and the clanking of the fax machine. "It's a madhouse here too."

"Well, hang on. I'll be there soon."

"How are you going to get here? I'd come get you but ..."

"Oh, don't worry about that. I got the truck back. Well, I will have the truck back as soon as they replace the window."

"They? Who's they?"

"I'm at a repair shop. You would like this place, Deb. It's all women, even the mechanics."

"Really?" Debbie sounded distracted.

"They tell me it won't take long to fix. About an hour. Then I'll be on my way. So do you need anything?"

"Funny you should ask. We need a mohel. "

"A? ..." Archie did a mental scramble. *The mohel was? ...* "Wait a minute. I thought that was all taken care of. Isn't Rabbi Davis going to do the ..." Archie almost said "deed" and quickly substituted "honor."

"Ohmigod, Archie, it's just awful. Rabbi Davis isn't here."

CHAPTER TWENTY-TWO

POUGHKEEPSIE, NY, Friday, February 19, 1993

"There are road closures all the way from Newburgh International."
Debbie's voice was strained. "He can't get here; he can't get through
all the checkpoints. He was headed this way and traffic cops
stopped him and told him that only critical traffic and emergency
vehicles were getting through. They told him to turn around, go
home, and forget about going anywhere north on 9 until late
tonight."

When the blockage would then be southbound.

"Caryn's crying, Mom's hysterical. Elliot's pulling his hair out,
and Dad is talking about switching his party affiliation to the
Republicans, he's so upset. What are we going to do?"

"Look, this will all be over by this evening. The speech is at
three-forty. It can't go on forever. The President will leave, everyone
will leave, the roads will reopen. Can't you reschedule for later
tonight or even tomorrow?"

"No. At sundown the Sabbath begins and Mom says that we
can't do this on Shabbat because the baby was born at twilight.
That's like a kind of limbo." She sighed. "It's a long story. A very
long story."

"Oh."

"Oh, Archie, this is a disaster." Debbie sounded close to tears.

Archie had never heard her so upset, not even on her worst work day. "Well, uh, didn't you tell me that the baby's father can do the circumcision? Did you say that actually he should do it?"

"I did, and he's talking about doing it himself but think about it. You've seen Elliot with a knife."

Archie pictured the ragged slices of chicken from last Friday night's dinner and shuddered. "Good point."

"What are we going to do?"

"Take it easy, babe. Make yourself a mimosa or a Bloody Mary. Make one for everybody." *Except Elliot.* "Let me think. Where's the rabbi now?"

"At the temple. He's been calling around to see if there's anyone who can do it who has a prayer of getting here but he's striking out."

"OK, babe, don't panic. Where's this temple?"

Debbie rattled off an address. "Do you know where that is?"

"If there's a road leading to it—"

"You can find it. I know, Sweetie. What are you going to do?"

Archie had no idea. "Just leave it to me," he said with unexpected bravado. Next he'd be racing into the men's room and popping buttons in his haste to rip off his shirt and reveal a superhero uniform underneath. Instead, he hustled into the service area. All four bays were filled. Power tools buzzed, mallets binged, air compressors wheezed. Radio music struggled to compete. *What was that they were listening to? Opera?*

One of the mechanics spotted Archie. "Hey, customers aren't really allowed in here," she said. "Insurance and OSHA rules."

"I just wanted to see how it's coming," Archie replied. The Kenworth's passenger door stood open and he could see the window had yet to be replaced. A few seconds later, Andrea appeared in the truck's doorway. "In a big hurry, I see," she said, wiping her hands on her coveralls. "I've just about got those wires fixed. Window's next."

"Truckers," one of the other mechanics muttered. "Always in a hurry. Fella, you know, if we're going to do this right, we need time to do it."

"I'm sorry, it's just–something just came up."

"Got a load that can't wait? What is it, ice cream?" She laughed.

"It's winter, it'll keep. Chill out, Trucker," said another mechanic and she laughed too.

"Actually, I'm due at a brit and I'm bringing the mohel."

The laughter stopped and Archie figured the ladies had no idea what he was talking about. From the distant radio, a diva wailed some aria.

"A brit?" Andrea said. "Your son?"

"My ... my nephew," Archie replied. "Or will be, if I can pull this off. It's my fiancée's nephew. If I can get the rabbi there in time, it'll—"

"Your in-laws will think you're a total mensch." She pressed a fist to her chest and sighed. "Oh, romance. "Girls, do you hear this?" Andrea shouted from the Kenworth's steps. "Rikki, Phyllis, give me a hand here."

Two women holstered their tools and jogged over to Archie's truck.

"Rikki girl, you finish repairing those stripped wires under the dash. Phyl, honey, give me a hand with this window. Archie, step back there, that's a good boy."

"Say, hand me that New York State map that's there on the seat," Archie called up to Rikki.

He moved away and stood with his back braced against a wall while a scene no less frenetic than had transpired in the Mid-Hudson Regional Emergency Room played out. The three women buzzed around the Kenworth like hummingbirds. It was like watching a time lapse movie sequence.

He unfolded the map and found enough detail in the Poughkeepsie insert to plan his route.

Rikki stood in the truck's doorway holding her tools high as if she had just scored a touchdown. "Done," she cried.

Andrea darted to a workbench, returned with a shop towel and a spray bottle which she handed to Phyllis. "If you'll just get that window cleaned up ... atta girl." She pried Archie from the wall and with her hands on his back steered him toward the office. "Let's get you settled up and you're good to go."

Archie signed the work order and one credit-card swipe later, returned to the Kenworth.

A smiling crew stood alongside the truck. Archie shook their hands as he mounted the steps. "I can't thank you ladies enough."

"Just come back to Amazon when you can, we'll fix that headliner," Rikki said.

Phyllis jabbed her index finger. "And we want an invite to the wedding."

Archie threw back his head and laughed. "Andrea, thanks again."

"*Mazel tov*," she replied. "Now get going."

A few minutes later he was headed east. Morning rush-hour commuters having arrived at their destinations, he had little traffic to contend with on surface roads. He nearly drove right past the temple which wasn't at all the type of building he expected. He realized he had been looking for something steepled and church-like. A single-story masonry structure with a white-colonnaded portico, Temple Emanuel could just as easily have been an elementary school. *Not much happening on a Friday morning, judging from the few cars in the parking lot.* The black Subaru positioned in the slot "Reserved for Rabbi" looked somehow restless to Archie, like a racehorse stalled at the starting gate.

Archie pulled open the heavy oak door ornamented with carvings and reliefs of a Star of David, the two tablets of the Ten Commandments, what appeared to be a sturdy tree in full leaf, a heraldic lion, and other symbols. He stood for a moment in the vestibule. Soft overhead lighting glinted off slabs of varnished wood bearing hundreds of two-inch by ten-inch brass plaques. Arranged in columns and rows, the plaques were inscribed with names. "In Memoriam," declared the bronze sign centered over the wooden slabs. Each of the little brass plaques had a tiny light bulb to its left. Most of the bulbs were dark but a few glowed.

Scores of photographic portraits adorned the walls. Name plates described some as rabbis, others as board presidents from years past. Archie grinned. If nothing else they documented the changes over the decades in men's hairstyles, ties, and suit jacket lapels. No women were pictured except in the most recent grouping of photos. Only one woman had gained the top board position. *The ladies at Amazon Truck Service would not be pleased.*

Glass showcases displayed ornate goblets, paired scrolls draped in velvet and topped with silver finials, candelabra, huge bound volumes in English and Hebrew—

"Excuse me. Archie, right?"

Archie turned to face the man behind him. "Yes, Rabbi Davis. Debbie Stenowitz's friend."

"Right. What are you doing here?"

"I was having some work done on my truck. Debbie said you're running into trouble trying to get to Salt Point for the brit."

The rabbi rolled his eyes. "*Oy gevalt.* I never had such a problem like this. I'm at wit's end. I've been calling all over but the only way to get a mohel there in time would be for a superhero to fly him there."

"I've worked my way out of some mega traffic jams, Rabbi. I thought I'd see what I can do. Want to give it a try? I can't promise that you'll make it back until very late."

"That's not a problem. I already arranged for a layman to pinch-hit for me."

"Well, then, if there's anything you need, I suggest you go get it and we'll hit the road."

The rabbi patted Archie's arm. "Be right with you," he said and trotted down the hall.

"I'll meet you in the truck," Archie called. He hurried outside to give the truck a thorough inspection. He had hauled some pricey cargo in the past but none quite so valuable as this.

The rabbi appeared at Archie's side bundled in an overcoat and fedora, and carrying what looked for all the world like a doctor's bag.

"Hold onto the grab bar, OK? Sometimes the steps can be slippery," Archie said as he guided the rabbi into the truck's passenger side. "OK, buckle up."

The rabbi shimmied in his seat and looked right and left. "Wow, this is, well, big." He scanned the dashboard. "I'll bet you've got more controls here than an airplane cockpit. This is really something. I had no idea."

Archie smiled with secret satisfaction. To the uninformed, truck driving looked like an easy job, but there was way more to it than simply holding a steering wheel.

They met no interference on the East-West Arterial headed to the junction with Route 9 and Archie took that as a good sign. Maybe the authorities were cutting slack for commercial traffic.

As they neared the junction, traffic slowed such that Archie could barely get out of LO. The stop-and-go had him braking and shifting, braking and shifting. He had been in traffic like that for hours in California. It was exhausting and he was already running out of steam. A cup of coffee and a couple of donuts at Amazon Truck Service were not the fuel that the waffle special and milk that he didn't get at the T&C would have been. The image of the smorgasbord Miriam Stenowitz had put out a week ago imposed itself on his brain and his stomach rumbled. The Tylenol he took had about worn off but he was reluctant to take another, worried about whether the drug would impair his driving abilities. Today of all days he needed to be able to respond at his peak.

Traffic slowed to a complete stop. Blood-orange "DETOUR" signs sprouting from the road's snow-covered shoulder like premature daffodils filled Archie with dread. All Archie could see ahead of him was a line of red brake lights. The chatter on the CB was all grumbling and swearing, and when the language got too blue for Archie's comfort given the nature of his passenger, he squelched it. "We don't always talk that way," he said.

The rabbi chuckled. "I've heard worse."

"I wasn't learning anything helpful anyway."

The rabbi sighed. "Yup, this is where I got stopped. When I finally worked my way up to where the officers were stationed, they had a U-turn set up and steered me right back east."

Archie grunted. They sat at idle then inched forward. A tenth of a mile ahead, strobing blue and red lights added wattage to the glowing brake lights. Archie prayed that they'd make it through the traffic and considered suggesting that the rabbi ask for a little divine intervention.

On foot, an officer approached the truck's driver's side and Archie rolled down the window.

"Sorry, sir," the officer said. "We're clearing the road. President Clinton will be passing through here shortly and we're removing any obstacles for his motorcade. We're looking to minimize the risk and avoid all possible complications. As an American citizen, I'm sure you want to contribute to the President's safety. We're diverting everything except emergency and essential traffic."

"See?" muttered Rabbi Davis.

"So if you'll kindly turn around," the officer said.

"But I've got to get to Salt Point. That's near Hyde Park. It's very important, Officer ..." Archie read the man's ID "... Katz."

"I'm sure it is but I'm afraid it will have to wait."

Archie sighed and reached to release the brake.

"Wait, wait a minute. You're that guy."

"What guy?" Rabbi Davis asked.

"The Hyde Park Hero," said the officer. "I just put it together. The Kenworth. Hyde Park. The story in the *Herald*. About the drug bust. There was a photo of you and your truck at a diner in Hyde Park. The caption says you're visiting family in Salt Point."

Well, they weren't family, not yet, but Archie wasn't about to debate the point. Maybe he could parlay all this sudden notoriety into something useful. "The family, yes. I came all the way from Tampa to help celebrate. A blessed arrival. A baby boy."

"Hey, congratulations.

"Thanks," said Archie. "In fact, that's my emergency run. The father, Elliot Jordan, and the baby are at my in-laws' in Salt Point. The Stenowitzes."

"Yeah, I know them. Marvin and Miriam."

"You do?"

"Yeah, they go to Temple Emanuel in Poughkeepsie. That's where I go, when I can. So what's the emergency?"

"Well, today, this morning, it's the baby's brit."

"The brit? It's this morning?"

"Yeah, the brit."

"Wow, talk about timing. I'll bet the guests are having a hell of time getting there."

"Well, when he was born, little Eli didn't know he'd be competing for attention with a sitting President. And yeah, everyone's getting stuck in the road closures. Including the rabbi here. Who's supposed to do the—"

Officer Katz peered into the cab. "Rabbi! Good morning." He gaped at Archie. "So they're trying to have the brit without the mohel?"

"That's my important delivery. I'm trying to get Rabbi Davis to the brit. That's an emergency, wouldn't you say? A sort of medical emergency." *The real emergency was going to be if Elliot decided to take knife in hand.*

Officer Katz stood silently, blinking. Please, please, please, Archie thought.

"OK, I've got an idea. Once you get to the junction with 9G, you can take that to Salt Point and bypass all this. We're controlling that route too but there's less traffic on it so it is moving. It'll take you south for a little bit before you turn east and then north."

"That's OK, 9G it is. I know how to get to Salt Point from 9G. It's just a couple of miles north on 9 to the junction. But you said—"

"Yeah, we're detouring traffic off 9. We're controlling on 9G too."

"So how?—"

The officer grinned. "I'm giving you an escort."

"You can do that?" asked Rabbi Davis.

"You won't get in trouble with your superiors?" Archie said.

"For the Hyde Park Hero?" Officer Katz shrugged. "Wait here a sec'."

"Not a problem." Without Officer Katz's help there wasn't anywhere he could go anyway except back to Poughkeepsie. Archie watched as the officer conferred with a clutch of officials. Officer Katz and two other officers moved aside the striped barriers blocking the road. Officer Katz wheeled a motorcycle up to the striped barriers blocking the road, mounted the cycle, turned, and beckoned Archie to advance.

"Wow." Rabbi Davis beamed. "I've never had a police escort before." He sat up straight and waggled his shoulders. "You'd think I was some kind of celebrity. Oh, wait, that would be you. Hyde Park Hero?"

"Didn't see today's paper?"

The rabbi shrugged. "Usually that's how I begin my day but I knew I had the brit this afternoon and I needed to get ready for that and get Friday night services squared away."

Archie filled him in as they crawled the few miles to their turn.

"Wow, a new grandson and a hero in the family. The Stenowitzes must be *plotzing*."

In the family, the rabbi had said. "Can I ask you a question?"

"Sure. People ask me questions all the time."

"It's kind of personal."

"Most of the questions that I get asked are personal. Discretion is my middle name. Ask away."

Archie cleared his throat. "It's about Debbie Stenowitz and me. We've been together for three years. You know, we're living together."

"Are you asking me if I disapprove of that?"

"No, that's not my question. I love her. I think she's, well, she's just amazing. I want to ask her to marry me."

"She seems like a lovely woman. I don't know her that well; it's her parents I'm acquainted with. So if you're asking my opinion—"

"Well, see, I'm not Jewish. Do you think that's a problem?" *The woman in the kosher deli certainly did.*

After only a moment's hesitation, Rabbi Davis replied, "Yes."

Archie's stomach hollowed out the same way it had when Yegor had shoved the gun in his face. "You do?"

"Allow me to clarify. Yes, it's a problem. Being Jewish is more than simply believing in a certain theological doctrine. It's a set of values, a way of being in the world. It's not something you share with her."

"So far that hasn't been a problem. Debbie says–how does she put it?–that she doesn't practice Judaism."

"Be that as it may, in many ways it's ingrained. Decisions that Debbie makes are driven by her Jewish upbringing. It could become a bone of contention. May I ask you a question? What's your religion?"

"I didn't have much of a religious upbringing. My dad was Lutheran and my mom was Catholic, but that's about as far as it went. Really, I grew up in a farming family. Farming was our religion."

Rabbi Davis chuckled. "Nicely put. Let me say that maybe it's not a problem now but it easily could become one. Debbie might change; people do. Judaism might not be important to her now but later in life, it could be. Look at her parents. They've been, well, a little casual about their Judaism. But now Eli comes along and Miriam doesn't want to leave a single stone unturned." He cocked his head toward Archie. "You could change."

"Get religion, you mean?"

The rabbi nodded. "It happens so often, it's almost a phase that people go through as they mature. Especially in midlife when they take a look back at where they've been and a look at what lies ahead and start asking themselves the big questions: "Who am I? Have I made the right decisions in my life? What's in store for me?" And there the two of you would be, going down roads that could be taking you away from each other. And of course there's the matter of children. Will they have a religious education and if so, what?"

"We haven't talked about that."

Rabbi Davis gave him a long look. "You might want to consider having that discussion."

Archie nodded, and downshifted as Officer Katz ahead slowed. "Maybe I should convert."

"Of course, if you want to. Be advised, though; it's not like rooting for a different basketball team. There are requirements. We have several rituals that we would perform that are more than simply ceremonial; without them the conversion would not be considered legitimate. For one, like little Eli, you would need to be circumcised."

"Oh, I wouldn't need that. I—"

"Yes, most male babies born in an American hospital in the last few decades were. But we ritually remove a tiny drop of blood. You also have to undergo immersion, a ceremonial bath."

"Like being baptized?"

"Yes, and no. They're related ... that's a long story. But a *mikveh* is different."

"How? Is it a bath in boiling oil or something?"

The rabbi spluttered. "Oh, no, no, no. Oh, don't even get that rumor started. No, it's a bath in natural water, as in not a chlorinated swimming pool, to achieve a state of ritual purity. It's quite a pleasant and moving ceremony. And we would also like to see you pursue a course of study. Even with all that, there are denominations that simply won't recognize the conversion."

Archie thought about the woman at Kosher Outpost and wondered if she would approve.

"Even if you did, it's not a panacea," the rabbi said. "There's still, as I said, that fundamental difference in world view that you might never share."

They traveled in silence for a few minutes.

"So you think we should break up," Archie said.

"Only you can decide that. The official party line would be 'yes.'"

"I get that," Archie said. "I'm not asking the United Council of Rabbis, if there is such a thing—"

"There is. It's called—"

"I'm asking you. I'm sure in your line of work you've seen a lot of couples come together, and a few come apart. What do you think?"

"I'm flattered," Rabbi Davis replied. "OK, my opinion? I think you and Debbie should talk about this. A serious talk. Don't let her blow it off. She might try. It might mean that she has to confront issues that she would rather avoid. Religious beliefs are not intellectual, they are emotional, visceral; people often act or react from a place other than their head. You both need to be courageous, get to the heart of the matter, explore how you really feel even if it means risking that you will find that you disagree. And if you decide to stay together then you must continue to talk, because as I said, your feelings may change."

"Thanks," Archie said, not the least bit reassured. He liked to think that he and Debbie had a good line of communication. He tried not to laugh at the sudden recollection of when they had first gotten in the clinch. Debbie paused the action and very matter-of-factly asked him about STDs. But the rabbi was right. This was uncharted territory.

Archie spotted road signs announcing the imminent exit for Route 9 and put on his turn light. Officer Katz too flashed his turn signal and just in case Archie missed it, signaled with his left arm, then pointed toward the exit. Archie felt the tension in his jaw and shoulders loosen slightly when they turned onto 9G. It, too, was lined with traffic cones and official vehicles but as Officer Katz had promised, traffic was moving, if slowly. "OK, it shouldn't be long now," Archie said to the rabbi. "This ought to be a half-hour trip. With this traffic, maybe it will be forty-five minutes."

He saw Rabbi Davis glance at his watch. "We have plenty of time. Sundown isn't until 5:36."

"5:36. Not 5:35 or 5:37?"

The rabbi chuckled. "Nope. 5:36."

"Let's let Debbie know we're on our way. They're all probably going out of their minds."

"How are you going to do that? Pull off and find a phone somewhere?"

"Oh, no. I've got a cell phone. Well, assuming I can get a signal. Hand me that phone, there, would you?" Archie pressed the button to bring the screen to life and glanced back at the road. He flicked his eyes at the phone and pressed the Menu button to access his address book. Another glance at the road and then back to the phone to find the Stenowitzes' number.

This will never catch on, he thought. Using the thing was way too much of a distraction from driving. Unlike the CB which he could operate hands-free without taking his eyes from the road. He got the phone dialing and handed it to Rabbi Davis. "Here, you talk to them. I need to pay attention to the driving."

"Oh, hello?"

Clearly it was the day for miracles. The rabbi had gotten a human and not the answering machine.

"Yes, hi, this is Rabbi Davis. Yes, Elliot, hi. How's everyone? Did you go ahead ... no? Oh, OK. I'm calling to let you know that it looks like I'll be able to make it after all." There was a pause and the rabbi laughed.

Elliot probably had just expressed his immense relief.

Giving half an ear to the rabbi's conversation, Archie refocused on leaving plenty of following distance between his truck and the motorcycling Officer Katz in front of him. With this congestion, the cop might have to stop short at any time. Rear-ending the man would give him poor thanks for his assistance. Sure enough, the cyclist's brake lights flashed. Archie downshifted to a crawl. Up ahead, vehicles were bumper to bumper.

"Yes, we figure we're about forty-five minutes away. So please apologize to everyone but we will get there. Who's 'we'? Oh, Archie Harlanson and I."

"Tell them I'm going to need a place to put the truck," Archie said.

"Right." Rabbi Davis conveyed the information to his listener. "OK, see you soon." He held out the phone. "Now what?"

"Just press that button there to turn it off." *Hmm, forty five minutes might have been optimistic. Something up ahead had traffic hosed up.* He turned up the CB and caught a clue as to what was causing the back-up. "Oh no."

"What?"

"I can't believe it." Apparently, up ahead, someone was hauling an oversized load, some heavy equipment. "You know, that guy had to get a permit for that. They could have denied it." He recalled the highway department conference. *Hadn't they resolved not to grant oversize load permits for the day?*

"We'll still make it, won't we?"

Archie did some quick calculations in his head. At the miles-per-hour they were now clocking it was going to be close. "Yeah," he said and was about to issue a new ETA when the motorcycle's brake light flashed. *Was the officer just going to pull off to the side or was he planning to turn?* Archie spotted a sign for another junction. *Maybe Katz had an alternate route in mind.*

Officer Katz's brake lights went on and stayed on. Archie braked. Officer Katz dismounted the cycle, set the kickstand, trotted over to Archie, and signaled for him to lower the window. "Here's what holding up the parade. There's a—"

"Piece of heavy equipment being moved. Yeah, I heard."

"The pickup truck pulling the trailer broke down. They're trying to fix it but they're blocking the road. The officers at the scene are able to route some vehicles around the mess but with the shoulder the way it is, it's slow going. They don't want yet another vehicle getting stuck in the snow."

The rabbi's face crumpled with worry. Archie sighed and rested his forehead on the steering wheel.

"Wait," he said, lifting his head. "You said the towing vehicle has mechanical difficulty. But the trailer's OK?"

"As far as I know."

"Can you check?"

"Sure." Officer Katz activated the radio at his shoulder, had a brief conversation that involved a lot of numerical codes and police-speak. "Yup, the trailer's OK."

"Well, if you can clear a path for me to get there, maybe I can tow it out of the way."

Officer Katz stared open-mouthed at Archie then slapped his forehead. "Duh!"

Archie laughed. "Right?"

Officer Katz got back on his radio and more chatter followed. "OK, it's going to be a squeeze. We're going to halt southbound traffic so you can get through and around."

"Roger that."

"Let's get moving." Officer Katz returned to his vehicle. The rescue operation required a lot of stopping and starting. The officer had to dismount to explain to the motorists what was happening. From where Archie sat, he could see that some drivers felt it necessary to step from their car to argue the situation, expressing their reluctance to cooperate with pointing fingers and arms akimbo. Officer Katz responded with squared shoulders, legs spread, and feet firmly planted. Precious minutes ticked away as Archie crept down the road.

"Look at the time," the rabbi said.

Archie didn't want to.

"Should we call the Stenowitzes and tell them we're not going to make it?"

"Have faith, Rabbi," Archie said and then wondered if that was appropriate. "It's not over yet."

Finally they reached the scene of the breakdown. It was a hot-shot operation, a Dodge Ram with a flatbed load consisting of a skid-steer loader. The towing vehicle sat with its hood up. Archie breathed a sigh of relief. At least the two vehicles weren't jacked; they were in alignment. If they could get the truck and trailer uncoupled and if he could get in front of the trailer, Archie could couple the Kenworth to it. That's a lot of ifs, he thought.

No one had bothered to secure the scene. "Wait here," he said to the rabbi. He set the brakes, gathered up his emergency equipment, and exited the truck then set about placing the reflective triangles where approaching traffic could see them. He couldn't bend at the waist without pain and had to squat. He chugged over to the hot-shot driver. "Any idea what the problem is?"

The driver shook his head. "I've checked everything I know how to check. It just quit."

"OK, well let's see if we can get them unhooked. Then we can at least get them out of the way so the traffic can get moving again."

Officer Katz, the other lawmen, and the hot-shot driver looked around. "There's room on the shoulder for the truck until a tow gets here but not the trailer," said one of the other officers.

"Hey, there's a gas station on the left a few miles up the road," said another. "Can you get the trailer there?"

"If I can get them coupled and the trailer's OK, I don't see why not," Archie replied. He looked a question at the hot-shot driver.

"Works for me," the man replied.

Archie and the hot-shot driver worked to get the two vehicles disconnected. Lawmen and citizen volunteers teamed up to push the disabled pickup onto the shoulder. Archie examined the trailer and didn't find any problems with it. He headed back to the Kenworth. "I'm going to need more room," he shouted to the men up ahead. He would have to place his truck well in front of the trailer before he could back up to couple with the trailer. The officers rallied, directed him to use the oncoming lane to pull around the wreck, and held traffic at bay until Archie could get into position.

The rabbi twisted in his seat at Archie's right to watch as he jockeyed into place, a procedure made a little easier with guidance from the hot-shot driver on the ground.

"My truck's got a fifth wheel with locking jaws," Archie explained as he worked. "I'm aiming to get under that trailer and get the kingpin—that shank there on the underside of the trailer?—centered in the middle of the jaws."

"A little like trying to thread a needle," said the rabbi.

"Using mirrors. Because the needle is behind your back," Archie replied.

"Yeah ..."

Archie got the two vehicles hooked together and moved ahead slightly to test the connection. It felt secure so he braked and parked the truck, turned off the engine, and exited to eyeball the coupling. He gave himself a mental thumb's up and made the final air- and electrical-system connections.

The hot-shot driver raised the trailer supports while Archie collected his reflective triangles.

"You going to wait here for the tow truck?" Archie asked.

The hot-shot driver nodded.

"OK. I'll let Officer Katz know when I've dropped the trailer."

"Thanks, man. I sure am glad that you came along. Sorry for the hassle."

You have no idea, Archie thought with a glance at his watch. "Officer Katz, we're ready when you are."

While Katz conferred with the other officers at the scene, Archie returned to the driver's seat. He turned to the rabbi and said, "Assuming we can get the rest of the way without any complications, we'll still make it."

The rabbi pressed his palms together, closed his eyes, and murmured a Hebrew phrase.

"A prayer for good luck?" Archie asked.

"Well, luck, that comes and goes. More like 'may we be successful in what we're trying to achieve.'"

"That'll work."

CHAPTER TWENTY-THREE

SALT POINT, NY, Friday, February 19, 1993

The perilous tight maneuver from the turnpike onto Hibernia Road came into view and Archie slowed. He got only half a sigh of relief. Despite the pleas that he and the rabbi had made, there was no place to park the Kenworth. In the driveway, a guest's sedan stood next to a white van backed up to the garage door. *Was that Nosh by Naomi's vehicle?* Archie hoped at least the caterer had made it on time.

Archie pulled as far off the road as he could and set the brake. "I'm going to have to find a place to put the truck, but why don't you go on ahead?" he said to the rabbi. "They're probably all—"

"On shpilkis."

Yup, that about covered it.

The rabbi unlatched his seat belt, grabbed his bag, and opened the door.

"Careful, there," Archie said. "I'd hate to have gone through everything we did today just to have you slip. Climb out backwards, like going down a ladder, OK?"

The rabbi nodded and exited the truck. "Catch you inside," he said from the ground and hurried down the cleared path to the front door.

Archie was about to release the brakes and go in search of a place to park when the Stenowitzes' front door opened. A woman he didn't recognize beckoned the rabbi inside. From the front step she held up her hand, signaling for Archie to wait. She trotted up to the truck. Archie rolled down his window.

"Hi, Mr. Harlanson," she said. "I'm the next door neighbor. One house down on the right. Go ahead and park in my driveway for now."

"Thank you." Archie moved the truck a few yards down the road. He secured the vehicle and before leaving, fished the pain pill bottle from his pocket and swallowed one dry, resisting the temptation to down them all. His wound was screaming and with any luck, he'd be relieved of any critical duty for a couple of hours. No time to change his shirt or search for a tie, but he could grab the sport coat. He tucked the bottle into the jacket pocket and his fingers encountered a small lump. He didn't have to pull it out to know what it was. From its velvety texture he knew it was the gift box containing the friendship ring that he bought in Rhinebeck and never got to present to Debbie. *Well, today wouldn't be the day either. Today it was all about Eli.*

Archie eased into the jacket and trudged back to the Stenowitz house. He mounted the stairs and raised his hand to knock when he noticed the door stood ajar. He wiped his feet on the welcome mat and entered the foyer.

Warm air wafted toward him bringing the aromas of smoked meat, onion, citrus, vanilla and cinnamon, and fresh bread. He continued down the hallway. The spot on the wall reserved for a portrait was no longer vacant. The picture lamp spotlighted a huge blowup photo of infant Eli.

From the animated sound of people greeting Rabbi Davis, the ceremony was taking place in the living room. Archie headed that way.

"Pssst! Archie. Mr. Harlanson."

Archie turned to his right. From the kitchen doorway, Naomi beckoned. "Thank God you made it."

"And I see you did too."

"Oy, for a minute there I didn't think that I would. Glad I got an early start. From what I've heard from the later arrivals, the roads are a nightmare."

Archie eyed the platters of food arrayed on the kitchen countertops. "Look, I haven't eaten all day. You wouldn't happen to have—"

Naomi held up a finger. She grabbed a crocheted potholder, opened the oven, and pulled out a tray. "Mini-knishes. I'm just keeping them warm." With a napkin she plucked a knish from the tray and handed it to him. "This should hold you. Hang in there. We'll be eating as soon as the brit's over and it's not a very long ceremony."

"Good to know." Archie wolfed down the tidbit in one gulp.

He hadn't even entered the living room and was already considering leaving while he could. In his jeans, boots, and flannel shirt, he was underdressed for the event. The men wore suits, prayer shawls draped over their shoulders, and skull caps. The women were in dresses and heels. Aftershaves and perfumes competed with the food aromas from the kitchen.

Some of the dining room chairs had been brought in to provide extra seating. The armchair and an armless chair stood side-by-side against the far wall along with a TV tray alongside bearing a glass decanter and a goblet. Rabbi Davis took some instruments from his bag and laid them on the tray.

"Archie!" Debbie elbowed her way through the gathering toward him.

So much for leaving undetected.

She threw her arm around him and kissed him. "My Super Man! I can't imagine what you went through to get here. You'll have to tell us all about it but right now—"

"I know. We're burning daylight," Archie replied, channeling John Wayne again. "Debbie," he whispered, "I'm not dressed."

"Dressed, shmessed, don't worry about that. You're here, that's all that matters. Come on." She took his hand and pulled him into the room.

Marvin and Miriam turned in his direction.

"Archibald," said Miriam. "You found our neighbor's house all right?"

"Yes, thank you. That worked just fine."

"Great," said Miriam. "OK, we're all here. Let's get started. Linc, remember—"

"No photos until after it's all done. Don't you worry, Miriam."

Linc was here? Well, Archie figured, the man was going to need a story for next week's *Valley Voice*.

Dapper in a suit worthy of the nation's highest court, Elliot mouthed "Thank you." His forehead was creased with wrinkles so pronounced that Archie thought they might become permanent. Caryn somehow managed to look both weary and radiant.

Caryn handed Eli to her mother who passed the baby to Marvin. Marvin gave the baby next to Elliot's father, Frank, who laid Eli on the dining room armchair.

"This is the seat of Elijah," Rabbi Davis intoned. "May Elijah stand at my right and protect us."

"Archie, would you please take Eli and hand him to Elliot?" Debbie said.

Me? Archie thought. Had he actually spoken the words they would have come out a squeak. Debbie took his elbow and led him across the room. He leaned over the chair. The baby looked up at him and blinked. With the care he would use hoisting the most fragile cargo, Archie scooped the baby up with both hands and turned to Elliot, whose forehead now was smooth, his eyes bright, and mouth turned up in a smile.

Elliot's father, Frank, sat on the dining room chair next to the one that had been named for "Elijah." Elliot handed his son to Frank. Rabbi Davis tore open a small packet like the alcohol wipes that Archie had in his truck's first aid kit.

"Antiseptic," Debbie murmured. "It's not really necessary, all his implements are sterile, but it's reassuring to everyone else."

While the rabbi gave Frank instructions on how to sit and cautioned him not to move during the procedure, Elliot unwrapped a knife from the nearby table.

After all this, was Elliot going to do the surgery anyway? Archie wondered, and was reassured when Elliot handed the blade to Rabbi Davis. "I appoint you my messenger," Elliot said.

Rabbi Davis swabbed the surgical site and recited some Hebrew. Everyone leaned forward but no one took a step or even breathed, it was that quiet. Archie realized that even he held his breath. The only sound was Eli chirping baby noises.

Elliot then pronounced some more Hebrew and the others chorused yet another phrase.

Marvin held the baby while the rabbi said something that included "Eli." Archie figured it was a naming ceremony. Rabbi Davis dipped his pinky into the goblet and placed a couple of drops of wine on Eli's lips.

The men clapped each other on the back and said "mazel tov." The women crowded around Caryn, hugged her, and cooed over Eli. Archie would have expected the baby to cry or fuss but he didn't. *Stunned into silence, or maybe that was the effect of the wine.*

Debbie sidled over to Archie. "Well, what did you think? Oh, Archie, are you crying?"

"Me?" Archie squeezed his stinging eyes hard.

"Ah, Sweetie." Debbie planted a generous kiss on his cheek. "Don't go away, I'll be right back," she said. Rejoining her family, she hugged her sister.

"I'll be right here," Archie managed to push through a surprisingly tight throat. It had all been unexpectedly moving. He felt like some sort of time traveler, beamed back to an ancient age to witness a potent ritual. Its symbols were so compelling that even the uninformed observer couldn't fail to be impressed by their gravity.

Archie took a deep breath, cleared his throat, and held out his hand to Elliot. "Do I say congratulations?"

Elliot laughed. "You say mazel tov. It means 'good luck.' Well, more like "God favored us.' Just a general, all purpose, 'well done.'"

"Mazel tov, then," Archie said. He circulated among the guests mazel-toving everyone, which brought out beaming smiles. Linc clicked away with his digital camera. Guests' instant cameras appeared as if by magic and groupings formed and reformed for dozens of photos. Debbie pulled Archie into a few of them.

He was grateful to see Naomi, the caterer, confer with Miriam then scurry towards the kitchen. His stomach rumbling and mouth watering, Archie followed her thinking that if he offered to help, he could sneak another tidbit.

As Archie and Naomi laid food platters on the table, Miriam and Debbie ushered guests toward the dining room.

"I believe it's Shabbat, isn't it, Rabbi?"

Rabbi Davis agreed and helped to steer people towards the table. Naomi circulated through the crowd with a fingerbowl and a small towel. Everyone in turn dipped fingers into the bowl, which Archie discovered held plain water, and dried them. Miriam performed the same ceremony with the candles and bread that she had the previous Friday. The rabbi sang a song in Hebrew. Glasses of wine in hand, the guests recited a phrase in unison. It sounded familiar and Archie made a mental note to ask Debbie about it. Uncertain if he could have alcohol with the painkiller, he took a token sip from his glass.

Not a moment too soon, Miriam invited her guests to help themselves and the eating and drinking began in earnest. It was all Archie could do not to shovel food in with both hands. Every once in a while, the rabbi or one of the other guests would break into song and anyone whose mouth wasn't full joined in. As they moved around the table, the guests dropped money into a small box placed at one end. The ornate silver box bore Jewish symbols and a Hebrew word. *Gifts for Eli?* Archie stuffed in a twenty.

Elliot clinked a spoon against his wine glass. "It is my privilege and honor to speak about what happened here this afternoon," he said in a strong voice that no doubt stood him well in the courtroom. As he progressed through his little speech, though, his voice would catch.

One by one, Debbie's relatives and her parents' friends approached Archie to thank him for his role in fetching Rabbi Davis, and between bites, pressed him for details about the drama at the police station.

Archie drew Linc aside. "I didn't know you were going to be here."

Linc grinned. "Miriam was really pleased with the profile that I did of her in the *Voice*. She's gotten feelers from some galleries that want to talk about showing her work. She was very complimentary of the way my photos came out and asked if I would shoot this event. So I got what I needed of the President and hot-footed it over here."

Whether it was the pain pill or the long day he had put in, or the combination, Archie felt his energy fade. *Was it too soon to ask about leaving?* He was about to go check with Debbie when the doorbell chimed.

Miriam frowned, looked around the room, and said to Marvin, "Who could that be? Everyone's here."

Marvin shrugged.

"Stay with your guests. I'll go see," Naomi said, and headed for the corridor toward the door. A moment later she returned. "Uh, Mrs. Stenowitz, I think you'd better come.'

Her frown deepening, Miriam excused herself and waved to Marvin. Debbie followed, turned, and beckoned Archie.

Cold air swept down the hallway. The open door framed a man in a black overcoat. His bare head was closely shaven. Over Marvin's and Miriam's heads, Archie got a glimpse of the street. Hibernia Road was ablaze with the headlights and warning flashers of dark sedans bristling with officialdom.

Archie's freshly-filled stomach turned. *Had the Hyde Park police come to take him back into custody or worse, the feds? Here? Now?* He strained his neck looking back towards the dining room, searching for Elliot.

In the doorway, the caller held up a badge. "Mrs., uh, Stenowitz?"

"I'm she."

"Sorry to disturb you, Ma'am. Would Mr. Archibald Harlanson be here?"

Archie said, "I'm Archie Harlanson." *No point in denying it since Miriam turned and stared right at him. Where was Elliot?*

"If you don't mind, Ma'am, may we come in?"

Wasn't there something about them not being able to arrest you unless you stepped outside? But too late. Miriam looked a question at Marvin who said "OK" and stepped back.

The overcoated man turned and waved to the street. Vehicle doors opened, two men climbed out, and made their way up the path. As each man entered the house, he paused and scanned his surroundings, badge held in an upraised palm then nodded to the man behind him. Leaving the Stenowitzes standing by the door in bewilderment, the men entered and fanned out through the house. One man returned from the second floor and said, "Clear." "Clear," stated the one who had headed toward the living room.

"Clear," the first man shouted toward the street, and mumbled into his coat sleeve.

"What the hell is going on here?" asked Elliot.

More car doors opened, more men emerged, and trooped toward the house. As they passed the porch light, each one revealed himself to be equally stony-faced, dressed in a nearly identical overcoat, and holder of an identification badge.

Except for one man who needed no ID.

President William Jefferson Clinton stepped through the doorway.

"The homeowners, Marvin and Miriam Stenowitz," said the first of the advance men. "And this, sir, is Archibald Harlanson."

Archie was as speechless as the Stenowitzes. Even Elliot was at a loss for words.

"We apologize for interrupting your evening," said President Clinton, "but we could hardly leave town without personally thanking Mr. Harlanson."

"P-p-please come in," Marvin said. "We're, uh, having a party."

"Can we get you anything?" Miriam asked. "You have had a busy day, sir." As if someone had thrown a switch, Miriam shifted into hostess mode. "Please, come join us." She all but took the President's elbow and towed him down the hallway. "Naomi, please, make up a plate for the President."

A stunned silence greeted Bill Clinton as he entered the dining room. The only one who spoke was little Eli.

"Oh, a new baby," said President Clinton. "No wonder you're having a party." He looked around and Archie heard him murmur "Skullcaps. Prayer shawls. Candles" to one of his aides. "Oh, wait," he said. "A brit. You had a brit today. Mazel tov." He drew closer to Caryn. "What's your boy's name?"

"Eli," Caryn stammered.

"Eli." The President leaned down and kissed Eli's forehead. "Welcome to the world, little man. We're going to do everything we can to make it the best possible world for you to grow up in." The President turned to face his stunned audience. "Well, I don't want to keep you from your evening but we did want to thank this man personally. Archibald Harlanson, at risk to your own safety you prevented not only a potentially embarrassing incident, but one that would unnecessarily detract from the important work with which the citizens of this United States have charged us. For that we wish to bestow on you the Presidential Citizen's Medal."

President Clinton held out his hand and an aide pressed a small deep blue box into it. The President opened it, withdrew a gilt medal suspended from a blue ribbon, and pinned it to Archie's sport coat. "Thank you." He held out his hand for a shake. Archie found the president's hand warm for a man who had just come in from the chill of a winter's night.

"It was my ..." Archie was going to say "pleasure" but it hadn't been pleasant. "My duty, sir, as a citizen."

"It's citizens like you that make this country great and an honor to serve as your president."

"Excuse me, sir, but could we get a photo?" Linc asked, practically salivating.

No sooner had the President agreed than everyone crowded in. Linc's camera flash strobed like a street warning light.

"Well, we'd stay, but we have a busy itinerary," said the President. "But thank you for your hospitality."

As expeditiously as they had arrived, the President and his entourage trooped down the hallway. As they passed the kitchen, Archie heard Naomi say, "Gentlemen, some nosh for the road?" and he heard someone—the President?—exclaim "Oh, knishes. Yum!"

They filed down the walkway and into the waiting cars. From his limo, President Clinton turned and waved. The cars pulled away, plunging Hibernia Road into mid-winter darkness.

For a moment, the gathering stood in stunned silence then all at once burst into conversation. Archie caught comments about Clinton's presidency and campaign, about the brit, and about the local uproar that the town hall visit had created.

"Congratulations, man," Elliot said. "You deserve it."

"I feel like I should share it with you. If you hadn't rounded up the cops, who knows how that would have turned out."

"You had it under control. You knew something wasn't right about that Bingo guy from the beginning." Elliot grinned. "National hero. That's really something."

"Should get me back in good graces with the feebies and the HPPD, wouldn't you say?"

Elliot laughed. "Ya think?"

Hugging his camera with all the affection that Caryn had for Eli, Linc said, "I'm sticking with you, fella. If this keeps up, I'll be set for stories for life."

Debbie sighed and shook her head. "I shouldn't be surprised, but I am just stoked."

"Go ahead. Be surprised. I am." Archie slipped the blue box into his pocket and pulled out another. "Here. I've been trying to give you this all week."

Debbie lifted the lid. "It's beautiful," she said, but her brow was furrowed. "But you already gave me something for Valentine's Day."

"This is different. This is a promise ring."

Debbie's lips parted and her eyes widened. She looked left and right. "After this crazy week, with my crazy family, do you really want to be promising anything?"

"I do." *I do.* It sounded good and it felt right. *The Rhinebeck jeweler was right.* Archie wasn't going to need any practice at all saying "I do."

With a tilt of her head and narrowing of her eyes, she said, "What are you promising?"

Good question. Archie thought a minute. "I promise to keep an open mind. To listen. To be flexible." Out of the corner of his eye, he saw that he had caught Rabbi Davis's attention.

"But you already do that. That's what I love about you."

"Then it will be a promise that's easy to keep."

Debbie bit her lower lip. She took the box and held it open. "Then I promise not to present too many challenges."

Archie threw back his head and laughed. "Oh no, no, no. The challenges are what make you 'you.' Keep 'em coming."

Debbie smiled.

"Well, then. I promise to ask you to marry me. You know, when the timing is right. When you're ready."

"OK, then." She held out her left hand. "And I promise to say 'yes.' You know, when you ask me." She waggled her fingers.

Archie slipped on the ring.

From his left came a burst of applause. Archie glanced across his shoulder. The Stenowitzes and their guests had crowded near and now clapped and cheered.

Elliot held out his hand and Rabbi Davis clapped Archie on the shoulder. "Mazel tov."

Eli tucked in one arm, Caryn hugged her sister with the other.

"I never meant to upstage Eli's big day," Archie said to Caryn.

She raspberried her lips and waved away the apology. "No such thing as too much joy. You brought us great *naches*. I am so happy for you two."

Marvin and Miriam appeared at his side. Marvin's face was smooth, the lines of tension eased, and Miriam's eyes were bright with unshed tears.

"You have made my girl very happy," Marvin said, and Miriam kissed Archie's cheek.

His tongue loosened by fatigue and the pain pill, the words were out before Archie could hold them back. "I have to say, I thought you didn't like me."

"No man will ever be good enough for our daughter," Miriam said. "But you—"

"You're a mensch." Marvin smiled and Miriam gave Archie a hug.

Andrea at Amazon Truck Service had suggested that Archie should aim for menschhood. *Looked like he'd pulled it off.*

Mazel tov. Well done. Archie felt all aglow and it wasn't from a sip of wine on top of too little food. From Super Man to national hero to future son-in-law. Not bad for a week's work.

Yes, Tom Cochrane had it right; life was a highway, one with sharp turns, detours, sudden downgrades, and road blocks. But Archie was definitely on it for the long haul.

ABOUT THE AUTHOR

"What if?" Those two words all too easily send Devorah Fox spinning into flights of fancy. Best-selling author of *The Lost King, The King's Ransom, The King's Redress* and *Detour* in The Bewildering Adventures of King Bewilliam epic fantasy series she also co-authored the contemporary thriller, *Naked Came the Sharks* with Jed Donellie, the *Masters of Time:* a SciFi/Fantasy Time Travel Anthology, and *Magic Unveiled,* An Anthology. Publisher and editor of the BUMPERTOBUMPER® books for commercial motor vehicle drivers she is developer of the Easy CDL test prep apps. Born in Brooklyn, New York, she now lives in The Barefoot Palace in Port Aransas on the Texas Gulf Coast with rescued tabby cats and a dragon named Inky and writes the "Dee-Scoveries" blog at http://devorahfox.com

Connect online:

Email: devorahfox@aol.com

Facebook: https://facebook.com/DevorahFoxAuthor

Twitter: @devorah_fox

Smashwords: https://www.smashwords.com/profile/view/mbapub.